Bellman & Black

Also by Diane Setterfield

The Thirteenth Tale

BELLMAN & BLACK

DIANE SETTERFIELD

BOND
STREET
BOOKS

DOUBLEDAY
CANADA

Bond Street Books and colophon are registered trademarks of Random House of Canada Limited

Library and Archives Canada Cataloguing in Publication

Setterfield, Diane, author
Bellman & Black / Diane Setterfield.

Issued print and electronic formats.
ISBN 978-0-385-67950-3 (pbk.).-- ISBN 978-0-385-67951-0 (epub)

I. Title. II. Title: Bellman and Black.

PR6119.E88B45 2013   823'.92   C2013-902635-5
                                             C2013-903034-4

This book is a work of fiction. Names, characters, places and incidents are products of the author's imagination or are used fictitiously. Any resemblance to actual events or locales or persons, living or dead, is entirely coincidental.

Jacket design and illustration by Connie Gabbert
Lines from *Crow Country* by Mark Cocker are used with the author's permission.

Printed and bound in the USA

Published in Canada by Bond Street Books,
a division of Random House of Canada Limited,
a Penguin Random House Company

www.randomhouse.ca

10 9 8 7 6 5 4 3 2 1

For my parents Pauline and Jeffrey Setterfield who, amongst other things, have taught me everything I needed to know about catapults.

You will have seen rooks.[. . .]
Don't be put off by any sense of familiarity.
Rooks are enveloped in a glorious sky-cloak of mystery.
They're not what you think they are.

Mark Cocker, *Crow Country*

I HAVE HEARD it said, by those that cannot possibly know, that in the final moments of a man's existence he sees his whole life pass before his eyes. If that were so, a cynic might assume William Bellman's last moments to have been spent contemplating anew the lengthy series of calculations, contracts and business deals that made up his existence. In fact, as he approached the border with that other place – that border towards which we will all find our path turning sooner or later – his thoughts were drawn to those who had already crossed into that unknown territory: his wife, three of his children, his uncle, cousin and some childhood friends. Having remembered these lost, dear ones and being still some moments from death, there was time for one last act of remembrance. What he unearthed, after it had lain buried some forty years in the archaeology of his mind, was a rook.

Let me explain.

Will Bellman was ten years and four days old and the glory of his birthday was still fresh in his veins. He and his friends were in the fields that ran between the river and the woods, fields where the rooks descended, flapping and swooping, to jab robustly at the ground in search of leatherjackets. Charles, inheritor-in-waiting of Bellman's Mill, was Will's cousin. Their fathers were brothers – and though that sounds simple, it wasn't. Fred was the eldest son of the baker. His mother was from dairy people. He was said to be the best-fed boy in Whittingford, and he certainly looked as though he had been weaned on bread and cream. He had white teeth and solid flesh over his strong bones, and he talked about the bakery he would take over one day. Luke was one of the blacksmith's offspring. There would be nothing for him to take over: his older brothers were too numerous. His bright copper hair could be seen a mile off; at least, it could when it was clean. He kept a safe distance from school. He didn't see the point. If it was a beating you wanted, you could get it just the same at home. Unless he was exceptionally hungry he kept a safe distance. from home too. When he couldn't feed himself by scrounging, he scrumped and when he couldn't scrump, he thieved. A boy had to eat. He was passionately devoted to William's mother who sometimes gave him bread and cheese and once a chicken carcass to pick.

The boys lived different lives at first, but something had drawn them together at the beginning of this summer, and it was their age. All had been born in the same month of the same year. The power of the symbolic anniversary had acted upon them like a physical force, and as the days of August slipped by, it was not only friendship that drew them back, day after day, to these hedgerows and these fields. It was competition.

They ran races, climbed trees, engaged in mock battles and arm-wrestling matches. Every yard run made them faster, every upper branch attained won them a broader horizon. They egged each other on, never refused a dare, took greater and greater risks. They laughed at grazes, bruises were badges of honour and scars trophies. Every minute and every day they measured themselves against the world and each other.

At ten years and four days old, Will was pleased with the world and with himself. He was a long way from being a man, he knew that, yet he was no longer a little boy. All summer long, woken early by the stony cawing of the rooks in the trees behind his mother's cottage, he had felt his power growing in him. He had outgrown the kitchen and the garden: fields, river and woods were his territory now, and the sky belonged to him. He still had a lot to learn, but he knew that he would learn it as he had everything else so far in life – easily. And while he learned he could enjoy each day this new and exultant sense of mastery.

'I bet I can hit that bird,' Will said now, indicating a far-off branch of a far-off tree. It was one of the oaks close to his home; the cottage itself was visible from here, half screened by hedges.

'You can't!' said Luke, and immediately he called to the others, scrambling up a bank and pointing into the distance. 'Will says he can hit that bird!'

'Never!' the other pair called, but they came running to see the attempt all the same.

The bird, a rook or a crow, was well out of range, on a branch half a field away.

Will pulled his catapult from his belt and made a great show of searching for a stone. There was a mystique around the best missiles for catapults. A reputation for recognising the right kind of stone was prized, and lengthy conversations were had comparing them by their size, smoothness, texture and colour. Marbles were superior of course, but rare was the boy ready to risk the loss of a marble. William's private hunch was that any roundish, smoothish stone was as good as another, but he knew the value of mystification as well as any boy, so he took his time.

Meanwhile, it was his catapult that interested the boys. He entrusted it to his cousin while he hunted the missile. Charles handled the weapon casually at first, then, feeling its fine balance, studied it more closely. The two prongs extended from the handle in a Y-shape almost too perfect to be natural. You could search an entire forest and not find a Y like that. Will had a good eye.

Fred joined him in studying it. He frowned and the corners of his mouth turned down, as if he was inspecting a churn of disappointing butter.

'It's not hazel.'

Will did not look up from his hunt. 'Hazel cuts easily. But you don't have to use it.' He had sharpened his knife, climbed, sawed patiently to excise the shape he had spotted. The elder was of an age to be strong, young enough for springiness.

The sling was familiar: Will had reused his old one, cut from the tongue of an outgrown shoe. Lines of small, neat slits made with a sharp blade allowed the leather to be stretched so that it made a bed for a small missile. But one element of the catapult was entirely novel. At the level where the sling was attached, Will had carved shallow inch-wide grooves. In the centre of each groove were tied the narrow strips of leather that attached the sling. But above and below this knot, string was wound. It lay neat in the groove, above and below the leather laces. Charles ran his fingers admiringly over it. It was deftly done, but he couldn't see the reason for it.

'What's this for?'

Luke reached out and ran an appraising finger along the winding of string. 'Stops the sling riding down, does it?'

Will shrugged. 'I'm finding out. It's not shifted so far.'

Until today the boys had not known that a catapult so perfect could exist. They had always thought of catapults as things that were good or bad by the will of the gods, things of chance, of hazard. To use one was to pit your chances against fate, fifty to one you'd miss. There was nothing accidental about Will's catapult. It had been made, fashioned, engineered.

Luke tested the give of the leather strips. They were supple enough, but he couldn't resist the chance to contribute something to this enviable catapult. He spat onto his fingertips and applied the wetness lovingly to the leather strips.

By the time Will had identified the stone that satisfied him he was surprised the bird was still there. He took back his catapult and loaded it. He was adept. His eye was good, his hand steady. He practised a lot.

The bird was too far away.

Turning their attention from the weapon to the target the boys grinned and shook their heads. Will's boast was so ludicrous that he was half laughing with them. But then his ten accumulated years of observation, of growth, of strength and of power readied themselves in him and he fell deaf to the noise of his companions.

While his eye traced the arc – the impossible arc – between missile and target, his brain calculated, calibrated and instructed its tools. His feet shifted, his weight settled squarely, the muscles in his legs, back, shoulders prepared, his fingers altered their grip minutely on the catapult and his hands tested the tension. He drew the sling back.

At the moment of launching the stone – no, just before: it was the second when it was too late to stop it – he knew a moment of perfection. Boy, catapult, stone. Brain, eye, body. He knew certainty, and the missile was released.

It took a long time for the stone to fly along its preordained trajectory. Or so it seemed. Time enough for William to hope that the bird, flapping into life, would rise upwards from the branch. The stone would fall harmlessly to earth and the rook's granite laughter would taunt them from the sky.

The black bird did not move.

The stone reached the apex of its arc and began its descent. The boys fell silent. William was silent. The universe was still. Only the stone moved.

There is still time, William thought. *I could cry out, and startle the bird into taking off.* But his tongue was thick in his mouth and the moment stretched out in time, long, slow, paralysed.

The stone completed its journey.

The black bird fell.

The boys stared in puzzlement at the empty branch. Had it happened? It can't have! But they'd seen it . . . Three heads turned as one to stare at Will. His gaze was fixed on the branch where the bird had been. He was still seeing it fall, trying to make sense of it.

Fred broke the silence with a great bellow, and three boys went haring over the field in the direction of the tree, Luke stumbling over the tree roots and furrows, always the last. Belatedly, William ran too. He came upon them crouching under the tree. They shuffled and shifted to make room for him to see.

There, on the grass: the bird. A rook. Juvenile, still black of beak.

It was true, then. He had done it.

He felt something move in his chest, as though an organ had been removed and something unfamiliar inserted in its place. A sentiment he had never suspected the existence of bloomed in him. It travelled from his chest along his veins to every limb. It swelled in his head, muffled his ears, stilled his voice and collected in his feet and fingers. Having no language for it, he remained silent, but felt it root, become permanent.

5

'We could bury it.' That was Charles. 'A ceremony.'

The idea of a ritual to mark the extraordinary event found favour. But before they could agree what to do, with a tentativeness that provoked laughter, Luke took hold of the tip of a wing and gently splayed it. A ray of light breaking through the foliage fell upon the dead creature and the black was suddenly not black: inky shades of blue, purple and green were released. This was colour that did not behave as colour should. It shifted and shimmered, alive with vividness that played tricks on the eye and the mind. Every boy wondered for a moment whether perhaps the bird was not dead after all – but it was. Of course.

The boys murmured and once again turned to look at Will. This beauty too belonged to him.

Emboldened, Luke picked the bird up.

'CRAA!'

He lunged the cadaver towards Fred, towards Charles – not in Will's direction – and the two boys stumbled back, exclaiming in alarm, laughing with relief. Then it was Fred who larked about with the dead creature, manipulating its wings, imitating flight, cawing and croaking with gusto. Will laughed weakly. There was the aftermath of turbulence inside him. His lungs were tired.

Before long Fred found something unpleasant in the slackness of the small body. They all did. It was the limp hang of the head, the way the feathers would not go back into place. In disgust Fred tossed the body away.

All thought of a burial was now forgotten and they turned their attention from the bird to the stone that had killed it. That stone had a value now. They spent a long time looking, picking up one round pebble after another.

'Too big,' they agreed.

'Wrong colour.'

'It didn't have that mark, there.'

The stone would not be found. Having accomplished its miracle it had divested itself of its uniqueness and was lying somewhere about, indistinguishable from any number of similar stones.

6

In any case, Charles suggested, and for once they all agreed, it wasn't really the stone. It was Will who had done it.

They told and retold the story, acted it out for each other. With imaginary catapults they killed whole parishes of imaginary rooks.

Will stood by. Like any ten-year-old hero, he took more than his fair share of teasing and shoving. He smiled, sick at heart, proud, abashed, guilty. He grinned and shoved back without conviction.

The sun sank low and the sky cooled. Autumn was coming, and they were hungry. It was time to go home. The boys parted.

Will lived closest, in only a few minutes he would be in his mother's kitchen.

On the brow of a bank of earth something prompted him to turn around. He looked back to where the bird had fallen. In the few minutes since the boys had left the place, rooks had come. They circled above the oak, fifteen or twenty of them. More were arriving from all directions. They stretched across the sky, loose skeins of dark marks, converging on this place. One by one they descended to alight in the branches of the tree. Ordinarily such a congregation would be accompanied by the noise of stony chatter as the birds flung sound at each other like gravel. This gathering was different: it took place in intent and purposeful silence.

Every bird on every branch was looking in his direction.

Will leapt off the earthbank and raced home, faster than he had ever run before. When he had the door handle in his grasp he dared to look behind him. The sky was empty. He stared at the branches of the tree but at this distance and with the late sun in his eyes it was hard to know whether he was seeing rooks or foliage. Perhaps he had imagined that many-eyed stare.

For a moment he thought one of his friends had returned to the oak. A boy, standing where he had stood in the shadow of the oak. But the figure was too short to be Charles, too slim to be Fred, and had not Luke's red hair. Besides, unless it was an effect of light and shade, the boy was clad in black.

With the next blink, the boy was gone, on his way home through the woods, probably.

7

Will turned the doorknob and went inside.

'What's got into you?' his mother wanted to know.

William was quiet that evening and his mother thought him pale. Her questions elicited little in the way of answers and she understood that her boy was old enough to have secrets now.

'Just think. In a week's time you'll be away at school with Charles.'

He leant surreptitiously into her side when she stood by him to pour his soup and when she put an arm around him he lingered instead of reminding her that he was ten now. Was her fearless boy nervous of leaving her for Oxford? That night, although it was not cold, she warmed his bed and left his candle burning. When she came to kiss him an hour later she stood and watched his sleeping face. How pale he looked. Was he really her son? They change so quickly.

Only ten and I am losing him, she thought. And then, with a pang, *Unless perhaps I have lost him already.*

The next day William woke with a fever. For half a week he stayed in bed being tended to by his mother. During this time, while his blood grew warmer and warmer and he sweated and cried out in pain, William applied his ten-year-old genius and power to the greatest feat he had ever attempted: forgetting.

He very largely succeeded.

&

A rook is a familiar enough creature until you actually look at him.

His plumage is among the most extravagantly beautiful things nature can produce. As the boys saw that day, a rook's feathers can shimmer with dazzling peacock colours yet factually speaking there is no blue or purple or green pigment in a rook. Satin black on his back and head, on his front and towards his legs his blackness softens and deepens to velvet black. He is not just black, he is blacker than that. His is a luxurious superabundance of blackness never seen in any other creature. He is the essence of blackness.

So whence the glorious colour?

Well, the rook is something of a magician. His black feathers are capable of producing an entrancing optical effect.

'Aha!' you say. 'So it is only an illusion.'

Far from it. The rook is no theatrical conjuror with his top hat full of tricks, deluding your eye into perceiving what is not. He is quite the opposite: a magician of the real. Ask your eyes, *What colour is light?* They cannot tell you. But a rook can. He captures the light, splits it, absorbs some and radiates the rest in a delightful demonstration of optics, showing you the truth about light that your own poor eyes cannot see.

Nor is this spellbinding display of flamboyance the only trick he has concealed in his feathers. Though it is exceedingly rare, a handful of witnesses have seen this spectacle: on a bright summer's day, turning into the sun, a rook alters from black to angelic white. Mirror-bright he dazzles and glories in his whiteness.

Given his beauty and the dramatic and magical alterations he can bring about in his appearance, you might wonder why the rook is to be found in common fields, grubbing for larvae. Why are these supreme creatures not owned by princesses, housed in gilded aviaries, fed dainty morsels from silver trays by liveried servants? Why do they spend their time with cows when they are surely the more natural companions to unicorns, griffins and dragons?

The answer is that the rook lives as he wishes. When he wants the entertainment of human company he is more likely to seek out the drunken poet or the wild-eyed crone than a damsel with a coronet. He is partial to a bit of dragon liver or unicorn tongue when he can get it though, and he wouldn't refuse griffin flesh if it came his way.

There are numerous collective nouns for rooks. In some parts people say a *parish* of rooks.

PART ONE

Verily, the rook sees far more than we give him credit for seeing,
hears more than we think he hears,
thinks more than we think that he thinks.

Revd Boswell Smith, *Bird Life and Bird Lore*

1

Six days out of every seven the area along the Burford Road re-
sounded with the clattering, booming, clanging, rattling, thundering
noise of Bellman's Mill. The shuttles that hurtled back and forth were
the very least of it: there was also the churning, crashing roar of the
Windrush as it turned the wheel that powered all this hectic toing
and froing. Such was the racket that at the end of the day, when the
shuttles were brought home to rest and the mill wheel ceased to turn,
the ears of the workers still rang with the vibration of it all. This
ringing stayed with them as they made their way to their small
cottages, was still there as they climbed into their beds at night and,
as often as not, continued to sound through their dreams.

Birds and other small creatures stayed away from Bellman's Mill, at
least on working days. Only the rooks were bold enough to fly over,
seeming to relish its clamour, even adding a coarse note of their own to
the music.

Today though, being Sunday, the mill was peaceful. On the other
side of the Windrush and down the high street, the humans were
making noise of another kind.

A rook – or a crow, it is hard to tell them apart – alighted with
aplomb on the roof of the church, cocked its head, and listened.

Oh come and dwell in me,
Spirit of power within,
and bring the glorious liberty
from sorrow, fear, and sin.

In the first verse of the hymn, the congregation was tuneless and as
disorganised as a herd of sheep on market day. Some treated it as a
competition where the loudest wins all. Some, having better things to

do with their time than sing, rushed to the end as quick as they could, while others, afraid of getting ahead of themselves, lagged by a safe semiquaver. Alongside and behind these singers was a mass of mill workers whose hearing was not what it had been. These created a flat background drone, rather as if one of the organ pedals had got stuck.

Thankfully there was the choir, and thankfully the choir contained William Bellman. His tenor, effortless and clear, gave a compass bearing, according to which the individual voices found north and knew where they were going. It rallied, disciplined and provided a target to aim at. Its vibrations even managed to stimulate the ear-drums of the hard of hearing, for the dull drone of the deaf was lifted by it into something almost musical. Although at 'sorrow, fear and sin' the congregation was bleating haphazardly, by 'Hasten the joyful day' it had agreed on a speed; it found its tune 'when old things shall be done away', and by the time it reached 'eternal bliss' in the last verse it was, thanks to William, as agreeable to the ear as any congregation can expect to be.

The last notes of the hymn died away and soon after, the church door opened and the worshippers emerged into the churchyard where they lingered to talk and enjoy the autumnal sunshine. Among them were a pair of women, one older and one younger, both abundantly decorated with corsages, brooches, ribbons and trims. They were aunt and niece they said, though some whispered otherwise.

'It makes you wish every day was Sunday,' the young Miss Young said wistfully, of William's voice, and Mrs Baxter, overhearing, replied,

'If you wish to hear William Bellman sing every night of the week, you need only listen at the window of the Red Lion. Though' – and her undertone was audible to William's mother standing a little way off – 'what is pleasant to the ear might be less so to the soul.'

Dora heard this with an expression of benign neutrality, and she turned the same face to the man now approaching her, her brother-in-law.

'Tell me, Dora. What is William doing these days, when he is not displeasing souls who loiter at the window of the Red Lion?'

'He is working with John Davies.'

'Does he like farm work?'

'You know William. He is always happy.'

'How long does he intend to stay with Davies?'

'So long as there is work. He is willing to turn his hand to anything.'

'You would not prefer something more steady for him? With prospects?'

'What would you suggest?'

There was a whole story in the look she gave him then, an old story and a long one, and the look he returned to her said, *All that is true, but.*

'My father is an old man now, and I have charge of the mill.' She protested but he overrode her. 'I will not speak of others if it angers you, but have *I* done you any injury, Dora? Have *I* hurt you or William in any way? With me, at the mill, William can have prospects, security, a future. Is it right to keep him from these?'

He waited.

'You have not wronged me in any way, Paul,' she said eventually. 'I suppose that if you don't get the answer you want from me, you will go to William directly?'

'I would much sooner we could all agree on it.'

The choristers had disrobed, and were leaving the church, William among them. Many eyes were on William, for he was as agreeable to look at as he was to the ear. He had the same dark hair as his uncle, an intelligent brow, eyes capable of seeing numerous things at once, and he inhabited his vigorous body with grace and ease. More than one young woman in the churchyard that day wondered what it would be like to be in the arms of William Bellman – and more than one young woman already knew.

He spotted his mother, widened his smile, and raised an arm to hail her.

'I will put it to him,' she told Paul. 'It will be for him to decide.'

They parted, Dora towards William, and Paul to go home alone.

In the matter of marriage, Paul had tried to avoid his father's mistake and his brother's. Not for him a foolish wife with bags of gold, nor love and beauty that came empty-handed. Ann had been wise and good-hearted – and her dowry had just stretched to the building of the dye house. By being sensible and choosing the middle path, he had ended up with a harmonious domestic life, cordial companionship and a dye house. But for all his good sense and solid reason he chided himself. He did not grieve his wife's passing as a loving husband ought and in painfully honest moments he admitted in his heart that he thought more of his sister-in-law than was proper.

Dora and William went home.

The rook on the church roof gave an unhurried flap, lifted effortlessly from the roof and soared away.

'I'd like to do it,' Will told his mother in the small kitchen. 'You won't mind?'

'And if I do?'

He grinned and put an easy arm about her shoulders. At seventeen, there was still novelty in the pleasure of being so much taller than his mother. 'You know I wouldn't hurt you if I could help it.'

'And there's the rub.'

A while later, in a secluded spot screened by sedges and rushes, Will's easy arm was around another shoulder. His other hand was invisible beneath a mass of petticoat, and the girl sometimes placed her hand over his to indicate slower, quicker, a change of pressure. Clearly he was making progress, he thought. At the start she had kept her hand over his all the time. The girl's white legs were whiter still against the moss, and she had kept her boots on: they would have to make a run for it if they were disturbed. Her breath came in sharp gasps. It still surprised Will that pleasure should sound so like pain.

She fell abruptly silent and a small frown of concentration appeared on her face. Her hand pressed so hard over his it was almost painful and her white legs clamped together. He watched closely, fascinated. The flush on her cheeks and chest, the quiver of her eyelids. Then she relaxed, eyes still closed, and a small pulse beat in her neck. After a minute she opened her eyes.

'Your turn.'

He laid back, arms behind his head. No need for his hand to teach her. Jeannie knew what she was about.

'Don't you ever think you'd like to come and sit on top of me and do it properly?' he asked.

She stopped and wagged a playful finger at him. 'William Bellman, I mean to be an honest married woman one day. A Bellman baby is not going to get in my way!'

She returned to her task.

'Who do you take me for? Do you think I wouldn't marry you if there was a baby coming?'

'Don't be daft. Course you would.'

She caressed him, gently enough, firmly enough. It was just right.

'Well, then?'

'You're a good boy, Will. I'm not saying you're not.'

He took her hand and stopped it, propped himself up on his elbows to see her face properly.

'But?'

'Will!' Seeing he would not be satisfied without an answer, she spoke, hesitant and tentative, the words born straight from her thoughts. 'I know the kind of life I want. Steady. Regular.' He nodded her to go on. 'What would my life be if I were to marry you? There's no way of knowing. Anything might happen. You're not a bad man, Will. You're just . . .'

He lay back down. Something occurred to him, and he looked at her again.

'You've got someone in mind!'

'No!' But her alarm and her blush gave her away.

'Who is it? Who? Tell me!' He grabbed her, tickled her, for a minute they were children again, shrieking, laughing and play fighting. Just as quickly adulthood repossessed them and they set to finishing the business they were there for.

By the time the leaves and the sky came back into focus above his head, he discovered his brain had worked it out for him. It was respectability she wanted. She was a worker, unimpressed by the easy life. And if she was killing time with him, while waiting, it meant it was

17

someone who hadn't noticed her yet. There were not so very many candidates the right age, and most of them you could eliminate for one reason or another. Of the remainder, one stood out.

'It's Fred from the bakery, isn't it?'

She was appalled. Her hand flew to her mouth, then, more aptly but too late, covered his. The smell of both of them was on her fingers.

'Don't tell. Will, please, not a word!' And then she was crying.

He put his arms around her. 'Hush! I won't tell. Not a soul. Promise.'

She sobbed and hiccoughed and then was quiet and he took her hand in his. 'Jeannie! Don't fret. I bet you'll be married before the year is out.'

They washed their hands in the river and parted, heading off in different directions in order to arrive home by different paths.

Will walked the long route, upriver and over the bridge, down the other side. It was early evening. Summer was clinging on. It was a shame about Jeannie in a way, he reflected. She was a good sort of girl. A rumble came from his stomach and reminded him that his mother had some good cheese at home and a bowl of stewed plums. He broke into a run.

2

William extended a hand. The hand that met it was like a gauntlet, thick pads of skin as unyielding as cowhide. Probably the man could hardly bend his fingers.

'Good morning.'

They were in the delivery yard and even in the open air the stink coming from the Spanish crates was high. 'Unpacking, counting and weighing all go on here,' Paul explained. 'Mr Rudge is in charge, he's been with us – how many years is it?'

'Fourteen.'

'Six men here with him today. Some days more, some days less. It depends on the deliveries.'

Paul and Mr Rudge talked for ten minutes, underweight crates and settling and the Valencia supplier and the Castilian one. Paul followed the order of the work: the crates were levered open and tipped up, the fleeces dragged out – their stink with them – to be attached to the hook; then all the business with the weights, the fleeces rising, suspended like grubby clouds and when the balance was found, Rudge – talking to Paul all the while, speaking of Valencia and Castile as though they were places just beyond Chipping Norton – noted the weight and signalled for the next. Then the fleeces returned to earth to be carted away for cleaning. William studied the work, all eyes, keen to take in every detail. And as he watched, so he was watched in turn. None stared openly, all appeared to be looking at their work. But out of the corners of their eyes and out of the backs of their heads, he felt their gazes all over him.

Paul and his uncle followed the donkey to the next stage.

'Let me introduce my nephew, William Bellman,' said Paul Bellman. 'William, this is Mr Smith.'

A rough hand in his. 'Good morning.' William watched. William was watched. And so it went on all day.

The wool had to be cleaned, dried and picked. William concentrated hard. Willying, scribbling, oiling, carding, slubbing: he tried to commit it all to memory.

'Sometimes it goes on from here to the dyehouse, to be dyed in the wool, but since it can also go as finished cloth, we'll leave it till later.'

There came an introduction with no handshake. In the spinning house the eyes that scrutinised him were all female ones – and they were not shy of looking either. He gave a half-bow to Clary Rigton, the most senior of the spinsters, and giggles burst out in the room, immediately repressed.

'Onwards!' Paul said.

To weaving, where the shuttles travelled so fast the eye could scarcely keep pace and the cloth grew so fast you might believe the rattling rhythm alone was enough to beget cloth. To fulling, with its urine and hog's dung fumes, filth to clean filth. To the tenterfield, cloth stretched out on frames, yard upon yard of it, drying in the fine weather . . .

'Unless it's wet, in which case . . .' and off they strode again. Paul opened a door on the air house. 'Self-explanatory, really,' and gave William a glimpse of a long, narrow room, perforated all along the walls. 'And once it's dry, the cloth next passes . . .'

On they went.

'. . . to finishing,' but they were not finished at all, for finishing meant scouring and more fulling and more drying and raising, where William was too dazed to do more than stare as the cloth passed through a machine and emerged with a haze of fibre on its surface, like felt.

William's nostrils were on fire with the smell of it all and his ears were ringing with the noise. His feet ached for they had crossed the site a hundred times, from north to south, from east to west, from field to yard to house to shed, one building to another, following the cloth.

'Shearing,' Paul said, opening another door.

The door closed behind them and William was stunned. For the

20

first time that day, he found himself in a place of hush. It was so quiet in the room that his ears seemed to vibrate. There were no hands to shake. The two men – equal in height, in stature – barely glanced up, so great was their concentration. They worked their blades along the cloth from end to end, in a silent and precisely choreographed ballet and where the blades passed over the cloth, they left not so much as a memory in the pile. The haze was cut away, it drifted like down, slow to the floor, and what was left behind was perfect and firm and clean and sound: finished cloth.

William didn't know how long he stared at it. He was in a numb reverie.

'Mesmerising, isn't it? Mr Hamlin and Mr Gambin.'

Paul looked at his nephew. 'You're tired. Well, that's enough for one day, I should think. There's only pressing after this.'

William wanted to see the pressing.

'Mr Sanders, this is my nephew, William Bellman.'

A handshake. 'Good evening.'

Sheets of heated metal had been inserted between pleats of folded cloth and were cooling. Along the wall packaged lengths of cloth awaited dispatch.

'There,' said Paul as they came away. 'So now you've seen it all.'

William's eyes were glazed with looking.

'Come on. Get your coat. You look worn out.'

William held his coat between his hands. Cloth. Made from fleeces. It was nothing short of miraculous.

'Good evening, Uncle.'

'Good evening, William.'

Before he was quite out of Paul's office, he spun on his heels.

'The dyehouse!'

Paul lifted a weary hand in the air. 'Another day!'

'So, how was it?'

Dora understood not one word in three of her son's reply.

He hardly chewed her food before swallowing, but nineteen to the dozen he talked, and his mouth was full of billies and jennies and burling rooms and double giggs and fulling stocks and she knew not what else. 'Rudge does deliveries, and Bunton has charge of cleaning. The senior spinster is Mrs Rigton and—'

'Was Mr Bellman there? The old Mr Bellman, I mean?'

He shook his head, his mouth full of food.

'Mr Heaver is the fuller and Mr Crace is in the tenterfield . . . No. Is that right?'

'Don't speak with your mouth full, Will. You know, your uncle doesn't expect you to know everything on the first day.'

In fact the chop and potato was already cold, but that hardly mattered. William ate without tasting. In his mind he was still at the mill, seeing it all happen, working out how it all fitted together, every process, every machine, every man and woman, all part of the pattern.

'And the others? Everyone else? Did they take to you, do you think?'

He gestured to his mouth and she had to wait.

She never learned the answer. He swallowed, closed his eyes and his head began to nod.

'Up to bed, Will.'

He jerked awake. 'I said I'd go down the Red Lion.'

She looked at her son. Red-eyed, white with tiredness. She didn't know when she'd seen him happier.

'Bed.'

And he went.

3

So had they taken to William Bellman at the mill?

A nephew was an object of curiosity and William's arrival was much discussed.

The first result was the resurrection of the old scandal surrounding his father. What was known was this: Phillip, brother of Paul, had run away to marry Dora Fenmore against his parents' wishes. She was pretty enough to justify his actions, poor enough to explain theirs. A year later he ran away again – this time leaving his wife and baby son behind him.

Seventeen years being neither a very short nor a very long time, Phillip was remembered and misremembered in equal measure. The story itself was weighed and picked and cleaned and oiled and spun and woven and pounded with hog's dung until it bore about as much resemblance to reality as a cloth cap to a sheep in a field. By the hundredth retelling Phillip Bellman himself could have eavesdropped without recognising his own story. With every retelling the roles of hero and villain, betrayer and betrayed were shuffled, sympathy being reallocated accordingly.

The truth of the matter went like this:

When he married, Phillip was perhaps not so much in love as he believed, but only dazzled by beauty and in the habit of taking what he wanted when he wanted it. His father was always hard on him, and Phillip fully expected him to harden his heart against the couple. However, he counted on his mother to smooth things over for him. Mrs Bellman was a foolish woman who, to spite her husband and for other private reasons, had indulged her younger son too much. She surprised him, though, by being not the least bit indulgent in the matter of his marriage. What he had not calculated for was the jealousy of his mother's love. When his father sent them to live in a small cottage inconveniently situated on the edge of the town, Phillip's considerable pride was hurt.

With the birth of his son, Phillip expected his parents' severity to soften. It did not. His reaction was spiteful: there were three male names in the Bellman family: Paul, Phillip and Charles. Heedless of the price his son might pay for his act of familial vengeance, Phillip chose none of them: he named his son William, out of nowhere, for nothing and for nobody.

Banished from the comfort of the parental home and short of money, he discovered he had paid too high a price for beauty. Love? He could not afford it. Three days after the christening, while his wife and infant were sleeping, he crept from his house by night, stole his father's favourite horse, and left Whittingford to go who knows where and do who knows what. He had not been seen or heard of since.

There was no reconciliation between Dora and her parents-in-law. She raised the child alone. Neither party cared to broadcast the details of the falling-out within the family, and since the only one who knew all the ins and outs of it was gone, that left ample scope for gossip.

The truth is one thing, the imagination of a mill's storytellers quite another. *If a father gives a child a name that is not a family name, there has to be a reason*, people said. It was tempting to cast Dora in the light of wayward wife. There are always men ready to imagine a quiet and pretty woman a wicked one. There was a serious impediment to this though: William had the square, unstill hands of Phillip Bellman, the long stride of Phillip Bellman, the easy smile of Phillip Bellman and the noticing eyes of Phillip Bellman. He was, indisputably, his father's son. He might not have had the Christian name you expect of a Bellman, but he had Bellman written all over him.

'Spitting image!' said one of the old hands, and there was not a single dissenting voice.

When the tale had been told so often that the tellers had exhausted every variation, the gossip changed direction. It was proposed and quickly agreed that a nephew was not a son. A son was an easy thing to understand. It was straightforward. Direct. A nephew on the other hand was on the slant, distinctly diagonal, and it was hard to know

24

what it might mean. The new Mr Bellman had taken his nephew under his wing, that was clear as day, but old Mr Bellman, so it was said, had no high opinion of the lad. A nephew, once you came to think on it, was a walking uncertainty. It could be anything or it could be nothing at all.

Theories wandered far and wide and at the end the only thing that could be pronounced with confidence was spoken by Mr Lowe the dyer, who was the one person who had not yet seen him: 'He is not heir. He is not master over us.'

4

'Mr Lowe,' said William, extending a hand. 'I'm William Bellman.'

The man spread his palms and William saw that his hands and arms were black to the elbow. He'd shaken hands yesterday with calluses, scars and burns. He couldn't see what harm a bit of staining would do, but the lack of warmth in the man's eyes told him not to insist.

Moreover, it appeared Mr Lowe had no intention of speaking.

'My uncle showed me the work of the mill yesterday. You may have heard.'

An incline of the head. As if to say, I have heard and I am not greatly interested.

'We did not come to the dyehouse though. I hoped you might have a few minutes to show me what it is that you do here.'

The man raised an eyebrow. 'We dye.'

'Of course.' Will smiled. The other man did not. Presumably he had not intended humour.

'Perhaps you would prefer me to come back some other day.'

A muscle twitched in the man's face. A tic or a communication? Whatever it was, it wasn't an invitation.

Will knew when he wasn't wanted.

In the courtyard crates were being offloaded.

William approached Rudge.

'Need a spare pair of hands?'

'You again? Haven't you seen enough yet?' This was better. Rudge was smiling as he extended his great leather glove of a hand. They shook.

'I'm here to work today.'

'With these hands?'

Will knew what work was; he'd chopped enough timber and scythed enough hay.

Rudge handed him a jemmy and for half an hour Will levered crates open. Then he lugged fleeces. Then he attached them to the hook. The men were reticent, awkward at first, but the work left no room for the intricacies of sentiment. He was a pair of hands, there with the next fleece when the first was weighed, and as he found his place in the process they forgot who he was and called 'Next!' and 'Ready!' to him with the same ease they had for each other. 'Here!' and 'Ready!' he called back, as if he had never done anything else.

When his palms got sore he rubbed grease in and bandaged them – 'like a hundred little knives, a fleece is, when you start out,' they told him – but worked on, till the delivery was cleared, and when they were done and he said goodbye, all the men could say about him was that he'd put his back into it.

In the next days and weeks, Will did every job that a pair of willing hands could do in the production of cloth. In the spinning house, the women laughed and flirted – as did he – but he also sat for long hours at a jenny and blundered with his bag of fluff till his hands were sore. That was nothing new! Every job he did found a new patch of tender, uninjured skin to torment. Over and over again his yarn broke, a thousand times he found himself spinning thin air, but by the end of the day he had spun a length of thickish, uneven yarn.

'I've seen worse from a beginner,' Clary Rigton admitted, and a saucy, dark-haired girl who'd been giving him the eye added, 'And for a man, it's a blimmin' miracle!'

In the fulling stocks, he inhaled a lungful of noxious fumes from the seg barrel and fainted clean away. He came to his senses, nauseous and gasping for air. When he got his breath back he laughed at himself, and said to the apprentice who had helped him outside, 'You're brother to Luke Smith, aren't you? Is he still arm-wrestling?' He knew it was not by accident that the lid was whipped away just as he came by, but by the end of the day he was in with the apprentices enough to have a game of cards with them, and he even made a penny from it.

In the tenterfields William crouched low to be taught by rough-handed children how to stretch the wet cloth on the lower pegs of the frame for drying. He barrowed wool from here to there and back again with Mute Greg. He decanted fermenting seg into the fulling stocks. He was not too high to feed the donkey and shovel shit.

At the other end of the scale, nor was William too low to meet the millwright. He stood beside the northerner, watching the millwheel turn, all ears. There were different types of wheel, undershot and overshot, high breast, low breast. Will asked a question, then another. The millwright explained, first in general terms then, encouraged by the boy's enthusiasm and general intelligence, in greater and greater detail. The diversion of rivers to create reservoirs of energy, the calculation and management of flow so as to engineer a continuous, regular supply of power, all the ingenious means by which a man might harness nature to multiply his own efforts.

When the man went to speak with Paul in the office, William remained standing by the wheel. Hands in pockets, blank-faced, he stared at the water and the turning wheel. He went over and over the science of it all, time slipping by unremarked, and it wasn't until Paul tapped him on the shoulder – 'Still here?' – that he came out of his absorption.

'What time is it?'

And when he learned, he swivelled and took off at a run.

'Got to see someone,' he shouted over his shoulder. 'Red Lion.'

By the time the month was out William Bellman had participated in nearly every aspect of the mill's work. He could not weave like a weaver, nor spin like a spinster. But he had operated every machine, even if only for an hour, and he knew how it was powered, what maintenance was necessary, what might go wrong with it and how to put it right. He knew the language: both the formal names for things and the ones the workers invented at need. He knew the system, how one job fitted with another, how the teams managed between them. He could put a name to every face: whether overseer, senior man or apprentice. He had looked everyone in the eye and there was no one he had not spoken to.

There were only two jobs he hadn't done. In the shearing room Mr Hamlin – or it might have been Mr Gambin, they were as like as brothers – teasingly offered his blade.

William shook his head with regret. 'You make it look so easy!'

Shearing was, quite likely, the most highly skilled job in the mill, and the one in which you could do the most damage by doing it badly. 'If I tried for thirty years I could not do what you do.'

And he had not worked at the dyehouse.

As time went on and the millhands saw more of William, their difficulty in placing him grew no less. He had attended the same school as Charles: to hear him speak, he was more of a gentleman than his uncle. On the other hand, when he caught his wrist on the hot edge of a pressing plate he swore like a fuller's apprentice. There was confusion over how to address him: some called him William, some called him Mr William. William himself seemed not to care and answered with the same easy willingness to both. He had the same manner for everyone; he smiled and shook hands indiscriminately.

'He's got no airs about him,' an admiring spinster told her sister. 'He never talks down to us. At the same time, he never butters up.'

So where did he fit? Master or hand? William was a puzzle and no mistake – but he was a puzzle they were getting used to.

5

'He's doing well,' Paul told Dora. 'Did you hear what Crace at the tenterfield said about him? If there's a way of getting the sun to shine all night, trust young Will to find it.'

She laughed.

Paul liked to lay these compliments about her son at Dora's feet.

William was taking his time in the vestry. Too cold to wait in the churchyard, Dora stood at the back of the church; it was scarcely warmer but at least it was out of the wind that made your ears ache.

'He's not afraid of hard work. And he's picked up the technical side of things remarkably well. The millwright mentioned what a clever lad he is. I believe he'd have stolen him away given half a chance.'

'And now that he's in the office?'

'Ned Haddon was unsettled by it all at first. He knows perfectly well I don't mean my own nephew for the fulling stocks, and must have been wondering what it means for his own position. But I don't see William sitting at a desk scratching paper all day, do you? He needs a wider canvas than that.'

'William has taken my recipe for fruitcake for Ned Haddon's mother. We had a basket of walnuts in return.'

Paul smiled. 'He has a way of getting on with people. And Ned is settled again now.'

'Does he get on too well with some?'

'The spinsters?'

She pressed her lips together.

'If I heard anything that worried me unduly, I would put a stop to it. He's a young man, Dora. You know what young men are.'

Dora glanced at him, the ghost of his brother was suddenly present, and he wished he could take back what he'd just said.

'This talk of card playing . . .' she went on.

'Is there talk of card playing?'

'So I have heard.'

'I'll speak to him. Leave it with me.' His brother's spectre diminished. 'William is a fine young man, Dora. Don't worry.'

'And Charles? How is he?'

Now it was Paul's turn to look worried. 'Oh, the same as ever. Supposed to be studying but I hear word that he is too busy painting to be bothered with exams.'

'Painting is better than card playing, I think. And there are no spinsters to tempt him there.'

'Temptation takes many forms. Charles is keen to travel. My father does not wish him to go, of course.'

'He wants him at the mill. It is only natural.'

There was a chill in her words, and who could blame her. His father wished for the grandson that was absent from the mill, and begrudged the one that was there.

Paul sighed. 'I am afraid it does not come naturally to Charles to wish to be there. Not at present, anyhow. And now I have probably said too much.'

William emerged from the vestry with the other choristers.

They made friendly farewells, found their family members and, wrapped up against the advent chill, separated into pairs and little groups for the icy walk home.

'What kept you so late in the vestry today, Will?'

'Talk. Fred is engaged to be married.'

'Fred Armstrong from the bakery? Who is the girl?'

'Jeannie Aldridge.'

His mother gave him a look out of the corner of her eye. 'I thought at one time you were keen on Jeannie Aldridge.'

William shrugged and made an indeterminate noise that might have meant *Yes* or *No* or *What was that, could you say it again please*, but that probably meant, *It's none of your business, Mother*.

6

Paul was not worried about the spinsters. He had the notion William sought his romantic escapades outside the mill. As for the card playing, well, that was foolish of him. He would have to speak to him about that. The boy would understand why it had to stop. Paul just hoped his father hadn't got to hear about it.

That very evening the topic of William arose at one of the regular conferences held between the old Mr Bellman and the new.

'He's not pulling his weight, eh? This William of yours,' Mr Bellman senior said.

'He seems to be doing all right to me.'

'That's not what I've been told.'

Once a week old Mr Bellman did his rounds and it was understood from the colour of his questions that he was not unwilling to hear criticism of William. There were those who, out of loyalty to the old man or out of mischief, were willing to oblige.

'What is it you've heard?' Paul sipped his whisky.

'Standing around, hands in pockets, staring into space, while others work.'

His father looked fiercely at him. It was an expression that had frightened Paul as a child, and led him to believe that his father was all-powerful. Now, translated onto this thin, lined face with rheumy eyes, the same expression only saddened him. 'And I do not like what I hear of his behaviour with the spinsters. And the boy has been a distraction to the apprentices. He draws them into gossip and idle mischief.'

Paul took a sip of whisky and tried to speak mildly.

'Is it possible, Father, that you've been speaking to people who have an axe to grind against William? There are jealous souls at the mill, as elsewhere.'

His father shook his head. 'He was seen standing idle for over an hour, staring at the Windrush like – like a lady poet.'

'Ah.' It was hard not to laugh. 'That will be the day the millwright came. He gave Will a lesson in engineering and Will was memorising it.'

'Is that what he told you? He won't be able to explain away his insubordination so easily, I'll be bound.'

'What insubordination is this?'

'He has been rude to Mr Lowe.'

'And Mr Lowe told you this?'

Paul was incredulous. Mr Lowe was so miserly with words that his apprentices held competitions to see who could draw more than ten words out of him on any one occasion. On those rare occasions when one of them did, the victor won a jug of cider at the Red Lion, the cost shared by all the others. How many words would it have taken Lowe to complain to his father about Will? What had brought this about?

'He is a distraction, Paul. How is the work to be finished on time if the apprentices are not at their work?'

Paul frowned. Things had gone slowly of late in the dyehouse.

Seeing his son's hesitation, the old Mr Bellman pressed home his advantage. 'Have you looked into the samples cupboard lately? I was there on Friday afternoon, but *you* go! See with your own eyes. I'm telling you, that boy's no good.'

Paul closed his eyes to curb his impatience. When he opened them again he saw afresh how old his father was. Fragility, folly and author-ity that clings beyond its time. Compassion moved him to speak more kindly than he felt.

'There is no need to call him "that boy". He has a name, Father. He is a Bellman.'

The face of the old man twisted beyond anger, into disgust, as he waved Paul's words away in a violent gesture of rejection.

It was a gesture and an expression that gave Paul reason to ponder. In his prime his father had been able to temper his anger, moderate his dislike of his younger son. Now that he was older, his feelings more frequently got the better of him. On and on his father went, listing the failings and weaknesses of William Bellman, and Paul let the voice go by like the Windrush, while he fished in a single spot.

He is a Bellman, he had said, and his father had swept the words away like so much rubbish . . .

But no one could fail to see that William was Phillip's son. It would be ludicrous to deny it.

There was another possibility and it slipped into Paul's mind now and found a space that it fitted into perfectly. It was so obvious, he couldn't even bring himself to feel surprised. In fact, he wondered why it had taken him so long to work it out.

His father's anger and his mother's unhappiness; the favouritism each had for one son . . . It wasn't William who was not his father's son. It was Phillip.

No wonder his father was so angry.

He thought about his mother, that foolish, unhappy woman he had ignored and neglected, and wished he had paid more attention to her. He thought about his brother – his half-brother – and discovered that he loved him and disapproved of him in just the same proportions as before. He thought about Dora and wished she could have had the luck to meet a better man than his brother; he came close to wishing that she had met *him* instead of his brother, but it was hard to see how that would have helped matters, and finally he thought about William. Was he a Bellman or not?

While Paul was still turning these thoughts over in his head, his father's account of William's faults and failings came to an end. He was waiting for Paul to respond.

'I'll look into it,' he heard himself say. 'Tomorrow.'

He went then to his own rooms.

William is my nephew and is doing well at the mill and I love him, he thought. *In some lights, it's actually very simple.*

7

'The samples?' William's face lit up. 'Yes, I did cut pieces from some of the samples. Let me show you!'

He pulled some crumpled strips of cloth from his pocket and laid them on the desk. They were in different shades of crimson: maroon, garnet, madder, cherry, brick, claret . . .

'This is the cloth that was left too long in the fulling. This one was from April. Remember the rain? It had to be dried entirely in-doors, with no sun on it at all. And this one – this is interesting, see – is one of Roper's specials. She makes a yarn that has less twist to it . . .'

So William could tell by the look and feel of a piece which cloth had come from which loom; he recognised the yarn from individual spinsters, he had the history of each piece clear in his mind. That didn't matter today.

'William,' Paul interrupted. 'Tell me. What have you done to upset Mr Lowe?'

'I've done a dozen things to upset Mr Lowe. Most of them he doesn't know about, I hope. What's he complaining of?'

'You are distracting his apprentices. That's one thing.'

'How else can I find out about dyeing? Mr Lowe won't tell me a thing.'

'Haven't you been here long enough to know that dyeing is a world unto itself, William? You can't go in expecting Mr Lowe to open up his secrets to you. There's an art to it. It's—'

'Alchemy, yes. That's what he wants you think!'

'William!'

His nephew looked pained.

'I've explained this before, William, so this is the last time. Mr Lowe's father invented a recipe for blue dye which is so clean that it means that we sell more blue cloth than any mill within a hundred miles. We are lucky to have Mr Lowe here at all. We got him when the outlook was bad over in Stroud and the mills were failing. They have made more than one attempt to get him back since things looked up. We cannot afford to upset him.'

William did not fidget or close his eyes or look away. He was listening, but it was plain he was not persuaded.

'If Mr Lowe does not want you in his dyehouse, you must respect his reasons. He doesn't want every Tom, Dick and Harry knowing his professional secrets. That is his livelihood at stake.'

'His crimsons aren't up to much,' William grumbled. 'In any case, it's your land, your building, your mill.'

'It's traditional. Dyers have always been their own men. They have their own ways. And they are too important to lose. I won't have Lowe going back to Stroud because you've upset him.'

There was a pause in which William's expression told him nothing was resolved. William opened his mouth to protest, but Paul raised a hand to stop him. 'Give credit where it's due, William. Mr Lowe knows what he's doing. If the crimsons are unstable, don't go laying it at Mr Lowe's door. It's the water makes them so.'

William shook his head firmly. 'So he told you that too. He's lying. It's nothing to do with the water.'

'You have only been here just under a year, William. I am warning you, watch what you say.'

'What he says about rain diluting the water is nonsense. He doesn't use water from the river. He uses spring water. It's consistent. Never changes.'

Paul hesitated.

'It's not alchemy. He wants us to think it is because it leaves him in the clear. He makes a good blue because he has the recipe; you're going to keep him on till the end of his days for his blue and he knows it. As for crimsons, what difference does it make to him how they come out? He can use old dye, chop and change the quantities at random, and when it comes out dull and brown, blame the water!'

36

He embarked on a gesture of frustration, caught sight of his pile of cloth strips and stopped. 'Look! Uncle Paul—'

Paul pushed the fabric firmly away. 'His blacks?'

'He makes a good black because with the iron in the water round here you couldn't fail.'

Could that be true? Paul had to admit, it might. The whole area was renowned for its blacks.

William fidgeted with the cloth he had separated from the rest. He looked as if he was making up his mind to something.

'His blue is good, Uncle. His black is good. The other colours are hit and miss because his dye cupboard is a shambles and he doesn't keep proper records.'

Paul put his head in his hands and William started to look like a man who had said more than he should.

'You have been into Mr Lowe's dye cupboard.'

'Yes.'

Paul felt weary to the core. He was more than willing to defend his nephew against his father but he needed William to meet him half-way. The boy showed no remorse, though, and had no sense of the boundary he had transgressed.

'You had help.' It wasn't a question.

William said nothing. A friend of a friend with a brother in the dyehouse, a few drinks in the Red Lion, money had changed hands. Subterfuge, distraction, the borrowing of a key.

'I'd have done it another way, if there had been another way. Mr Lowe gave me no choice.'

'Mr Lowe is very particular about the sanctity of his dye cupboard.'

'And now I know why.'

William said nothing but he took a piece of cloth from the black leather inlay of the desk, and stroked it flat against his palm. It was blood red, as fresh and clean as if a blade had just this second sliced his skin.

'Go home, William.'

'What? Now?'

Paul nodded.

'Am I to come back?'

'Take a few days off. I need to think it over.'

When he heard the door close behind him, Paul groaned.

8

Dora turned out her son's pockets to launder his clothes. Once it had been stones and pencils that made the holes in his pocket, now it was a penknife and other small tools that came in handy for freeing a tangle of yarn in the machinery or loosening a bolt. Today with his handkerchief she drew out strips of scarlet cloth. Some thick, some thin, of different textures, weights and shades. The colour varied from the lightest red to the darkest; most were evenly dyed, a few were patchy. The pieces were a few inches long and had been chopped with no great care. Whatever they were, with William no longer at the mill, they would not be wanted.

While William was out, Dora sat by her window to make the most of the last hour of light. She cut and folded the pieces of fabric into petal shapes, and put a couple of stitches in each to make them hold their shape. Then she started to join them, the smallest in the middle, increasing in size as she went.

This was an activity that reminded her of her past. More than once in her girlish days she had made flowers out of scraps of cloth to adorn a coat or a hat. She had been wearing a golden rose corsage on the day she met Phillip. She had made it out of an old apron that she had dyed herself with half a teaspoon of turmeric, and he had commented on it.

Dora did not breathe a word of criticism about her husband, nor any word of praise either. Indeed no word ever passed her lips about him, good or bad; it was a decision she had taken early on. Once you said a thing, it could never be taken back and would be taken up and repeated and altered and told again, no matter how misshapen and out of true. Better to say nothing. Others might conclude that she had simply forgotten all about Phillip Bellman, but the truth was that her feelings were as intense as ever, though they had changed. In the first days she had been beside herself with worry, believing her husband to be missing through some accident or injury. It was only when a month had passed with no word from him and no answer to any of Paul's thorough enquiries, that she accepted the fact of her abandonment.

Then she had grieved. All day long she had cared for her son, loved him and taught him the world and kept him from harm, while he taught her a merriment she otherwise came close to forgetting, but once he slept, she wept. The memory of those long nights spent grieving for happiness lost could still make her shudder now. She had never known pain like it. When had it slipped into anger? She could not tell. It must have been gradual. The feelings must have existed alongside each other in her heart for some time before she became aware that the anger was the uppermost.

First it was Phillip's family she had blamed. In her heart she had raged against Phillip's father who had punished his son's elopement with the imposition of what to Phillip had felt like hardship. He had hated the smallness of this cottage, the lack of servants, the humiliation of it. She had raged against his mother who had withdrawn not money but love. Eventually her rage turned itself on Phillip himself. He it was who had abandoned them. What spite against parents can justify a man abandoning his child? And she thought the journey of feeling would end there, but latterly she had come to feel that it was neither loss nor anger that preoccupied her, but sadness. The sadness of knowing that the happiest and best days of her life had been false. His love had not been real – nor hers. She had been dazzled by him: by his handsome face, and his compliments and – she was ashamed – by his money. No man had called her beautiful before, and in the face of his adoration, in awe at her own power, she had agreed to run away with him. The intensity of feeling was so great it had never occurred to her it might not be love.

The only thing that differentiated them was that she had been as good a mother to their child as she knew how to be, and if her efforts were worth anything at all, William Bellman would be a better man than his father. It was her redemption.

Now though, William was so miserable at being sent away from the mill that she could not even settle her thoughts with the prospect of her son's future success. Her son was all her life now, and the old griefs of her own lost happiness were as nothing compared to seeing her child in pain. He did not complain at Paul's treatment of him, but had gone straight back to his previous employer Davies the very next day, losing not a single day's work. But he missed the mill. It was his element, and he belonged there, and without it he was suffering.

Now, as she finished stitching her rose, William himself came in.

'Can you see to sew in this light, Mother? What pretty thing is that?'

'A rose. It is not for a woman my age. I will put it in a drawer until the day you bring your betrothed home.'

Seeing the dyed scraps she had used for the rose, he grimaced, before quickly covering his pain with a smile for her sake. Looming over her as tall and handsome as his father, her boy took the rose from her hands and held it to her hair.

'Wear it. Wear it in your hat when we go to the wedding, and I will be glad to have the prettiest mother in Whittingford on my arm.'

She was touched by his efforts to hide the extent of his unhappiness from her. After so many years of looking after him, it was still novel to have him wishing to protect her.

'Let me talk to Paul,' she told him. 'I can tell him that you were overcome by enthusiasm, that you have learned your lesson . . .'

A spasm gripped his face and he turned abruptly away. 'Yes. Please.' His voice was strained and muffled.

I'll be crying in a minute, she thought, as she took her hat from the peg and then realised it was too late for sewing now.

Behind her back she felt William turn and he gripped her shoulders in a brief, ferocious embrace. Then he was gone.

Had he learned his lesson though? The trouble with William was that his enthusiasm knew no bounds. When he once got it into his head to do a thing – and she was his mother, she should know – there was just no stopping him.

9

Paul turned away from the Windrush and into the high street. His thoughts had grown uncomfortable to him and he wanted the diversion of activity and people.

As he drew level with the church, he spotted William in his chorister's gown on the church steps. A crowd was milling in the churchyard and among them was Dora. Dora had a rose in her hat.

It would not do to meet them now. He had not yet made up his mind.

Nice day for a wedding. He had heard it was the baker's son marrying today. He didn't know the girl, but she was a sweet-looking miss, all smiles and blushes as her new husband shook hands with William, then embraced him with unusual vigour. William bowed to the pair, smiling, and Paul felt a paternal pride. He knew how much William wanted to be at the mill, knew what his error was costing him in heartache. Yet today his friend was marrying and he smiled and shook hands and only Paul – Paul and Dora – knew what the effort was costing him.

Paul missed William at the mill too. After one short year, he had come to rely on him. Wherever something went wrong – mechanical, human, administrative – there would be William, scratching his head, cudgelling his brains, putting his shoulder to it, begrudging neither time nor energy till the trouble was sorted. He smoothed out machines, misunderstandings, tangles of yarn, figures, paperwork. His deft hands, physical strength, ability to talk to the workers made him useful in situations beyond his years. *That's a job for William*, Paul thought a hundred times a day, and *William will sort that out*. Now each time he thought it, he had to ask himself, how will I ever manage without him?

But William had put him in an impossible position.

Paul had no liking for Mr Lowe. It was his father who had taken him on. Mr Lowe's authority in the dyehouse had come about during old Mr Bellman's time. There were a lot of fathers in the case, Paul reflected, unhappily. Mr Lowe made a good, clean blue because his father made a good, clean blue, and he, Paul Bellman, had never been into Mr Lowe's dyehouse because his father had never been into Mr Lowe's dyehouse, and habits and ways get fixed like that, father to son, and ever on.

And William? Fatherless son of a fatherless son, William was free of all that. He rose above habit, saw through tradition, understood things the way they were. The past had no hold on him. Perhaps that's why his vision of the future was so strong. Without the past to cast its long shadow, might you see the future more clearly? You could almost envy him.

Paul had been spotted. Dora was there, at his side.

'That's a pretty rose you have in your hat.'

'It is not the time to talk of roses. Paul, he may be smiling today but underneath it he is so unhappy. Is there nothing that can be done to put things right?'

He took a deep breath. 'Perhaps there is something.'

Dora was startled.

'Give me the rose.'

Bewildered, she raised her hand to her hat. 'This? But it is stitched on.'

She let him put his penknife to her hat to pluck the bloom.

'Fetch William.'

She signalled to her son to approach.

'These are all the same dye batch, I take it? Only the cloth is different?' Paul indicated the various petals.

'Yes.'

Paul applied the blade to the base of the brightest red petal and excised it. Peering through his looking glass at the cut edge of the petal, he could just make out that the cloth was red all the way through. The dye had penetrated to the very heart of the wool. He examined a few of the duller shades to compare. All had a core of white.

Now Paul and William began to talk. Fast and technical, so that she understood the excitement better than the meaning. Ann Roper and her low-twist yarn, and fresh madder from Harris's not Chantrey's, and air-drying, and double-dyeing, and record keeping . . .

'. . . and if we do all that,' William concluded, 'there's no reason why we shouldn't get consistent crimson, soft as this, bright as this every time.'

Dora looked from her son's face to Paul's. She didn't know quite what was happening and her poor rose had been so tortured and cut about that it was irretrievable, but she could see from both their faces that there was a chance everything was going to be all right again.

'And Mr Lowe . . .'

Dora held her breath and prayed for William to hold his tongue.

Paul's smile grew wary. 'What about him?'

'If he were to be brought to thinking it was all his idea . . . ?'

Paul took William's hand in his and squeezed it firmly. 'Just leave Mr Lowe to me, eh?'

10

'You want to give us a bit of warning next time!' said Rudge, coming into Paul's office.

'About what?'

'Bright red! Drills right into a man's brain, I can tell you. From right over the other side of the valley you can see it. Set my eyes all ajangle, I thought they were going to explode in my head.'

Paul went to see for himself.

It was a perfect day for drying. The sun was warm but not too strong, there was an even heat in the air and a soft breeze. The din of the fulling mill was something Paul was used to now; it hardly interfered with the pleasure he took in the blue sky and the green and gold irregularly shaped fields in the distance.

As he rounded the dyehouse and the view of the tenterfield opened up before him, Paul came to a sudden halt. To the left and the right, his long line of frames receded into the distance, and stretched along them, vivid as fresh-spilt blood, was yard upon yard of crimson cloth. For a moment that was all Paul could see, and he understood that Rudge was only half exaggerating when he spoke of exploding eyes. He felt a pleasurable excitement flood his mind and a quickening of his pulse; a smile rose irresistibly to his lips. Then he saw that he was not the only one.

Crace, his overseer at the tenterfield, walked the length of the racks, stopping here and there as if to gauge the evenness of the tension along the upper and lower cross bars, but it was clear enough that this was a pantomime for the boss's benefit: he was there for one reason only, and that was to relish the colour.

Paul hailed him.

'Have you ever seen a better crimson, Mr Crace?'

'I can't say as I have.'

'Nor I. Not here, nor anywhere.'

Leaning in the doorway of the dyehouse, Lowe himself had come out to see how his colour was drying.

'Bright enough for you, Mr Bellman?' he asked.

'Dazzling, Mr Lowe.'

Lowe inclined his head and returned to his dyehouse.

Paul's arrival had sent the dozen or so lowlier employees scurrying back to their work, but evidently the crimson was the talk of the mill and everyone who could was coming to take a look. Nor was it only the mill folk who took an interest. Along the far fence, clusters of people leant and looked, riders slowed, all come for the glorious spectacle of the new crimson.

'How does it look?' William was impatient.

'Congratulations,' Paul told him. 'We're going to do well out of it.'

His nephew's face relaxed.

'You did right not to go over yourself. Lowe is pretending not to notice that he is the star turn, but he is enjoying every minute. What's on your mind, Will?'

'The frames.'

'In the tenterfield? What about them?'

'We have the length for an extra one at the end of the tenterfield but the ground drops and the copse at the corner will cast a shadow so that's no good, and I can't see that Mr Gregory will sell us any of the east field, not for love nor money.'

Paul laughed. 'But does it matter? We rarely use all five as it is—'

'Yes, but when the orders start coming in for the crimson . . .'

'Hold your horses, William. We don't know yet what orders will come in for the crimson.'

But William didn't hear. 'So far as I can see, it's either buy up some land on the other side – there's nothing to cast shade on that length of field belonging to Mr Driffield, and he'd sell at the right money – or else build another drying house and do more drying inside. And with the quality of the colour, if we had the softness from indoor drying, we could raise our prices. I'd be in favour of that except for the time it'll

46

take to build it. Unless Mr Driffield would rent us the land for the time it takes to build the drying house . . .'

'Aren't you getting ahead of yourself?'

'What time is it?'

Paul consulted his watch. 'Ten to three.'

'He'll be on his way.'

The merchant would be arriving by the Burford Road. He would have an unimpeded view of the crimson cloth for a full ten minutes of his journey.

By five o'clock Paul had orders for a thousand yards of crimson cloth by the end of September and the same again a month later.

He went directly to Mr Driffield on his way home and arranged to rent a length of his field.

A year. All this the boy had brought about in a year. What could he do if he were given free rein?

11

Behind the scenes were arguments William was not privy to.

'Father, you made me manager of the mill. You must let me manage the mill. I intend to make William my secretary.'

'But Charles is to inherit! Your own son!'

'Charles has no interest in managing the mill. That is abundantly clear to me, as it should be to you. If we insist on him taking on a job in which he has no interest and for which he has – let us face facts – no aptitude, we can expect only one thing. The mill will fail. William is part of the family. He is willing and he is more than able. In two years he has learned more about the running of the mill than Charles who has barely put his nose into the place since the day he left school.'

'Charles will be interested soon enough. When he inherits—'

'Charles wishes only to travel and paint. He doesn't know how to speak to the men or the customers. He is bored by the money. When he inherits the first thing he will do is put a manager in. We do our best by the mill and by Charles by making sure that such a man is ready and waiting. Charles does not want to be at the mill. William wants nothing more. Why should not both of them lead the lives they wish? Both benefit? And let the mill thrive.'

Old Mr Bellman's views of the matter were unalterable and Paul would not be swayed. It was stalemate. In the end it was agreed that Charles would go off for the twelve months of travelling he had asked for, and that William would be invited to act as secretary to Paul for that year. At the end of which time . . .

Paul's father gave way because he saw the future as clear as a bell.

'When Charles comes back, he'll be ready for it. And when young William realises what's at stake, he'll soon take fright. All that work for a mill you can't call your own? He'll back off. Take my word for it!'

At the end of twelve months Charles, inspired by the palazzos and basilicas of Italy, refused to come home at all, and far from 'backing off', William was throwing himself into new projects and ventures and the Bellman mill was prospering as never before.

This had happened though:

Old Mr Bellman sneezed and then coughed. A summer cold, not uncommon, though it lingered and turned into something more serious. He had a fire lit in his bedroom on the first floor and spent the days with a rug over his knees, looking out over the fields where the rooks were coming down to jab at the earth with their stony beaks.

It was the maid who found him.

If in his last minutes he had reviewed his life – his unhappy marriage, his wife's infidelity, the revenge he took on her second son – and if at the last minute he had had a change of heart and realised that his domestic unhappiness was in part the result of his own harshness, then not a trace of any of this showed on his face. Rigid, glaring, set in a frown, his face was so much what it had been in life, that the maid spoke to him three times before she realised he was dead.

William was in London when it happened. A series of meetings with the India and General Company. 'Send me,' he had begged. 'They'll think I'm still green and it will put them off their guard.' He came back clutching a nice batch of orders to find that old Mr Bellman – he had never thought of him as Grandfather – was not only dead but in the ground.

'I'm sorry to hear it, Uncle.'

'Show me these orders.' Paul nodded. 'You've done well. These dates will dovetail nicely with the Portsmouth orders. Do you ever think of your father, Will?'

Will shook his head.

'You don't wonder where he is? Whether he is alive or dead?'

Will applied himself to the question, as though with effort he might find among his recollections some small overlooked instance of such curiosity.

He shook his head. 'Never.'

12

It came like this.

Dora Bellman felt tired. *That's unlike me*, she thought.

She took a bowl and went to pick blackberries. Perhaps the fresh air would stir her. In the distance, beyond the farmland, was the tenter-field: lengths of white cloth all in a row, and a few tiny stick men, moving between them. Not William; even at this distance she would know him. Was it a good drying day for them today? A strong breeze was stirring the treetops and the rooks were cawing in vulgar merriment as they roiled and tumbled on the high air currents.

The bowl was half full of fat berries and her fingertips were stained red when a vast fatigue came over her. The bowl fell; berries rolled on the ground. When her legs gave way, not wanting to fall onto the scattered fruit, she grasped at the hedgerow for support, but she slumped all the same, and scratched her hands. The blackberries bled into the fabric of her dress.

Astonished dismay: at spoiling her dress, at showing her calf, at dying.

Think of William . . . say a prayer . . .

First, though, she must rearrange her skirt . . .

Dora had time to rearrange her skirt.

It was the Misses Young who brought the news. Never before had there been a reason for them to come to the mill, and their appearance was so unexpected that only some out-of-the-ordinary occurrence could explain it. The possibilities were few, the look on their faces narrowed it down, and when they asked for William, the news was as good as out: Mr William's mother was dead.

But William did not know.

'Oh, William!' and 'William, dear!' exclaimed the Misses Young in sorry chorus, as they entered the room where he was.

William turned a surprised and half-amused face to them. The Misses Young. At the mill. Whatever next! In their funny matching dresses and their overdone hats, eyes wide and something unfathomable in the way they looked at him. For some reason the older Miss Young was clutching a white bowl stained with red. Had they come straight from their kitchen? How peculiar!

'How can I help you?' he prompted.

Two pairs of eyes fastened on him. Let him understand! Let him at least start to understand!

William was politely puzzled. Why were they goggling at him, as if they were waiting for something from him, when he was waiting for them?

Old Miss Young opened her mouth to speak, but the absoluteness of his ignorance made it hard to begin. Mutely she offered the bowl, like an explanation.

He was perplexed and did not take it.

It was Paul who understood. He recognised the terrible compassion that means only one thing and rose from his seat.

'Mrs Bellman,' he said.

Then the story was told. The Misses Young took turns in the telling, their voices fluttered and wavered, interrupted and overlapped, but the story emerged. A walk in the lanes – the wind getting up – such a wind, it nearly blew Susan's hat off – a shortcut home – turning the corner – something on the verge – Mrs Bellman! Poor Mrs Bellman! – and the blackberries – and this white bowl – look! – unbroken, miraculously unbroken.

William, like a bystander, witnessed his uncle receive the news. It seemed to him that the world had taken a wrong turning: it needed only a word or a gesture from him to set it on track again, but he was paralysed and his tongue was frozen and so, temporarily, he was unable to restore the world to what it ought to be.

Only when old Miss Young turned to him with the bowl, so that he might see for himself, was his tongue released.

'Yes,' he agreed. 'I see. Not a crack in it.'

*

51

That evening, and for the next few days, Paul kept his nephew under his wing. He ceded to the Misses Young in their wish to be helpful, and it was clear that Will would not go cold or hungry or lack for clean shirts. Paul's job was to find occupations for Will. It was not difficult. Decisions had to be made: Wednesday or Thursday for the funeral? Eleven o'clock? Which hymns? Letters had to be written to Dora's brother at Nether Wychwood and other relatives. And then there were the visitors. Singers from the choir, workers from the mill, drinkers from the Red Lion, spinsters whose fences he had mended, men with whom he'd once had a game of cards, butchers, bakers, candlestick makers and the sisters of all these, and the daughters. In fact, Paul had not realised so many pretty girls lived in the town. Was there anyone that his nephew didn't know? A hundred hands wanted shaking, a hundred tongues expressed their condolences. *Thank you*, said William, and *Kind of you*, endlessly.

Between his uncle and the helpfulness of the Misses Young and all these other people, William was never alone, not for an hour, except to sleep. He went to bed with the distant, certain expectation that over-night the world would put itself right. He slept for long hours: endless, dreamless sleep, which did not refresh, and when he woke the world bewildered him by persisting in its wayward course. He felt weighed down and dreary. A fog settled between him and his own thoughts, and behind it, unformulated, unexamined, was this: *How long before things go back to normal?*

His mother was dead: he had seen the body; yet this knowledge refused to find a settled place in his mind. It came and went, surprised him every time he chanced upon it, and there were a million reasons not to believe it. His mother was dead, but look: here were her clothes and here her tea cups, here her Sunday hat on the shelf over the coat hook. His mother was dead, but hark: the garden gate! Any moment now she would come through the door

The feeling that it was all a charade persisted and on the morning of the funeral he was more than anything irritated that it had come to this. He dressed in his Sunday suit and laced his good shoes, but nothing altered his expectation that the next caller at the door would be his mother herself. *All dressed up on a Wednesday? Whatever's got into you all?* As the procession of men left for the church, inside the cottage the Misses Young were making tea so that the women could do their feminine mourning in domestic comfort. *She will be here by the time I get back*, he thought.

William had sung at a good many funerals. He knew the service well. All the same, today everything appeared false to him. He was in the front pew and not the choir stall. The church was not the church he knew but a stage: Reverend Porritt masquerading as himself, the coffin an ugly prop. It was unsettling. When Dora Bellman's name emerged, in slack mournfulness from Reverend Porritt's lips, Will wanted to give him a punch on the nose.

At the singing, Will's voice cracked.

Something in his chest was restless. It expanded painfully inside him, pressed against his heart, compressed his lungs.

What on earth was the matter with him?

After a few bars of croaking he reduced his effort to a mumble, and without his shepherding the communal voice strayed and wandered most painfully.

And now a new discomfort. He wanted to scratch the back of his neck. Below his hairline, that place under the collar, a vertebra near the top of the spine, the one where the bone marrow stirs when someone has their eye on you . . .

Will wanted to rub the back of his neck, and he wanted to turn and see who was staring at him. *Don't fidget in church!* He could hear his mother's voice speaking the words. Today was hardly the day to disobey. He repressed the urge.

How did he come to be here, anyway? How could such a thing – such a stupid thing – have come to pass?

He sighed, exasperated, and his hand twitched with the urge to rub his neck, but the thing that was pressing his lungs and squeezing his heart turned the sigh into a cry, and he felt Paul's arm around his shoulders. His uncle was still supporting him as they walked from the church and into the open air.

At the graveside, fingers of lucid September sun pointed at the coffin and at the pit. Had Reverend Porritt and the coffin really seemed so unreal a moment ago? Look at them now . . .

The thing in his chest had grown into his throat and he couldn't swallow. It had locked his jaw. It was pushing from behind his eyes . . .

Clusters of mourners stood around the grave: Dora's brother and nephews were there, and some cousins, her neighbours and friends, people who had liked and admired her, those who had gossiped, those who had listened to gossip and those who had not.

It was the smallest of movements that caught Will's eye. Someone at the back. Just a glimpse. There and gone again – the merest impression . . .

The man who had been staring at him in church! He knew it!

Will shifted his weight a little, swayed to the left, trying to get a view of him. Nothing. The fellow must have moved. He leant fractionally the other way. Between two mourners a sturdy shoulder was visible. Was that him? Or there, that edge of a cape? But in the mass of black, among all the downcast faces, it was impossible to distinguish one man from another.

Paul, taking the swaying for faintness, grasped his shoulder more firmly.

The thing inside was rattling William. He could not keep his arms still, his legs vibrated dangerously under him. He was cold in his stomach, cold down his spine, his ribcage was locked, his throat was blocked, he couldn't breathe.

He closed his eyes in a slow blink.

Nothing will ever be the same again, he thought.

When he opened his eyes it was to the glare of sunshine and tears. Was that someone signalling to him on the far side of the grave? Some gesture, it seemed to be. Exhorting him? Encouraging? Will blinked and squinted. A raised arm, he thought. The wide drape of a black cloak, splayed fingers emerging from the cuff. Something glittering. Dazzled, he could look no longer. His eyes sought respite in the darkness of the grave. At the edge of his vision he was aware of the great sweep of the cloak, as it blacked out the sky and the sun, the mourners, everyone and everything, and last, William himself.

54

Later. By some tacit arrangement, it was his friends from the mill who had the care of him for the night. Will's mind was dull and blank already so he didn't see what help cider and whisky could be to him, but others knew better and they took him to the Red Lion. After three days of sympathetic ironing from the Misses Young, he welcomed the rougher way in which the men from the mill administered their consolation. There was a jug of cider on the table, and no sooner was it empty than it was filled. Fred from the bakery dropped in to clasp him in his arms and nearly lifted him off the ground. 'She was a good 'un, your ma. Can't stay. Must get home. Got a little 'un now, you know?' Hamlin and Gambin the shearers came in especially to shake his hand; their words were inaudible above the hubbub of the inn, but the sense was clear enough. *Thank you*, Will said, *Kind of you*. A jolting blow on his shoulder was Rudge's leather hand dealing out robust sympathy. Greg the mute made a delicate display of compassion, fingertips and temples expressing fellow feeling in a mime that came closer to touching Will than anything else. Some left and others came, and every minute, Poll the landlady was there, refilling the cider jug, giving him a pat or a stroke as if he were a nice stray dog, taken in at the Red Lion to be the inn's pet. In the commotion around him, men were smiling, men were laughing. At the edge of Will's mouth a muscle twitched. Some raucous shouting burst out, someone accusing someone of exaggerating . . . Will listened as men leant in towards each other to recount lewd and improbable stories about respectable women. 'On us, eh?' Poll ruffled his hair maternally as she refilled the jug for the goodness knows how many'th time.

The current was strong, Will let himself be carried by it.

The cider bore his mind to a silent place far from all the hubbub. When he was restored to his senses, it was to discover himself bellowing the words of a vulgar song. Hoarse his voice was, a rusty croak.

Someone leant over his shoulder to place a whisky in front of him. 'See if that mends your voice.'

He felt slow. He lagged a few seconds behind everyone else. He organised some words and spoke them to the blacksmith's son he'd known once. 'Luke! Thank you. Not having one yourself?'

Luke pulled a face. 'Poll's only serving me for ready money now.' His hair was dulled with grease, his skin yellow and stringy. 'Can't blame her.' He shrugged. 'All right, are you? Saw you keel over up the churchyard this morning.'

'Oh. You were there, were you?'

'Dug the grave. I've covered her up, nice and cosy.' A grimace, black sticks of teeth in his gums. 'Well, you know. Best I could.'

What to say? 'Thank you. Kind of you.'

'She was all right, your mother.' His good eye drifted, either to a place where Will's mother was still opening her pantry for a hungry boy or to nowhere. 'Well, I'll be off. Nothing worse than watching men drink when you've got a thirst on, eh?'

'Let me get you something.' Will stumbled up, swaying.

'No need.' He opened his jacket and Will saw a bottle. Something noxious and cheap.

'It'll kill you, you know.'

A farewell salute, another flash of the black stubs. 'And if not that then something else!'

Poll refilled the cider. Laughter. An arm thrown across his shoulder. Singing. Poll patted him and refilled the cider. Someone vaguely familiar said, ''e's all right now, an't yer, me old mate?' Singing. Poll refilled the cider and stroked his shoulder. Singing. Someone put a hand on his two shoulders and gave him a slight shake, to see if he fell to pieces. He didn't. Laughter. Singing. Poll refilled the cider . . .

All was silent. Will opened his eyes. No one. He was lying on the settle under the window of the Red Lion; the grey blanket draped over him had slipped to the floor and he was chilly. Outside the sky was growing pale. He put his feet to the floor and stood up with a groan.

A door opened. Poll's head appeared, strands of crinkled hair sticking out from her nightcap. 'All right?'

He nodded.

'You off?'

Another nod.

'I'll have that blanket back, then.'

He crossed the room to give the blanket to her, kissed her. In her little bed she pulled her nightdress up. The next moment he was inside her and with a few thrusts it was done.

'There,' she said. 'Take a bit of bread to eat on the way. There's some on the shelf over the big barrel, out the back.'

Will followed the hedgerow home. He broke off a piece of bread, mashed it in his mouth, swallowed. Hungry, he ate another piece, and another, then vomited wetly into a ditch. *Good*, he thought. He expected something vile to emerge in the cascade of fermented apple, something rank and bloody, a clot of something decomposing, darkly foul and liverish. But there was only this golden stream of pippin juice, and a gob of sweet froth to spit out.

Then he felt something else in his gut. Hard and painful. This will be it. He opened his mouth again, but it was only a sharp-cornered belch – CRAA! – that emerged.

A rook in the branches of the elm looked down askance.

After an hour's sleep William went to the mill. He sweated the rest of the alcohol out with heavy work. Against the clamour and the shouting there was no room for thought. The next day he sat for thirteen hours in the office, motionless except for his fingers tapping ceaselessly at the abacus, and caught up a backlog of numberwork for the ledgers.

The mill had its own energy, its own rhythm, and a man could give himself up to it. As the wool was drawn by the shuttle, so he was drawn by the demand of the work itself. Like a piece of the machinery, a wheel turned by the force of the river, he did what was necessary. He never tired, he rarely faltered, he moved from one task to the next without a break. Sleep was easy: he never remembered putting his head on the pillow, and the moment the sun was up he was up and on his feet.

Between the mill and his bed he made sure there were as few hours as possible. Sometimes he played cards. He won a bit; he lost a bit.

Sometimes he went to the Red Lion. Once or twice he stayed on when everyone else had gone home. 'Don't go thinking you can make a habit of this,' Poll warned him. On Sundays he sang in the choir – his voice clear and effortless – and in the afternoon he went fishing a few times with Paul.

'Are the Misses Young still cooking and cleaning for you?'

'Yes.'

'Hmm.'

He knew what Paul meant. The Misses Young had hopes. Hopes had a habit of growing into expectations.

'I'll get a woman to come and clean for me. Someone to leave me a dinner ready.'

'Good idea,' Paul said.

In early advent, William broke a teapot. He wasn't even using it, had barely touched it in fact, yet it toppled and fell plumb to the flagstones as if some vengeful spirit was trapped inside and knew only this way out. He swept up the pieces and buried them, then a gulf opened beneath his heart and a fearful vertigo took hold of him.

It wasn't the first time. This one you could understand: his mother's teapot, a burial, reminders of a loss he preferred not to think about. But the feeling – a sinking diaphragm, nausea stirring, darkness gaining on him – came upon him at other times. He couldn't predict these crises. It might be an unexpected interruption that set it off or the gap between one task to the next; it might be waking too early and being alone in the dark.

It was a hard thing to put words to: sometimes he experienced it as a great void, a universal and eternal nullness. Watching other people – Paul, Ned, Fred and Jeannie – he came to believe that he was alone in seeing it. At other times the black mood seemed to him as a dark and menacing thing inside himself, and that was worse. Something putrid, monstrous, was poisoning his blood and his thoughts. He was ashamed of it and glad that others did not see.

It was a source of puzzlement to remember a time when the world had seemed an entirely benign sort of place. He had rarely been ill and never for long; he had never gone hungry; he had been met everywhere with smiles and friendship; his efforts had been rewarded, his failings largely forgiven. Though he had been a boy who knew how to get into trouble, he had the useful knack of being as good at getting out of it. What little there had been to frighten or pain him was left behind in the forgotten days of childhood: as a man he saw no reason to be afraid. Now some great hand had peeled back the kind surface of that fairy-tale world and shown him the chasm beneath his feet.

Still he was not defenceless. He had his triad of weapons: sleep, drink and work – the most powerful of them all.

William had never shirked at the mill. But now he filled every minute of the day with activity. He lived in fear of idleness, sought out tasks to fill every chink and every nook of his waking day, and if something was finished five minutes earlier than he'd allowed, he grew fretful. He learned to keep a list of small jobs to fill those dangerous spaces in his day. Accompanying Paul to a meeting with a haberdasher in Oxford, he stopped off in Turl Street to purchase a calfskin notebook for the express purpose of writing these lists. He kept it close by him: in the office it was always on his desk; on site at the mill or travelling it was to hand in his pocket. He slept with it by his bed, reached for it the moment he awoke. When the monster reached its claw for him, sometimes just the touch of the calfskin cover was enough to hold it at bay while he armoured himself with work.

They came and they went, these crises, and he covered up for himself as best he could. When one passed, leaving him short of breath, heart beating like the clappers, he hoped it would be the last.

Outwardly, within three months of the funeral William was the same man he had ever been: energetic, smiling, full of life. Only Paul, his closest observer, noticed the change that had come over him: he was perhaps working a bit too hard. Paul encouraged him to rest, take a book upriver, ride out to visit his mother's brother, go fishing. But William resisted solitude as he resisted leisure. On the surface he was all ebullience and activity. Inside, hidden even from himself, he proceeded through life as though he had learnt the ground beneath his feet was mined and at any step his footing might give way beneath him.

&

The juvenile rook has a fine black beak. By adulthood the beak is craggy grey. Moreover, where it meets the face, it is bordered with a pitted, warty excrescence that is – I don't mince my words – ugly. Some say it is an incomplete fairy-tale vengeance: the spell destined to turn him into a stone statue of himself touched only his beak before he flew out of range. In fact, it is more to do with survival. Any tool fresh from the forge will look fine. Use it for a few years to hack the soil, break bones, hammer sea creatures against rock, and see how handsome it looks then. The beak of the rook is ideally adapted for survival and a pretty beak soon turns ugly.

The rook is a skilled survivor. His ancestors are ancient and have inhabited the planet longer than humans. This you can tell from his singing voice: his cry is harsh and grating, made for a more ancient world that existed before the innovation of the pipe, the lute and the viol. Before music was invented he was taught to sing by the planet itself. He mimicked the great rumble of the sea, the fearsome eruption of volcanoes, the creaking of glaciers and the geological groaning as the world split apart in its agony and remade itself. This being the case, you can hardly be surprised that his song has not the sweet loveliness of the blackbird in your spring garden. (But if you ever get the chance, open your ears to a sky full of rooks. It is not beautiful; it is *magnificent*.)

Because of his many centuries of experience the rook is tough. He will fly through a heavy downpour and in high wind. He dances with lightning and when it thunders he is first to go out on the rampage. He soars blithely in oxygen-starved air over the mountain tops and without a care in the world flies over the desert. Plague and famine and battlefield are all familiar to the rook. He has seen it all before, and knows how to make the best of it. For a rook is comfortable pretty much anywhere. He goes where he pleases and, when he pleases, comes back. Laughing.

Temperature, altitude, danger . . . The things that form barriers to humans are not barriers to rooks. His horizons are broader. This is why it is the rook that accompanies departing souls through a thick fog of mystery to that place where no air is needed and drought really doesn't matter. Having deposited in that place the soul that your body has relinquished, he returns, via other worlds and feasts of unicorn tongue and dragon liver, to this one.

There are numerous collective nouns for rooks. In some parts people say a *clamour* of rooks.

13

The months passed after Dora Bellman's funeral. Then more months. When almost a year had gone by, to fill an empty Sunday afternoon, William rode the seven miles to Nether Wychwood where his mother's brother farmed. On the way he rehearsed a conversation he meant to have next week with the plate supplier over carriage terms: what objections was the man going to come up with, and what would he say to head them off? By the time he clattered into the courtyard of the square, stone farmhouse, he was satisfied that he had found the way to present the matter so that the man would be sensible of the benefits both to himself and to the mill. Good.

He had seen something of his uncle's farm and they were sitting down to good bread and butter and seed cake, when they heard the kitchen door open and feet come running in. A boy of six or seven, out of breath and urgent: 'Our best cow has fell in a ditch and we can't get 'er out. Can Mr Thomas come? Straight away, if you please, and I'm to ask politely but be sure to bring him.'

Will rose in the same instant as his uncle and they put their bread and butter back on the plate, with only the first bite taken.

It was a deep ditch, a foot of brown water at the bottom of it. The bank had collapsed, and no wonder, it was three-quarters stones. What little earth it contained was thin and flavourless; nothing had wanted to root in it and hold the bank together. Will cast his eye around to get the measure of the situation. A fence had been erected – after some earlier slide, presumably – but now a recent, second collapse had taken half the fence with it. The cow, wedged on her side by the bank on two sides and by the landslide on the other, flailed her one free foreleg, interfering considerably with the efforts to save her.

Two young men about Will's age were digging out the collapsed soil and geology; closer to the alarmed animal they had to work with their hands. An older man, standing in the ditch, patted the animal's flank soothingly. He was strongly built, cut short by the muddy water that hid his lower legs, and his fair hair was dark around his face where the sweat had run into it. 'We can't budge her,' he said. Man or cow, it was hard to judge which knew the greater anguish.

Will took off his jacket and clambered into the ditch. 'Clear the landslide enough to work something underneath her and lift her out? Is that it?'

'Only way, I reckon.'

Will turned to the boy. 'Got more shovels?' Off he ran again.

They laboured. For the first hour they were hindered by the cow herself, flailing her free foreleg constantly, unable to recognise the help she had. Once they had got the leg strapped down – a harness, adapted, did the trick – the cow complained but they made faster progress.

The boy returned with shovels. Next Will set him to work hammering at the broken fence, working the posts free, while the men first shovelled and later with their bare hands reached under the cow, into the cold muddy water, to clear debris and stones. They worked in silence, except that every once in a while the neighbour straightened his back with a grimace, rolled his shoulders and murmured to his animal. 'Don't you fret, my lovely,' he told her. 'All will be well. You'll see.'

A cluster of boys, scenting drama, appeared on the bank and were fascinated. 'Back!' they were ordered, and five minutes later, 'Back!' again. But curiosity got the better of them. Nearer and nearer they edged, until the ground beneath their feet threatened to crumble and bring all the men's efforts to naught.

Will muttered a suggestion to the owner of the cow, and the man nodded. 'Boys,' he said. 'Run up to my wife at the farm. Tell her what I want, and she'll give you the tools. I want the cellar door off its hinges and brought up here, quick as you can.'

A job! A door to be taken off its hinges! Off they went.

In the third hour they got the fence posts under the cow and a sturdy door made its way horizontally over the field on a dozen legs. Six men raised the cow, two per post. It was out of the question to bring her up into her home field: the bank would only collapse under them. So they raised her to the wrong side, and laid the door across the ditch like a bridge, and the cow – 'See my lovely? Didn't I tell you so?' – when she had found her legs, needed little encouragement to cross it and return to her own field.

She looked about her with a surprised air, then put her nose to the grass and began to eat.

'She looks right as rain, to me,' Will's uncle said.

The men blew out their cheeks and arched their backs.

'Will, this is Thom Weston. Thom, my nephew Will.'

'Pleased to meet you.'

Hands were too wet and dirty to want shaking, and after what had passed, it was superfluous anyway.

'You'll come up home?' Thom Weston raised a closed hand and tilted it towards his mouth. An invitation.

At Thom Weston's farm a woman ran out to meet them. Nice, blue eyes with friendly creases round them, and not a bit of grey in her fair hair. A good-looking woman, only worried. 'Is she up?'

Yes, yes, she was up and out, she would go on all right now. No harm done only a lot of time lost and six thirsty men. Oh, and this is William Bellman, Geoffrey's nephew, over from Whittingford.

She smiled in relief and then at Will and her teeth were set straight but with gaps. It made you like her all the more.

'Rose!' she called into the house. 'Set the table. Bread and butter and get out the cured ham. And peel cake!'

In the kitchen the men stripped off their shirts to rub themselves dry and unlaced their sodden boots. Thom's wife stoked the fire and Thom was as good as his word and poured something warming generously into glasses.

'You are not riding back to Whittingford tonight, are you, Mr Bellman?' Thom's wife asked, looking at the wet garments that were draped all around the hearth. When she learned that he was, she called again. 'Rose! There is a young man here soaked from head to foot, who has to ride to Whittingford this evening. Before all the rest, take his boots. Let's see if we can't get them a bit dry before he goes.'

65

The chinking of plates and cutlery from the next room stopped and a girl appeared and leant against the doorframe. Fair hair, blue eyes, the spit of her mother.

'Shall we try something of Grandfather's on him, Rose? Would it fit?'

The girl's eyes measured him up. 'I think so.' She looked him in the eye. Her gaze was straight and steady. 'You'll not have to mind the smell of mothballs.'

'I don't mind.'

She turned to fetch the clothes.

'I'll bring them back next Sunday,' he told Mrs Weston.

From the next room, the girl looked over her shoulder at him and smiled. She had a nice gap between her teeth too.

Paul had told him yesterday everything he needed to know about the East India and General Company order for fine cloth, and today it was plain that not a word had gone in. Paul went over it a second time.

'Right,' William said. 'I understand it now,' and he settled down to the record book again.

'Anything wrong?' asked Paul.

'No.'

But William was out of kilter, Paul could tell. Something had unsettled him. Perhaps it was time to take him fishing again. In the peace of a Sunday afternoon perhaps his nephew would be coaxed into revealing what the trouble was. But when he proposed an afternoon on the river, Will looked alarmed. He couldn't go, he had something he had to do.

Well. He'd tried. Whatever it was, it would probably blow over. Anyway, even with only half his mind on the mill, William still did a fine job.

William's calfskin notebook went unopened for a week. There were no spare minutes in the day to be filled with tasks, because every minute was filled with Rose. Her eyes, her hair, her teeth – he could spend half an hour imagining running his tongue over those teeth. And then, the rest of her was exactly as he liked. She was well made, whether you looked at her from the front or behind or sideways on. After that first frank look, she had not lifted her eyes to his until they said goodbye. It was not coyness: she was too occupied to be coy, what with packing his boots with old rice to draw the wet out, slicing bread and ham, pouring tea and fetching cake, making wide-eyed faces at her baby sister, wagging a finger at the brothers who were out to steal each other's cake. But he knew by the way she didn't look at him that she was pleased he was looking at her.

As it turned out, the gap between Rose's teeth was every bit as pleasant to his tongue as he had imagined.

'Every time you smile, I see that gap and I have to kiss you,' he told her.

'That'll be a lot of kissing then,' she replied, 'because I smile all the time!' And it was true. She was smiling as she said it. He kissed her again.

How many Sundays had it been now? Three, including that first. Only a fortnight then, and a whole new world.

In a field, under a tree, they kissed and clung and petted. His fingers had found the way into her undergarments already, and hers into his. They were delighted with the thrills hands could give and receive, but yearned for more advanced pleasures.

'I want . . .' he said and, 'So do I,' said she.

The trouble was, having got her parents' cow out of a ditch he was indebted. That good woman, kind-hearted and so quick to think of his boots. Making her cross? It was unthinkable. He thought of the tender man who had spoken so soothingly to his terrified cow. No. It was a happy home, and William would not bring grief into it.

But, but, but. They couldn't go on as they were. Bliss, disaster, call it what you will, the thing was bound to happen sooner or later, they wouldn't be able to stop themselves. It was a predicament.

On Thursday, in the tenterfield, the solution came to him.

'Uncle Paul!'

Paul half rose in alarm as William burst in. 'What is it?' He prepared himself for news of an accident: someone burned or drowned, cloth scorched or torn or blown away.

'I must have the horse. I have to ride to Nether Wychwood.'

'Now? Why?'

'There's a girl. I have to marry her.'

'This minute? Surely not. Sit down.'

William didn't sit down. He didn't even remove his hand from the door handle, stood ready to be out the door the minute he had permission. But he did answer Paul's questions. Who are her people? And this Rose, what does she do all day? Why is it this girl that you must marry?

They rode to Nether Wychwood together. Paul saw that the Westons were good people. The Westons liked what they saw of Paul. Will and Rose sat palely on the settle, hand in anxious hand. The date was set for a fortnight's time.

14

The hopes of the Misses Young that had never matured into expectations, now died. Poll ruffled William's hair like a pet dog when Ned took him for a last bachelors' drink in the Red Lion. 'Nice girl, is she?' and on learning the answer, 'That's all right then.' The spinsters teased relentlessly until they made William blush, for once he was wed, they would never be able to tease him again. And everywhere he went in the mill, men shook his hand and offered congratulations or jovial warnings. Mute Greg presented him with a pair of figures, a bride and groom, that he had twisted himself out of straw.

William met Fred and Jeannie arm in arm in the high street, she buxom as a hen, he grown fat on bread and contentment: 'Good news, William. It's a sweet life!'

'And this is from Charles,' Paul said. It was a letter congratulating him, and letting him know that he was sending a gift for William and his new wife: a painting of Venice, to put on their wall.

And now, walking home after midnight, the night before his wedding day, he failed to see a form hunched low against a wall in the dark. The first he knew of it was when his foot caught and he went flying, hands out to save himself from a fall. The thing he had tripped over sprawled and grunted and something sounded: glass, a bottle tipping over.

'Luke? Is that you, Luke?'

'Who's that?'

'It's Will Bellman.'

The figure in the dark groped for something, there a tiny chinking noise and a murmur of satisfaction. The bottle was not broken, then. The smell of drink was strong off him and William was not certain that Luke knew who he was, nor whether he knew someone was there at all. He put a hand on Luke's shoulder – he was even

69

thinner than he had been as a child, if that were possible – and shook gently.

'Luke? You all right? What are you up to these days?'

There was a long silence, long enough for Will to think the drink had put him to sleep, before Luke came to himself and spoke.

'I remember . . .' Words failing him, Luke resorted to an impoverished pantomime with his shaking hands. Spitting in his palm – well, that was what it looked like – and fingertip meeting thumb with drunken delicacy, and a gesture, fine, stroking, meaningless. Luke expelled a few more syllables – catapult, it sounded like that, anyway – and chuckled in pleasure.

William waited but there was no explanation.

'I'm getting married tomorrow,' he said.

There was no sign that Luke had heard him. After another silence, William made up his mind to go, but Luke's voice came again: 'D'you remember? I remember . . .'

William turned. He walked home for his last night alone in his bed.

I am getting married tomorrow, he told the house as he entered it. I am getting married tomorrow, he told the candle, snuffing it out. He laid down his head and whispered I am getting married tomorrow to the pillow. And then, in the moment before he fell asleep, the thought came to him of a drunken night in the Red Lion: *I've covered her up, nice and cosy.*

But it didn't keep him awake. He was getting married tomorrow.

15

William Bellman no longer drank at the Red Lion. He played no more games of cards behind the fulling stocks. He had paid his debts, settled his slate. That part of life was over. At the age of twenty-six the young man had a regular income, health and the liking and respect of his fellow men. After five years of marriage, he had discovered more reasons to be in love with his wife than he knew on the day he married her, and when they argued they did it rapidly, effectively and made it up with good hearts. His daughter Dora was a healthy child, curious and quick to learn, and his baby boy, who in good Bellman tradition they had just named Paul, laughed at everything and grew strong.

Life was good to William Bellman. Even those who did not know him but only saw him in the street could not help but be struck by the impression he gave of himself: here is a man who is healthy, happy and successful said his gait, and even his clothes, from his hat to his boots, seemed to have a word to add about the positive qualities of their bearer.

William was not unaware of his good fortune, but being more given to action than contemplation, he enjoyed his happiness rather more than he thought about it.

Others were not so lucky.

There came a hammering at the cottage door early one winter's morning. William opened the door and snow blew in. It was Mute Greg, snow on his shoulders, shivering and with urgency in his eyes.

Was it a fire? Had there been a break-in? Were the machines wrecked? It could not be unrest among the workers: he'd have known. Other millers then, jealousy . . .

William piled his clothes on over his nightshirt and ran with Mute Greg back to the mill. When he was heading towards the buildings,

Greg took his arm and tugged. Not that way. He drew a circle with his hand in the cold air: the wheel.

There was no separation between the sky and the land. There was only snow. The only things not white were the oaks. In the upper branches were black clots of twigs, last year's rooks' nests. A few millhands awaited them. These were the men with no homes, who slept in the mill, huddled around the stove that heated the warming plates for the first part of the night. If it was bitter cold they moved then to the seg barrels, put up with the foulness of the stink for the fermenting heat.

William stood by them and they considered the wheel. Something was impeding its movement. A branch, most likely. Perhaps the weight of snow had made it fall. Or else Farrah's timber stack had toppled and a log had rolled into the water, been carried downriver, jammed the wheel. Or some desperate soul had stolen a barrel of beer and after drinking the contents had dumped the barrel in the river for fear of discovery.

Will took off his coat and jacket. Hesitation could only make it worse. He lowered himself in a single shocking moment into the water, and only frowned at its bitter sting. Quickly, before the cold could stun him absolutely, he waded to the wheel and peered at the dark shape through the splash and spume, trying to get a sense of its length and its lay. He must get a firm grasp on it in the first moment, before his hands were too cold to know what they were doing. He plunged his arms in to the shoulder, took hold and heaved.

The first effort achieved a minuscule shifting. At the second the obstacle came free. A hand flailed out of the water and gave William a thump on the mouth. For a second William thought it was his own fist, benumbed by the cold. He dragged the waterlogged cadaver to the edge; the men grasped the drowned man by his clothing, while Greg reached out a hand to Bellman. They came out of the water together, the dead man and the living, icy water streaming off both their bodies.

'What's going on?' It was Paul, come running, alerted by a messenger. 'Good lord! Who is it? Anyone know?' And then, more urgently,

'Get William home, quick, before he freezes to death. Get him dry. Get him warm.'

William felt a fire inside him. He could not carry his own weight, needed a man each side of him, his arms across their shoulders, and supported like that he could just manage to put one foot in front of the other.

Behind him, they rolled the body over.

'One of the Smith boys,' somebody said. 'Better send to the forge and tell his brothers.'

'They won't want to know. He never had much to do with them. Nor anybody.'

'He'll have been dead drunk and fallen in. That's what it is.'

Paul spoke. 'He dug the graves, didn't he? Poor fellow.'

William turned to look over his shoulder.

On the snow, a flare of brightness. Copper hair, washed clean by the Windrush.

An urgent rook in the treetops cawed a stony message that only the dead man heard.

Rose stripped William, rubbed him dry and draped blankets over him. She stoked up the fire. She boiled water and he drank honey water fortified with liquor. She heated more water for the tub, and he sat waist deep in it, while she poured bucket after bucket of hot water over his shoulders. She dried him again, dressed him in more layers of clothing than he knew he had. She dragged the armchair close to the fire and sat him in it.

First he was hot, then he was very, very cold.

The baby slept, but Dora, made curious by the unusual activity, got in the way. Rose scolded her, sent her away. He heard his daughter weeping.

'Let her come,' he said.

The child climbed onto his lap, and his painful fingers managed to wrap his blanket around her. Enchanted by the novelty of the snow and having her father at home by day, Dora rested quietly against him. He felt her breathing grow steady and regular. The solid weight of her against his thighs and belly. How warm she was!

William felt his eyes close. His body was paralysed by weariness, and as he approached the border of sleep, memory rose up in his unguarded mind: Luke at the Red Lion: *She was all right, your mother.* Some other time, late at night, in the street: *'D'you remember?'*

Unease brought William suddenly awake. At the moment of opening his eyes he registered a perception of something: a momentary darkening. Something had been there at the window, blocking the light. He had seen it – or if not seen then glimpsed. A dark figure, looking in at him. He stared in alarm at the window. There was no one there. Only a white landscape, broken only by the oak trees, stretching their black branches across the white sky. To get up and peer out would mean waking Dora and, in any case, his limbs were slow with sleep.

Dora shifted slightly in his lap.

Looking down, he met his daughter's steady, sleepy gaze. Gravely she raised her hand and he felt the mysterious touch of her fingertips drawing down his eyelids. Sweet child! His heart returned to its proper rhythm. How good it was to be warm. He could hear the fire crackling and billowing, smell the fragrance of something good in the kitchen.

He settled into his cushions and into the certainty that whatever the woes and troubles that beset other people, he, William Bellman, was immune.

There had been rooks once, in the oaks by the cottage, he remembered as he drifted into sleep. All through his childhood they had woken him with their cawing. All winter long the old nests were visible, like the ones by the wheel this morning. But they were gone now. Quite gone.

Luke was buried. His family did not care enough to dig into their pockets for their dead brother, so it was Paul who came to an arrangement with Reverend Porritt. 'Someone must do something for the poor fellow,' he said. William being in bed with a chill after his immersion,

Paul thought he would be the only one to attend; he was surprised to see that the young baker was also there.

After it was done and the gravedigger had been lowered into a grave of his own, Paul and Fred Armstrong shook hands.

'I hear it was William who pulled him out,' Fred said.

'It was.'

'Will you mention it, perhaps, when you write to your son in Italy?'

Paul was curious. 'Did they know each other?'

Fred hesitated, remembering a particular day in the fields. 'Perhaps not. Not really. We were just children.'

16

'I wonder whether we should put some ears in the inns on the Stroud Road?' William asked.

He might easily have used a more authoritative mode of speech. 'Let's send out the spies,' or, 'We must find out what the Stroud millers are up to,' but instead he 'wondered whether' and thus submitted his idea to Paul for approval.

Paul was touched by this verbal tentativeness. His nephew knew as well as he did that in knowledge, understanding and business sense they were on an equal footing. Ownership was another matter, of course. On those rare occasions when William and Paul disagreed, it was ownership that won the day. 'It's your mill, Uncle,' William would say, palms up, easy smile. But it wasn't often that he went against any idea of William's. These days, when his own judgement was at odds with William's, it was himself that Paul was inclined to overrule.

Nine years ago he had made William his secretary, and in those nine years the mill had gone from strength to strength. The books were full of orders. The millhands were efficient and orderly. Profits had risen and continued to rise. They were investing in new machinery, investigating ways of boosting the steam power, expanding. He couldn't have achieved it alone. Now, if William was concerned that the Stroud millers might be poaching hands, it must be with good reason.

'You know the right ears to send?'

'I have someone in mind.'

'Put them on it.'

William glanced at the clock. It was five o'clock. 'I'll arrange it on my way home.'

And William was happy at home too. Long gone the days when the young man worked late at the mill, squinting at the ledgers till it was too dark to see. He had another life now.

'What are your plans for Sunday, Will? Bring Rose and the children for lunch. It will be good to have some life in the house.'

'We'll come,' said William. 'See you tomorrow.'

Paul could have wished that William were his son. He might have looked at Dora and the two boys and wished they were his grandchildren. But he was careful with his desires. Wiser than his father, he knew that Charles would never marry, never return to Whittingford. No matter what reports reached his ears of Charles's life in Italy, he would always love him. Better for Charles that the gossip was in a foreign tongue and whispered by strangers who had not known him as a child. Paul Bellman loved his son and his nephew, but what he admitted privately was this: loving William was a much more straightforward matter.

After supper, William had Paul and baby Phil on his lap and Dora was leaning on his arm. They were playing with a puzzle, three carved bits of ash that could, with a bit of cleverness, be made to interlink. William was amusing his boys by being deliberately clumsy and failing to connect the pieces.

It was Rose who answered the door. A girl, Dora's age, out of breath, in the rain. 'My mother says, can Mr William come?'

'It's Mary, isn't it? Mrs Lane's girl?'

Rose went to William. 'You are wanted. At your uncle's house.' She brought his coat, frowning. 'I wonder what it can be?'

William did not seem concerned.

Perhaps it was nothing.

At the Mill House Paul's housekeeper was full of words. Too many, too fast and in the wrong order. Something that had been done as soon as possible, but yet was too late, too late. William was still failing to make of sense of it when she opened the study door and there was Paul, at his desk, back to the door.

'What is it then, Uncle?' he asked.

A gasp came from Mrs Lane's throat and she stopped in her tracks. Will stared at her.

'But he is dead,' she said. 'I have just been telling you. He is dead.'

He shook his head, half laughed. 'No, I was with him only two hours ago. He was perfectly all right.'

'That's right,' said Mrs Lane. Two hours ago Mr Bellman had come home from the mill, perfectly all right. And now he was dead. So quietly!

She attempted to usher him into the room, to look, to see. William would not be drawn.

'Mrs Meade will come for the laying out, but he must be got upstairs. Do you think we can manage it? The two of us?'

Paul's back was very still. William could see it now, something unnatural in the sit of him. He was not held upright from the inside, by his own power. Gravity's hold on him was delicately poised and death had come so gently to him that he had not slumped forward or back or to the left or right, but downwards only. A mere hand on that shoulder would be enough to destroy the balance and he would topple . . .

William sought something to steady himself, something to grip on to. He found it: a list of tasks.

'I will fetch men to move him. I will get word to Mrs Meade and to the vicar. I will write to Charles.'

Better now. The dizziness had receded.

'You look very pale, Mrs Lane. You have had a shock. I will have the housemaid make you a cup of tea. You are to sit down, until the others come.'

He left the room, turned on his heels to come back in.

'Where is the key?'

'The key?'

'To the mill?'

'Why . . . In his pocket, I suppose.'

William eyed Paul's tweed jacket. He could not touch it. He could not.

'The pocket of his overcoat, in the cupboard in the hall.'

So that was all right, then.

William instructed the housemaid to make tea, retrieved the key and left.

A gang of ragged rooks flew airily overhead, talking philosophy and laughing.

William went first to the clerk's house. There he raised Ned and his brother and sent them to his uncle's house. On hearing the news, Ned's mother offered to go to Mrs Meade's house and he accepted her kindness. He left a message at the vicarage door for Reverend Porritt to go to Mill House as soon as he returned. When these things were done, he ran to the mill. He had never unlocked the main gate before; he did it now.

In his uncle's office he looked out Charles's address and wrote a plain, informative letter to his cousin. He roused Mute Greg from his bed alongside the donkey and put the envelope into his hands. 'Take this to Robbins. It must go now, tonight, without delay.'

Next he looked through the charts and lists pinned to the wall, outlining the orders and productivity needed in the coming weeks. He went into the side room, and set his own schedule alongside his uncle's diary. Obviously his uncle's work would fall to him. It would be more time-efficient to take over his uncle's diary than to transfer the notes to his own papers. Those of his own jobs that could not be delegated he added to his uncle's workload, his own quick and jagged hand squeezed between his uncle's neater notes.

And the rest of his work? To whom would he delegate? He thought rapidly, listed the men it would be most important to have around him, the ones who knew his mind best, the ones he could rely on. He worked intently and with method. What was urgent? What might be left for a later time? What must be cancelled, postponed, rearranged? He made lists, notes, clipped them together in careful order.

William lost track of time, his mind engaged in the toing and froing between the overall business of running a mill and the detail to which it all comes down in the end. He was so absorbed that the hours were like minutes. His uncle's solicitor needed to know what had occurred.

The mill's local suppliers and customers should hear from William himself and be reassured immediately that everything was in hand, rather than chance upon the news and be plunged into uncertainty. The vicar: better the funeral be Wednesday. No need to give any reason. Was it seemly to organise a man's funeral in relation to the smooth running of a mill? Probably not. Yet for a vicar one weekday must surely be the same as any other. William couldn't see what harm it did to organise things in such a way as to minimise disruption.

Mute Greg returned. William gave him the dozen letters he had written, 'Now these, Greg. Quick as you can.'

William worked without recognising the case that came from losing himself in a project like this. His mind moved with satisfying smoothness from one detail to another, prioritising, organising, planning, deciding, instructing, calculating.

When he emerged from this state of absorbed concentration, it was early dawn. He went to rouse the sleepers at the stove in the pressing house and gave his instructions. 'Wait at the gate, and when these men arrive' – he named them: Crace, Rudge, a handful of others – 'send them straight to me.'

By seven o'clock the men were all present in his office. William could see from their faces that word was already out. He presented the fact of his uncle's demise, and the men presented their condolences. It was so unexpected; Mr Paul was a good man; God works in mysterious ways; only yesterday he had seemed well, etc. etc.

When everything had been said about Paul that needed to be, William suggested that the mill's work ought to be disrupted as little as possible by the unhappy event and indicated to each man what he had in mind to ensure continuity. 'Yes,' each one said, 'that should do it.'

'And you are my key men now,' he told them. 'I need your help to keep the hands steady and the work progressing smoothly through this period. It is only natural for the men to worry. Change always brings worry. But I know that there is no need for doubt or uncertainty. Your job is to convey that to the men in such a way that they feel the truth of it. Do you think you can do that?'

80

They looked at him. He was steady, confident, reliable. It was impossible to imagine anything going wrong.

'Yes, Mr William,' they nodded. 'Yes, Mr Bellman, sir.'

17

It was Wednesday. The day of the funeral. William was irritated. Since the death he had spent the best part of his time at the mill, planning and ordering and problem-solving. He had slept for a few hours at most. There was so much still to do.

What was a funeral? Only sitting and standing and singing and praying. Any fool could do it. His efficient working mind proposed delegating it a hundred times, and he regretted that he could not accept the idea. But it would not do. Someone must lead the mourning, someone must show himself in public, visibly, as the new Mr Bellman of the mill. As likely as not, Charles had not even received the letter yet, and even if he could have made the distance in the time, his presence would not have the same effect. It could only be Mr William, Bellman the nephew. It must be done.

After five good morning hours at the mill William raced home to change. The tub of water in front of the fire was cooling for it had been waiting for him this last hour and Rose, who had put out his best suit and a freshly laundered shirt, was vexed. But on the day of a funeral you do not grumble at the chief mourner.

When he was almost ready, she stood in front of him to retie the cravat his hasty fingers had rumpled. He was taut with tension, his impatience was palpable.

'You're overdoing things.' She looked at him for a few long seconds. He was thinking of something else, appeared scarcely to see her.

'Come home after the funeral. Are you listening to me?'

'Of course.'

'Good. Now, go. You'll be late.'

He was late – almost. Anxious faces were looking out for him. 'Here he is!' said Mrs Lane, relieved and cross. He took his place in the line of mourners and they proceeded to church.

During the service William rose and sat and knelt with the congregation, murmured amen where he had to and sang. His voice did its job, gathered and organised the voices of the mill workers in the congregation. He knew the songs by heart and all the while he was singing, he was thinking.

Stroud . . . Word had come. The ears he had planted in drinking places along the road to Stroud also had mouths, and the mouths had come whispering everything they knew to him. The Stroud millers had orders again. The hands they had laid off were welcome back, and they would match Bellman's wages. 'And they are tempted to go,' the mouth told him. 'At least, those that have family still over Stroud way.' William was disappointed but not surprised. If they went, it would mean losing some good men.

The simple answer was to offer more money. But what was to stop the Stroud millers matching his higher wages? It was easy to escalate salaries, a lot harder to rein them in again. There had to be a better way. He would think of one.

The strain of overwork and lack of sleep had put bags under William's eyes and taken the colour from his cheeks. His eyes were bloodshot. If he had a half-absent air about him all through the funeral, it passed quite naturally for grief.

Coming out of the church a knot of mourners formed in front of William. He was deep in thought, blundered, and in the minor collision that followed, someone turned. The face was instantly familiar. Head on one side, curious, the man gave William a stare: frank, ironic, questioning. William couldn't quite place him. It was a bit unsettling.

At the Mill House, William drank a glass or two with Paul's friends and neighbours and the most senior men from the mill.

'Who was the fellow at the funeral?' he asked Ned. 'I recognised him but can't put a name to him.'

'What did he look like?'

William opened his mouth to describe him, but was too tired to call the man's features to mind properly.

'He's not here?' Ned asked.

'No.'

'You are more familiar with Mr Bellman's friends than I am. If you don't know him it's hardly surprising that I don't.'

'I suppose not.'

William was among the first to leave the gathering. He gave his feet no conscious direction and, left to their own devices, they turned of their own accord towards the mill. They had made no promise to Rose. The mill was closed all afternoon as a mark of respect for Paul. It was an opportunity to get on with some paperwork in peace and quiet.

It was unusual for the mill to be still. William was used to the noise, the different machines, the shouting, the wheel, all with their own tone and rhythm, blending into a cacophony too familiar to be uncomfortable. It was strange on a weekday to hear the rooks cry overhead. He could hear the thumping of his own heart, the rush of blood in his veins. As he opened the door to his office, something black appeared to be perched on his desk. It seemed to rise, flapping, towards him.

William cried out and raised his hands to protect himself, but the thing receded.

It was only cloth. An open window, a draught he had made himself by opening the door, and a sample of fine black merino. Attached to it, in his uncle's hand, was a note: *Will – for Portsmouth? P.*

William reached to the ink and had already put pen to paper for an answer when he realised that his uncle was dead.

I have seen that man before, he thought. *He was at my mother's funeral.*

He had to grip the back of a chair to steady himself.

Many hours later William stood and left the office. The paperwork was untouched. He had sat all through the end of the afternoon and half the evening, not knowing what he did. His thoughts were as muddled as a barrowload of wool roving on its way to the spinning house. His chest, meanwhile, was overfull of beating heart and flighty breath and urgent jabbing sensations.

As he walked home, the sky that was losing its light seemed full of ill-defined menace. He wanted walls around him, a roof over his head and Rose's arms. He shrank from looking at the leafy canopies of the trees that rustled in the dark, and was relieved when he came to the door of the cottage.

'William Bellman, what has become of you? You gave me your word you would come home, and you have been at the mill for hours.'

Rose was too mindful of the sleeping children to shout, instead she hissed her anger. 'Have you forgotten you have a home? Have you given one thought to your children these last days? Have you once thought of me? Because we think of nothing but you, and this is how you repay us!'

Though she averted her face, hands plunged in a sink of water, he saw the gleam of tears on her cheeks.

He glanced at the table. It was late to be clearing the meal away.

'We *waited* for you. We *waited* though the children were hungry. We *waited* because you had been at the funeral and we wanted to *comfort* you!'

William sank to his knees in the corner of the kitchen. His fists rose to his eyes, the way his sons' did when they wept, but he did not weep. His shoulders shook, and the pain in his chest rose up and stabbed at the back of his throat, choking him, yet he could not weep.

He heard the soft placing of the plates Rose was washing, and then she was crouching beside him, drying her hands on a cloth. Her still-damp arms enfolded him and he felt her cheek resting on the top of his head.

'I'm sorry. The day of the funeral . . . He was a father to you, William. I'm so sorry.'

She fed him morsels of bread and cheese. She sliced late plums for him. She took him to bed where they made love with sudden intensity. Afterwards they fell instantly asleep in each other's arms.

The next morning William slipped out of the warm bed before dawn and went to the mill.

The mill lost not an hour in productivity. He did his uncle's job at the same time as continuing to do half of his own. Ned took on a good deal for him in the office, and he had Rudge and Crace and the others to do the rest. There were a few younger men he had noted: reliable,

85

intelligent, willing, and he let them know there were opportunities. The time it cost him to train them up to what he wanted was time he could ill afford. But it was an investment. In four to six months, he would reap the benefit as they grew into the roles he envisaged for them. And who else to teach them but him? A number of others he called and laid off. Shirkers, unreliable types, men you couldn't quite trust. If Stroud wanted men, let them first have the ones he selected for them . . .

Every day he made himself available to whoever wanted him. Essential that all should know this was not a captainless ship. Confidence was the essence of the matter. So all day long he made himself visible. He went wherever he was wanted. He answered questions, trivial and serious, brief and involved. He spoke to foremen, clerks, weavers, shearers, fullers, dyers, porters and spinsters. He never passed Mute Greg without a nod of the head and if he was near enough, the donkey received a reassuring pat. All must know the mill was in safe hands.

Only when the mill was quiet was there time to pore over the papers, to tally figures, check off orders, write letters. And when that was done, there were his uncle's personal finances to manage. He settled small debts out of his own pocket, saw that Mrs Lane had the housekeeping she needed, paid the gardener, spoke to the bank manager.

'How long will this go on?' Rose asked at the end of a week when William had worked seventeen hours a day every day. 'You'll wear yourself out.'

'Five more weeks,' he predicted.

'Really? As precise as that?'

He nodded. He'd worked it out.

Mind you, once this five-week period of stabilisation was over, he had other things in mind.

18

The man dismounting in the courtyard cut a curious figure in his foreign clothes and with his hesitant manner. From the office window William saw him hail one of the porters.

He doesn't even know his way, he thought.

A few minutes later Charles was at the office door.

'By the time the letter caught up with me . . . I came as soon as I could. Far too late, of course.'

William offered the conventional sentiments and Charles accepted them. 'I should offer you my condolences too,' Charles said. 'These last years you have been closer to your uncle than I ever was to him, though he was my father.' It was said without rancour, merely stated as a fact.

William offered his cousin a seat but Charles seemed reluctant to take it. He was tall and straight and well fed as ever; his muscles were the leisurely kind, William thought: his legs would be good for walking up hills to get a better view of the landscape. When William opened the ledger to show the mill's profits, Charles did not lay a finger on the pages, but clasped his soft, white hands firmly behind his back. He leant forward to show willing, not so much as to indicate any real interest. William pointed here and there – callused hands, dirt under his fingernails – setting out in layman's terms what had been done, was being done, to keep the mill productive.

'Yes,' said Charles. 'I see.' He failed to keep the tremor out of his voice. His eyes flickered over the tables of figures and the order records, and though William tried to be brief and use simple language, he knew Charles was seeing nothing, hearing nothing.

'The thing is,' he said, 'I've a few commitments in Venice . . .'

It had the sound of a rehearsed statement, something he'd been murmuring under his breath all the way from Italy. It must have

87

sounded all right, in his head, in carriages and on horseback and on the sea. The magic words that would get him out of his difficulties. William supposed it was only now, pronouncing the words in this office, that Charles heard how weak they seemed.

The cousins looked at each other.

'There's no need for you to stay if you don't want to,' William said. 'Everything's under control. I can keep you informed in Italy or wherever. No need to turn your life upside down.'

'No, no . . . So long as that's all right with you.'

William nodded. 'I'll take a salary.' He named a figure. 'Here are the profit figures for the last five years. We'll divide that fifty-fifty. I'd like to reinvest more in future than we have done lately, but I'm happy to do that out of my share of the profit and take any increase in profit in future years over and above the present level. I can guarantee you an income of . . .' He jotted the figure down, and passed it over. 'What do you think?'

The sum was much more than the allowance Charles had received from his father. It was more than he needed. He would be able to live exactly as he chose.

'That sounds . . .'

He tried to remember the kind of thing his father would have said, with his judicious and extensive language for talking about money and business, but he couldn't. Charles could discuss poetry and history and Louis XV furniture, and he could do this in English, Italian or French, but the plain English of business negotiation was quite alien to him. So he nodded.

The cousins shook hands.

Charles's face started to return to its normal colour. He was saved. William had saved him.

For five minutes Charles waited while William wrote out the agreement they had just reached. Relieved of the fear that he might have to spend the rest of his life imprisoned in it, Charles looked at the office as an outsider looks at another man's place of work, admiring the industrious impression it gave but understanding nothing. It was clear that William knew what he was doing. Twice someone knocked at the door with an impenetrable question, and each time William dealt with it in half a dozen words that meant nothing to Charles. Twice he made a note to himself in a smart calfskin notebook, then returned to drafting his contract without a hesitation.

The pen Charles signed with was the only item he touched all the while he was at the mill. William signed in turn and the two men shook hands again.

'Thank you,' Charles couldn't help saying. 'Now, what is this?'

A pencil outline in a childish hand, on the free page of William's notebook. A donkey. William smiled. 'My daughter amuses herself making pictures in my notebook, if she can't find anything else to draw on.'

Charles showed more interest in the donkey picture than he had in anything else since he had arrived. He flicked back in the book and found other sketches: a flower, a gate, a cat. 'How old is she?' he wanted to know. 'Does she have lessons?'

William realised that his cousin was a man of conversation. He was not used to work, to the clock, to the sense of measuring the hours ahead and dividing them according to the number of tasks to be completed within them.

'Call in at the house,' he suggested. 'Come today and eat with us. Dora will be pleased to tell you how old she is. If you are very good she will draw your portrait.'

When his cousin was gone, William took up his pen and fresh paper with great satisfaction. There was a project that had been close to his heart for a long time. Paul, aware of the level of investment required, had been cautious of the risk. William had read up on hydraulics. He knew the principles inside out, and enough of the detail to have been able to make some preliminary sketches himself. He had assessed the terrain and researched the experts in the field. With the right man, the risk was negligible – and he knew which was the right man. All the while the situation with Charles had been unresolved he had been unable to act. But now!

He wrote to the engineer, lost himself in the pleasure of making explanatory sketches. Several hours passed.

He looked at the clock. Supper time. He ought to go home.

On the other hand, it was the ideal moment to find Turner at his farmhouse and make him an offer for that bit of land that he couldn't refuse.

19

Charles found his cousin's wife to be a charming, capable person; just the wife a man such as his cousin needed. The children were lively, happy, curious souls. He sat in the small living room that he remembered from his childhood. His grandmother had not been pleased by his visits to his cousin's home, but his father had not discouraged it. Memories of his aunt, William's mother, came to mind, and he told some little stories about her.

Rose saw that her husband's cousin was surprised by the rapt attention these anecdotes aroused. 'We are learning more from you in a few minutes than my husband has told us in years,' she explained. 'Will you stay and eat with us? Dora will show you her drawings while I am cooking.'

It was light and there was warmth in the air. Charles sat in the garden with the young artist at work. She showed him page after page of sketches, each one just a few broken lines, interrupted, aborted, incomplete, and yet, to Charles's eye at least, distinctly avian.

Dora flicked through quickly, creasing the pages in her dissatisfaction.

'Careful.' He put out a hand to halt her. 'What's this?'

'A rook. He comes into the garden, over there. I see him from my window.'

Charles drew the book nearer to him. There were faults. No one had taught the child the correct way to hold a pencil and she applied too much pressure on the paper. Her efforts to draw feathers were naive. The bird had no eyes. Yet it was distinctly corvid. The claw grip on the branch, the angle of the legs, the balance and weight of the body were all there. There was enough clarity to convince, despite the inexperience.

'This bit is wrong,' she was saying, 'and this, here,' indicating with her pencil the very weaknesses he had seen for himself. Well, it showed promise that she knew where her failings were. She had an eye.

Charles knew where his failings were. There was the great one. The one that exiled him and brought him joy and which he could not bring himself to hate. And all the smaller ones, among which was his failure to be a great painter. Someone had told him once that the desire to do something well is a good indicator of talent. In his case he had found this not to be true. He was no artist. He loved it, he was a good judge of art, but his own efforts were feeble, no matter how strong the desire. He knew how to look at the world and he could conceive the work of art that would convey what he saw, but he had not the ability to execute it. At best he might have made a good teacher. A man of means does not teach girls to paint, though. It would be entirely ridiculous. What remained for him then was to be what he was: a collector. By buying art he enabled others, more talented than himself, to live and thus to paint. He lived at one remove from his passion, but he was largely reconciled to it.

Perhaps Dora had what he lacked. She was unschooled and haphazard in her approach but she was observant, her hand was accurate, she was unafraid of the paper.

'Look.' He took up a pencil and showed her how he held it. 'Then you can do this . . . and this . . .'

She took the pencil from his fingers and made her own attempt.

'I see. Like this.'

'That's it.'

And now, called out of nowhere by his twin on paper, the rook himself appeared, losing altitude rather gracelessly, but landing with a certain aplomb nonetheless. Charles was amused and moved to see Dora's face grow serious as she was absorbed in her observation. She watched closely as the bird pecked about inquisitively in the roots of the lawn, quite fearless of its human companions.

She did not attempt to draw, but only watched until, having exhausted its curiosity, the bird casually flapped and rose with muscular power into the air. Then she put pencil to paper.

The rook appeared anew on a fresh white page. He noticed that she had already assimilated the new way of holding the pencil, and you could see the improvements in the greater freedom of her line. When she had done all she could, she put her head on one side to consider her effort. 'It's better, isn't it? The way to draw a bird,' she explained as she passed the drawing to him, 'is to begin by looking really hard. Then, after it has flown away, you still have it, in your mind's eye.'

'A very good method it is, too.'

'Are you going back to Italy tomorrow?'

'I am.'

She turned her face fully to him and gave him a long and serious stare.

'Are you fixing me in your mind's eye?'

'Before you fly away.' She nodded. 'There. I've got you now.'

20

On the morning of his departure, Charles met his father's solicitor.

'I'll not be staying in England. I have commitments abroad,' Charles told him. 'William Bellman and I have come to terms over the management of the mill.'

He passed a copy of the contract he had made with William to the solicitor, who read. Coming to the part about William's salary, he put his hand to his chin and smoothed his beard. 'Generous salary. Still,' glancing at Charles, 'he's a capable man. You wouldn't want to lose him to a competitor.'

Charles's heart leapt. The thought hadn't occurred to him.

The solicitor read on. 'Fifty-fifty profit share . . .' He frowned.

'Yes?'

'Unusual.'

Charles was hardly in a position to judge.

'And your cousin will be making future investment in the mill, but will take any additional profit resulting. Unorthodox . . .'

Charles was considering what it would mean if William went to manage a competitor's mill. 'He is my cousin. We shouldn't overlook the family connection.' He half smiled to himself. That is how his father would have put it.

The solicitor reflected. 'Your uncle had a lot of faith in William Bellman. That's clear enough in the agreement that was signed when he made him secretary. Of course, if you were minded to reconsider the profit-sharing it would be an easy enough matter to review the contract with Mr Bellman. It sounds as if it were concluded in something of a hurry, and you had made that long journey and were doubtless still reeling from the news of your father's demise. If in the light of day you thought better of that paragraph, one might exert pressure on Mr Bellman to redraft . . .'

Exert pressure? On William? Charles baulked. In any case, he wanted to be in Oxford by three, a driver was waiting to take him to the coast for tomorrow's crossing.

'The contract is entirely to my liking.'

At the new note in Charles's voice the solicitor looked up.

'Well . . .' So that was it. Charles had got what he wanted by this contract. And whatever that something was, he wasn't going to let go of it. So be it. He hadn't been looking forward to wrangling with William Bellman in any case.

Talking it over with himself later the solicitor found that he was reassuring himself he had acted in his client's best interest. 'It's not as if it's going to be much, is it? Profits over and above the current level . . .' He shook his head. The mill was already running at full tilt. How much more profit could there possibly be?

Charles found himself ready to leave earlier than planned. The coach was there, why wait? He was not sorry to go. Italy was home now. The person he loved was there. He did not wish for anything here, neither the mill nor the house. He was glad to say goodbye to them both. All the same, it was curious to think that he need never come back now.

As it travelled out of Whittingford, the coach took him along the road that led to his cousin's house. He had scarcely seen William. But he could see the mill was safe in his hands. William was safe in Rose's hands. There was much to admire in William's life, though heaven knew, Charles couldn't live it, not for a single day. He had spent one unexpectedly happy hour here though: drawing rooks with his cousin's daughter. He wished – the thought was shockingly new to his mind, desire and its impossibility dawning on him in the same moment – that he could be father to a girl like Dora, and sit on sunny afternoons teaching her to draw in a garden.

Remembering the rook they had drawn, he turned and looked the other way. Over the bank, across the field and to the group of oaks, thickly foliated now as they had been when he was ten. There had been a stone that had drawn a perfectly arched line in the sky, with William and his catapult at one end of it and a young rook on a branch

95

at the other. It had seemed miraculous then. It presented itself to him as a miracle even now. Fred had been there. And Luke, who was now dead, he recollected; his father had written to tell him. Luke it was who had opened out a wing and released from the blackness those dazzling colours. They still dazzled now, so much so that he had to wipe away a tear.

Arriving early in Oxford he had time to go to Turl Street and buy sketch books and pencils. He made arrangements for them to be delivered to Dora, then his onward coach was ready and he began the next stage of his journey.

21

William thought about the Stroud men, who were trying to buy his hands, the weavers and fullers and packers he had trained and shaped so they fitted his mill like a dream. Everyone thought the answer was money, but it wasn't. Why pay higher wages for the same output? He was reluctant to pay money to stand still. Money should work harder than that.

He had a better idea.

One fine morning, William was in the kitchen when the boy came to deliver the bread. 'Tell your father I want to see him, will you? He can call on me here, this afternoon.'

At three o'clock Fred Armstrong the baker arrived at William's kitchen door.

The two men shook hands.

There was a time Fred Armstrong had been a familiar of this cottage. In the days of their boyhood, he and William had eaten apples here, on this step, before he went away to school with his Bellman cousin.

Thinking of it now, with William here, shaking his hand like a stranger, the memory seemed improbable: Should he call the man William? Some years back they had drunk together sometimes at the Red Lion. And now his childhood friend was manager of the mill – and a stranger. Perhaps he should say Mr Bellman?

Fred looked around at the packing cases. 'You're moving, I hear.'

'That's right. We'll be in the Mill House from tomorrow.'

'Is the bread all right? If anything's wrong . . .'

'The bread is good. I'd like more of it.'

They stood leaning over the kitchen table and William set out his plan. So many hundred bread rolls delivered every morning to the mill, by a certain time.

Fred was perplexed.

'This is how much I'll pay you for it . . .' William scribbled the figure on a piece of paper. It was a large sum, large enough to cause Fred to raise his eyebrows. 'That's a unit price of . . .' and William added the price per roll.

The baker took off his hat and scratched his head. 'It can't be done.'

'Can't it?'

'It's not a question of price. I've only got two boys working for me, and it'd need another two ovens to make this quantity.'

'Sit down.' William nodded at a crate.

Side by side the mill manager and the baker bowed their heads over a sheet of figures. Whatever they might have been in the past, they were sound men of business now. They calculated reductions that could be made in the cost of the flour given the larger orders that would be placed, added in the cost of the two new ovens. How many extra workers would the baker need? The cost of that.

'I've a man who sees the lads who come to the mill asking for work. Anyone that looks suitable for a bakery job, he'll send them along.'

Line by line, figure by figure, the whole impossible deal was worked out, from the loan that William would make Fred for the new ovens, to the temporary return of Fred's father to the bakery to see them over the early days. Every difficulty was resolved, every obstacle levelled. And finally, the extra profit that Fred could expect to make '. . . in a week . . .' the pencil jotted '. . . a month . . .' another squiggle '. . . and per year . . .' The final flourish.

By the time the deal was concluded with a handshake, Fred had found his footing with William again.

'Your cousin Charles was in Whittingford a little while back?' Fred mentioned, making small talk before taking his leave.

William nodded.

'And as for Luke . . .'

William was inspecting a crate, ticking something off a list.

'It was you pulled him out of the mill race, I seem to remember?'

William nodded so vaguely, his eyes elsewhere, that it was clear he wasn't really listening.

98

'Well, if you're moving house tomorrow, you'll be busy.' He knew what it was like. He was a busy man too.

They shook hands again and Fred went home.

'That's the second good turn Will Bellman's done me in life,' he told Jeannie later that day.

'What was the first?'

'I'd not have dared court you back then if he hadn't talked me into it. I wasn't much of a one for knowing how to talk to womenfolk, if you remember.'

Jeannie remembered. And while she remembered a day on the riverbank, her naked legs concealed by the sedges, her husband remembered the day a perfect catapult launched a stone on a perfectly curved trajectory across the sky and brought down a perfect black bird that had glints of purple, amethyst and blue in its blackness.

'He's moving his family into the Mill House tomorrow,' he told his wife. 'Charles the cousin's not interested in running the place himself, apparently.' And at supper, when the memory was still on his mind, 'I always knew he'd do well, that Will Bellman.'

A baker in a small town cannot order two new ovens without it being talked about. Word got out. William was going to give breakfast to his workers. The dairy man would be delivering milk as well. The competitors laughed. Had the man gone soft in the head?

William was taking a risk, he knew that. How much sickness and absence could be eliminated by the provision of one bread roll and a glass of milk per day to four hundred workers? How many families convinced to stay at Bellman's instead of leaving for Stroud?

It wasn't certain that it would work, but then nothing was certain in life. You dealt in probabilities, and Bellman's calculations told him his plan would probably work. You had to be bold.

In the event he found he had, if anything, underestimated the impact his bread rolls and milk would have. Fewer absences, less sickness, increased productivity. And it became easier and easier to take people on. The queues of people wanting work at Bellman's Mill grew longer and longer, and only his cast-offs could be tempted to Stroud.

With that problem solved, he could concentrate on boosting the power. With the railway bringing coal and his plans for creating a reservoir on Turner's field, he could as good as double capacity. The engineer was starting on Monday.

22

Phil dragged one of the red felt bags to the table and Paul carried the other over his shoulder like a thief with his swag. Dora brought the big bowl, and their mother Rose the flagon. When everything was ready on the kitchen table Phil and Paul climbed onto chairs. William untied the knots that drew the bags shut and the boys took one each.

'Ready, steady, go!'

There was a great clinking and chinking as the coins spilled out of the bags and the boys hurrahed as loud as they could. Phil groped into the bottom of his bag in case there was a stray penny, but there wasn't, while Paul considered the coins that came three-quarters up the sides of the bowl. 'Here's a really dark one, look,' he said as he stirred the money with his fingers.

The next moment was Dora's. Conscious of her responsibility, anxious to lose not a single drop, she tipped the heavy vessel and poured. The tang of vinegar hit them all at the back of the nostrils, except Paul who was prepared, fingers clamping his nostrils shut.

'Can we stir?' the boys wanted to know.

William eyed Rose. He was inclined to be indulgent on these weekly occasions.

'Their hands will smell of vinegar all night and all day,' she said, but she knew it brought her husband pleasure to see his children so happy. 'All right then.'

And the two boys put their hands in and mixed and stirred the vinegar and coins as if it were a Christmas cake. When Paul judged the coins sufficiently mixed, William locked the bowl in a metal box with a big key and the boys were made to wash their hands three times.

No matter how hard they scrubbed with soap, the smell of vinegar lingered. They fell asleep with the tang of it still in their nostrils, looking forward to the next day when the best part would come. On waking, the vinegar smell was the first thing they were aware of and they wriggled out of bed full of anticipation.

Even Dora who was older and had participated in the ritual a hundred times never tired of seeing the darkened, cloudy vinegar drain away through the holes in the colander, leaving the coins so bright and shiny they looked newly minted. After rinsing in several changes of water, Rose set Paul and Phil to drying the coins and sorting them into denominations, with Dora to supervise and catch the stray coins that wanted to roll onto the floor.

Today William drew his daughter aside. 'How old are you now, Dora?'

'I am ten. You *know* I am ten.'

'What a fine coincidence! I happen to need a helper this afternoon, and it must be a person who is at least ten.'

She didn't dare believe what she thought he was asking. 'Do you want me to help you with the pay day?'

It was her mother who generally helped with the pay day, but heavily pregnant, Rose now sometimes needed to rest in the afternoons. So to the intense chagrin of Paul and Phil, when Susie and Meg carried the table from the hall to the porch outside, Dora was allowed to sit behind her father and count out the coins from the tray while her father wrote down the amounts paid out next to every man's name in the ledger.

All afternoon she counted – so much for the fullers, so much for the spinsters, this big pile for her favourites, Hamlin and Gambin the shearmen – and made not one mistake, though the work was fast and there was a lot of chat and joking to distract her. When the final worker had been paid – Mute Greg was the last, he had an extra amount for his donkey – Dora was perplexed. There was one coin left over on the tray. It was supposed to work out to the penny. Doubtfully she looked at her father.

'Who have you forgotten?' he asked.

'Nobody!' she said. 'And there is no job that is paid a penny a week.'

He kissed her troubled little face.

'What about the little girl who counts out the money? Is she worth a penny a week?'

She scolded him for making her believe she had made a mistake, he accepted his telling-off gracefully and, having got the upper hand, Dora took advantage and negotiated further pennies for her fellow coin cleaners. 'You wouldn't want them going to clean money for some other mill, would you, Father?'

'No, I wouldn't,' he had to agree.

'She drives a hard bargain,' he told Rose later, laughing, as he undid his wife's shoes that were pinching her ankles.

'And me?' his wife asked. 'What do I get? I carried the flagon of vinegar, remember?'

'Do you want a penny too? I don't know how long I can afford to keep running the mill at this rate.' He feigned reaching into his pocket for a coin.

'A kiss will do for me.' She laughed, showing the gap in her teeth.

'You can have a thousand. And cheap at the price!'

He leant over her rounded belly and kissed her.

Then he kissed her again.

'I don't know how I would manage without you,' he murmured, late that night, his fingers patiently untangling a knot in her hair on the pillow.

'Mm,' she agreed sleepily. 'Did you wash your hands? I can still smell vinegar.'

They fell asleep but not for long.

Rose woke with a sharp cry in the night and some hours after that the new baby arrived. A little girl, Lucy.

23

It was a good painting. Perhaps it was better than good. The subject was well executed. The bird looked out at the viewer with a dark eye glinting with intelligence and character, and behind it was a landscape that was sure to be Italian, though to Charles's mind it recalled the Windrush. Should he buy it?

He was off his usual track. He had come to Turin because the house he called home was unendurable to him. The young painter who had shared it with him for the last year and a half had gone. 'I have to get married,' he had explained. 'I have my parents to think of. My life is not like yours.' Charles had wept. What had he expected? It wasn't the first time. It wouldn't be the last. Everyone got married in the end. But this pain was worse than the last. He had entertained unrealistic hopes. He couldn't bear the loss of them.

So he had come travelling, and here he was in Turin, in a gallery, looking at a painting that reminded him of another home he couldn't bear to be in.

The painting reminded him of a day in his childhood. There had been a rook then. A catapult. His eyes glazed momentarily with tears as he thought of William, his easy happiness, his facility, the way his life fell into place as naturally and as simply as could be. He thought of Dora, his cousin's little girl. Of blackness and colour.

He would buy the rook painting for Dora.

He pinched his tears away and turned to the owner of the gallery. Would he deliver the painting to him at his hotel? Later today? *Grazie.*

A few hours later the receptionist at the hotel took delivery of the painting and beckoned a boy to take it up to the English *signor*. When his knock went unanswered, the boy assumed Signor Bellman was out and unlocked the door. In this way Charles's body was found.

Word came from Italy. A strange letter in a strange language. William had to fetch a man from Oxford to tell them what it said.

'But we had no word he was ill,' Rose protested. 'Was it an accident? What did he die of?'

The translator coughed gently. 'The letter does not state the cause.'

William showed the Italian out.

'Did my cousin die by his own hand?' he asked at the door in a low voice.

The stranger moistened his lips. 'The letter leaves room for the reader to draw such a conclusion.'

Charles had written a few times since his brief visit after his father's death. Rose took the letters from her desk, and read parts of them aloud. Charles had had some verses published in a magazine, though it wasn't a very significant magazine. He had visited a particularly lovely part of Italy and he described the mountains in some detail. He had bought a small French table on a trip to Paris. The workmanship was second to none, but it didn't fit in the space he had envisaged for it.

William did not like the pages in his wife's hand. Black ink on white. A dead man speaking through his wife's lips. He could not find the words to tell her so.

She put the letter down with a sharp little cry. 'Oh, William! To think! He was no older than you!'

He was three weeks older than me, William thought.

William left Rose to her reading and went to his abacus.

A week later a second letter arrived. This time the words were English. They were strung together in a strange order: legalistic sentences with baroque flourishes you had to read twice. The gist was clear enough.

For a man of wealth, Charles had not lived particularly extravagantly. He had liked wine and cigars moderately; he had liked paintings and furniture a great deal, but the house he had leased was a small one and he had furnished and decorated it accordingly. Otherwise his expenditure had been modest.

Charles's furniture had been left to a named individual who was described as a 'painting friend'. It was a generous bequest though not scandalously so.

The money, the mill and the Mill House went to William.

Dora was to have the paintings.

24

There was a part of William's mind that counted. It counted whether he wanted it to or not. He could not stop it. He was three weeks younger than Charles. Twenty-one days exactly. They had news of Charles's death six days after it occurred. That left fifteen days. William tried to keep busy, he tried to distract himself with work from the eternal abacus in his mind, but to no avail.

He counted down the days and the day arrived. *I am the age my cousin was on the day of his death.* It being Sunday, there was no immersion in noise and activity at the mill to soothe him. In his chest something hopped and cavorted irregularly, adding to his anxiety.

'Rose!'

The children stopped the ball game. Paul turned to Dora. She would know whether they were right to be alarmed: she was eight.

It came again, this time in a great roar, *'ROSE!'*

Dora dropped the ball. 'Look after Lucy,' she told the boys.

Paul and Phil took up sentry positions, next to their sleeping baby sister, and Dora ran over the lawn to the house.

Dora found her father by following the sound: he was whimpering as if in pain and gasping helplessly on the floor of the study. Face white as a candle, he twitched and trembled all over.

'Mother isn't back yet,' she said tentatively. 'And Mrs Lane is out.'

'The chimney!' His voice was shaky.

She looked at the chimney. The remains of last night's fire was dead in the grate.

'Listen!'

Dora listened. Her hearing was acute. She heard the ticking of the clock in the hallway. The far-off rush of the river. The creak of the floorboard as she leant forward. The movement and resettling of her hair around her ears as she turned her head. The rapid in and out of her father's breath.

'There's nothing,' she said, and in the same moment he burst out: 'There!'

And actually she had heard something. In the instant she had spoken, all but drowned by her own voice, something soft and indistinct, as close to silence as it is possible for a sound to be.

She approached the chimney piece and rested her ear to it, intent.

Her father was gasping in panic; she put a finger to her lips to quiet him, and he watched her, wide-eyed.

It came again. A muffled sound of movement accompanied, this time, by a hushed fall of powdery soot that sent a jolt through her father's body.

'There is a bird trapped in the chimney.'

He stared at her.

'That is all it is.'

He could barely stand but she made him get up, led him to the drawing room, and settled him in the big armchair with his feet up. She fetched a blanket and tucked it gently round him. She put a hand on his forehead and smoothed his hair back.

'There,' she said. 'All right now.'

Back in the study she shut herself in and stood on a chair to open the sash windows as wide as they would go. While she waited, she entertained herself with the abacus and added, 'Give Dora a penny,' to the list of jobs in her father's notebook.

With a gritty rush of soot something black burst into the air. A panic of wings, flapping collision – thud! – against ceiling, window, wall. Then a wing-stir of air brushed her cheek and, miraculously, the stunned bird found the open window and was gone.

Fine grey plumes of coal dust still drifted gently in the room. The tang of soot was at the back of Dora's throat and on her tongue.

And look! How sad! How beautiful! The bird had left pictures behind: blurred impressions of plumage imprinted on the wall and the ceiling. There was one, ghost grey, on the window.

She climbed back onto the chair to close the sash. Face close to the glass, she studied the soot burst. Here were delicate and precise reproductions of feather parts: a central shaft and serried barbs. Here was the calligraphic mark of a feather tip. Father mustn't see it.

The marks on the ceiling and walls were out of reach, but at the window Dora rubbed the bird away with her sleeve. It left a black mark at her wrist.

Poor creature.

Not hoping to see anything, Dora looked for a moment at the sky. There was nothing there.

She watched a moment longer.

A few weeks later Dora sat with her mother, looking at pictures. They had Mary with them, who was Mrs Lane's daughter and Dora's friend. She was helping carry the pictures to different rooms in the house, when they had decided where to put them. Some paintings the girls found pretty, others were rather dull. Together they pulled another out of the crate and unwrapped its sackcloth cover.

'Oh!' Dora exclaimed. She was looking at a rook, gleaming black.

'You like that one, do you?' Rose was puzzled by her daughter's taste.

'He's looking at me!' Dora laughed. 'Can't you see? I think he's laughing.'

She held the painting so that her mother and Mary could see it clearly. Rose tipped her head on one side, unconsciously imitating the bird, and smiled. 'I don't know how you can see he is laughing. Not with that beak! Where will we put this one, then?'

Dora's face changed. 'Father doesn't like birds.'

'Doesn't he?'

And Dora took the sacking and wrapped it round the painting and tied it with a length of cord. 'I will hide it under my bed. Until I am grown and married and have a house of my own.'

Rose, who thought the painting rather strange, did not disagree.

25

The mill was doing well. The breakfasts had proven their worth. Productivity was up. The cheaper coal from the new railway meant drying was less dependent on the weather: Bellman's new drying houses heated by coal-powered steam pipes made the cloth softer too and therefore he could command a higher price. And with the reservoir he was planning on the field he'd bought from Turner, productivity would be less susceptible to changes in water level. When rainfall was low, they need only release some of the pent-up water into the race to maximise the water power for those parts of the process that used it. Reducing the impact of unpredictable alterations in power would allow him to forecast output and guarantee delivery dates in a way that reassured customers and increased orders . . . Yes, it was all going just the way he liked it.

New customers were coming to him all the time. He was able to replace some of the machinery that was growing old and outdated, bring in new and improved feeds to the carding machines. He had made a few astute loans to other mill owners. When they ran into trouble – as he expected them to – he would be the first to know about it. He had his eye on expansion beyond Bellman's Mill itself.

There came news one day of an accident at Rose's parents' farm. A horse carrying her brother's child had reared up. The child had fallen and suffered nothing but bruises, but Rose's mother, dashing to help, was struck by the animal's hoof. She now lay senseless in her bed.

Could Rose go and nurse her mother?

Mrs Lane agreed to take care of the children and Rose went.

After six days she sent a message to William. Her mother was dead.

He rode in the morning to the farm and took his place with his father-in-law and brothers-in-law for the funeral while Rose and her sisters wept at home.

It had been arranged that William and Rose would return to Whittingford together the following day; tonight they would sleep at the farm. Rose had nursed her mother for six days and nights and grieved for two. She could not cry for her tears were all used up. Aching with sorrow and exhaustion the only comfort left to her was sleep – and the presence of the husband she loved. She blew the candle out and turned towards him. He lay by her side, still and tense as a stranger.

'There was a man at the funeral,' William said, in the darkness, 'and I don't know who he was.'

Rose understood that he was expecting a response. 'Was he one of those that came back here afterwards?'

'No.'

Why was he asking her, then? What was the point of asking a woman about a person she hadn't seen? The men were at the funeral. Why not ask them? She didn't say all this. 'My brother will know, I expect,' she told him.

There was an edge of sharpness in her voice. She forgave herself for it instantly and because her feelings were generous, she forgave William for his inconsiderate question at the same time.

She reached an arm for him, wanting comfort. 'What was it like when you lost your mother?' If she could make him remember his own grief, perhaps then he would know to comfort her . . .

'He was there too. At her funeral.'

In his voice was a note she knew: it was taut, unrelenting. Her heart shrank. She could expect nothing from him tonight.

'He was in black.'

She frowned in the dark. 'Of course he was in black, William. Like two dozen other people.'

Rose drew back her arm. He hadn't noticed her hand upon his chest, had not placed his own over it, nor turned to take her in his arms.

If she could not have his hand stroking her hair, then she would sleep. She must have at least that.

She turned her back and settled her head on the pillow.

'He was at Paul's funeral too.'

She said nothing. Sleep was not far away.

'It should be possible to work it out. Who is there who knew your mother and my mother and Uncle Paul? There can't be so many people who knew them all.'

Her eyelids grew heavier. The muscles in her neck and shoulders softened. Her jaw relaxed . . .

William began to fidget. The sheets were too high or too low. He was too hot and had to open a window. Now there was a draught.

Rose sighed. 'What did he look like, this man?'

She listened vaguely to William as he tried to give a description of the man whose countenance was so distinctive yet so unwilling to be defined by mere words.

It seemed to Rose that he really didn't know what the man looked like. 'Was he taller than you or shorter?' she prompted him wearily. 'Was he bearded? Was he fair or dark?'

The information was scant. He was about William's height. Whether he was clean-shaven or bearded – now that William knew he ought to be able to remember but for some reason he couldn't. But he was dark. No doubt about it.

Sleep is possible, she thought. *If he would only be quiet and let me sleep!*

She knew William well enough to understand that where there was a problem, he wouldn't rest till he had a solution. But his description was so vague. It could almost be anyone. And her mother was dead and all she wanted was to sleep.

'I suppose it might be my Uncle Jack.'

'What does he look like? Describe him to me.'

'About your height. Dark hair. He used to be bearded in the old days. I can't say for sure now.'

'How would your Uncle Jack know my Uncle Paul?'

'I believe he lived in Whittingford as a young man.'

'Ah! So he'd have known my mother?'

'More than likely.'

He sounded better now. Her husband tossed in the bed once more, a definitive, once and for all shifting. At last! *Now*, she thought, *he will sleep*.

And he did.

Rose waited for the night to bring her the same comfort. It didn't. Her mother was dead, and she was in a strange bed with a strange man who was her husband. She was now too exhausted to sleep – and too heartbroken to weep.

26

Opening her mail one morning at breakfast, Rose frowned.

'Trouble?'

'My uncle has died.'

William's spoon paused over his porridge. 'Which one?'

'Uncle Jack.'

William did not examine the surge of satisfaction that flared in him. 'When is the funeral?'

'Thursday. But don't feel you must. You are so busy with this reservoir. I haven't seen my uncle since I was a child; no one will think anything of it.'

William swallowed his porridge. 'I can take half a day and go over.'

Enjoying the superiority of the living, William found himself rather looking forward to the funeral. His dislike of the man he had never spoken to faded now that he was dead, and he rode out to Upper Wychwood Church with a lightness of spirit that he didn't associate with funerals.

At the church gates someone seemed to be waiting for him. It was the man in black. William felt a prickle of astonishment. The fellow's eyes glanced over in William's direction and in them was an expression of amusement that William thought quite unsuitable for the occasion. He seemed simply entertained by William's bewilderment, quite as though he knew of William's mistake and had been waiting to be merry with him about it.

William was horrified as the fellow made towards him, as if to greet him. At the very moment he was expecting the man to open his mouth and speak – *Just the man I've been waiting for!* the words were written all over his face – some other funeral-goers arrived at the church. The man in black had to hop back out of the way to let them pass, and as they went he got swept up with them, somehow, but not before turning his head and making a jaunty gesture in William's direction. *Another time!* it seemed to indicate. *No hurry!*

Anyone noticing would have said the gesture was filled with good-will and fellowship.

William was incensed.

&

There is a story much older than this one in which two ravens – which are nothing but large rooks – were companions and advisors to the great God of the north. One bird was called Huginn, which in that place and time meant Thought, the other Muninn, which meant Memory. They lived in a magic ash tree where the borders of many worlds came together and from its branches they flew blithely between worlds, gathering information for Odin. Other creatures could not cross the borders from one world to another, but Thought and Memory flew where they pleased, and came back laughing.

Thought and Memory had a great many offspring, all of whom were gifted with great mental powers, allowing them to accumulate and pass on a good deal of knowledge from their ancestors.

The rooks that lived in Will Bellman's oak tree were descendants of Thought and Memory. The rook that fell was one of their many-times-great-grandchildren.

On the day that Will Bellman was ten years and four days old these rooks did what needed to be done to mark their loss. Then they departed from that dangerous place. They never returned.

The tree still stands. Even now you can go and see it – yes, right now, in your time – but you will not see a single rook alight in its branches. They still know what happened. Rooks are made of thought and memory. They know everything and they do not forget.

Since we are on the topic of ravens, the collective noun for ravens is an *unkindness*. This is somewhat puzzling to Thought and Memory.

27

'Lovely!'

Bellman and the chief constructor and the engineer were standing together watching the diverted water fill the reservoir. Where it entered it splashed and frothed in surprise at its new direction. At the further end it was more settled, still and tame. It was a magnificent sight. Thousands of gallons of water stored up against future drought, enabling the mill to stay productive no matter what the water level. It insured profits against chance, hazard, uncertainty.

A boy came running from the mill, out of breath.

'It'll have to wait,' Bellman told him, 'I'm busy here.'

Twenty minutes later the boy was back, apologetic. 'Mrs Bellman insists that you come straight away. She has told me not to return without you.'

Bellman frowned. He wanted to stay and watch this more than anything in the world. It was a dream he had cherished for many years. He had stood and watched the mill wheel turn, the very first time he had met the millwright, and known then what was needed. And now it was here!

But Rose wanted him. Knowing what was happening today, she wouldn't have sent for him for no reason.

The moment he walked into the hall, an acrid, scorched smell filled his nostrils and he pulled a face.

Before he could go in search of the source, an entirely altered Rose ran down the stairs. Her hair had escaped from its pins and strayed wildly; her face was taut and white.

'Thank God you have come!' the strange Rose said, in a strange Rose voice. 'Lucy has the fever.'

'Have you sent for the doctor?'

'He has just left. We are to isolate her,' Rose said, indignant. 'We must keep the others apart from her.' So far she had mastered herself but now, abruptly, tears sprang to her eyes. 'Oh, William! We have cut her hair and put it on the fire!'

So that was the dreadful smell.

Rose wiped the tears away with an angry sleeve and he consoled her briefly. 'It will grow again. Where is she?'

On being told that even he was not to have contact with his infant daughter, Bellman put the ladder up against the wall and climbed to the level of the nursery window. Inside, Mrs Lane, who had offered to nurse so that Rose could look after the other children, was leaning over the cot.

He rapped his nails on the window, and Mrs Lane turned.

The child in the bed was not the Lucy he knew. The whiteness of her skull took him by surprise and she seemed thinner, but surely that was not possible: he had seen her only yesterday. Her willingness to believe the world a happy place was still strong enough to make her stare at her father in anticipation of pleasure, but when she realised he would not come in and stop the pain in her head, she screwed up her face and wailed again.

It was a good, loud wail. He and Rose had made robust children with strong hearts and big lungs. She would pull through. Good girl!

He took a step down the ladder, forced himself to take his eyes from her imploring face, and returned to the ground.

Rose shuddered. 'I cannot bear her to suffer so. I must go to her.'

'Let us do just what the doctor said. Lucy is a strong little girl. Mrs Lane is a good nurse. Everything will be all right.'

'Will it?'

He took Rose's hands in his and looked – calm, steady – into her face until her trembling anxiety diminished.

'Yes,' she said, with a deep breath and a faint smile. 'Of course it will.'

*

118

Doctor Sanderson returned that evening. He visited the patient and spoke to Mrs Lane. He came to William and Rose in the drawing room.

'I have done everything possible. I am sorry I can do no more. There is still prayer.'

Now Rose would not be dissuaded and went to her child.

William was taken aback. He had always thought Sanderson a good doctor. He had the best reputation of all the Whittingford doctors. He immediately sent a messenger for one of the others, but a note came back: there were many in the town with fever, and the doctor would be busy with them all night long. He would not be able to attend Lucy before tomorrow morning.

While William was reading this, his housekeeper's daughter came in. She had clearly been crying though she was making efforts to contain her tears. 'Mrs Bellman says that it won't be long now. It is time to pray.'

He nodded curtly and walked with her to the sickroom. 'Why did not Susie or Meg come to tell me?'

'They have gone, sir. They are afraid of the fever.'

The moment he was in the room, William embarked upon an interrogation of Mrs Lane. Had she done this, and had she done that, and how often and for how long . . . 'I do not suggest that you have failed in anything,' he explained, 'on the contrary, I am quite sure your care has been everything it needs to be. It is only so that I may know what the treatment has been.'

His questions were involved and Mrs Lane was hard-pressed to answer them and see to the dying child.

'William,' Rose chided, in a murmur, and when this had no effect, '*William!*'

He looked at his wife in surprise.

'All we can do now is help her to pass. Stop distracting Mrs Lane and kneel with me. Let us pray for her everlasting life.'

He had never heard his wife speak with such authority, and he knelt at her side, put his hands together and joined her in prayer.

All the while he watched. It was scarcely his Lucy any more. The fever had melted the flesh off her. What remained was a scrawny, pallid creature, with sunken eyes, that was racked with convulsions and knew nothing of their presence. He observed every detail.

His wife did not remove her eyes from their child either, he saw. But her gaze was doing something other than look. She barely blinked and in her eyes was a power that went far beyond mere observation. He understood that something was happening in the intensity of that unwavering stare, but he did not know what it was.

The child died.

William – bewildered – rose and left the room. In the drawing room he paced. An unendurable restlessness possessed him. He could not rid himself of the feeling that there was something he had to do. Lucy was gone, he kept thinking, and he must go and fetch her. She could not have gone far in the time, she was only an hour away. He must saddle his horse immediately! A hundred times he suppressed the instinct to go to the stable, a hundred times it reasserted itself. And when it wasn't the stable it was this: Lucy was broken. Some part of her had failed, wanted mending. He had tried the expert, and the man had been no good. He must do the job himself. When had he ever failed? Where were his tools? I will soon have her working again, good as new.

She is dead, he told himself over and over, but his brain persisted. Nothing is impossible. All things are retrievable. Broken things can be mended. If there is a way to make the sun shine all night, William Bellman will be the one to find it.

He paced and paced, looking for a solution. He did not find one, but he could not stop looking until it was morning – when there was a new problem. Paul and Phillip were sick.

Now he could be of use.

William rode to Oxford to consult the doctors there. When he came home he brought nitre and borax and salts and acetate of ammonia and nitrate of silver with him. He unrolled camel-hair brushes from a roll of paper. He had oil of lemon and oil of persimmon. He had a waxy balsam that made everything smell of cloves. He instructed Rose and Mrs Lane in the mixing and measuring and application of these preparations.

'Shave the head entirely,' he instructed. 'We did not shave the baby close enough. The head must be kept elevated, wrapped in silk that is first soaked in lemon oil. The feet are to be warmed by application of the clove pomade and covered in warm water cloths. No leeches, no bleeding. Feed them only on barley water and rice water for the first three days. After three days only meat broth and chicken, and the chicken to be sealed dry in a jar and boiled. Their bladders to be opened every six hours and the bowels every twenty-four. Every evening, nitrate of silver to be brushed onto the throat ulcers . . .'

He noted everything. He made lists and timetables in his calfskin notebook. He checked off every opening of bladder and bowel. Nothing happened in the sickroom without his making a record of it in his book.

At first the boys were puzzled by illness. They looked at their father from the other side of a wall of pain, bewildered that their father stood writing in his book, when he had only to reach over the division and lift them clear of it. They struggled, shrank, agonised.

William scrutinised his notes for patterns, indicators of improvement. Tentatively he altered timings, dosages. Was there an improvement now? Was it too soon to judge?

When he wasn't in the sickroom he was in and out of every room in the house. What things had belonged to Lucy? What toys had she played with? What blankets had she used? What cushion had she rested on?

'Burn it!'

They lit a great bonfire in the garden that never went out, for there was always something remembered that had to be burned. The boys' clothes. Their books. Their mattresses. And what had he worn, when he kissed and cuddled them? Burn it! And Rose, what had she worn? Every room in the house was gone through, every cupboard and every drawer examined; this doll and this hat and this ribbon, 'Burn it! Burn it all!'

In his sons' bedroom he pulled boxes from under a bed. Buried beneath books and toys and balls, all the beloved junk of a boy's life, a pair of rudimentary catapults. He hurled them from the bedroom window to the astounded gardener, stoking the flames outside.

'BURN THEM!'

Shaking, he stood, hands on the window frame, getting his breath back. When he could breathe again, he went back to the sickroom, and took up his calfskin notebook.

First you had to watch. Only by watching could you understand. Only when you understood could you intervene. Sickness was a mechanism like any other. Close observation would always suffice to elucidate the workings. It was just a matter of time.

William went to bury Lucy. The service was short; it had to be: there were too many to be buried. The stranger in black bowed to him sympathetically, but William barely registered him. He went home to learn that his boys had died, within a few minutes of each other.

Rose, praying at their bedside, looked up at him with overbright eyes, a flush on her throat.

'My love,' he told her, 'you are sick.'

'You had better fetch the scissors, then.'

She unpinned her hair. She drew the scissors out of their leather sheath and cut her hair. She threw it on the fire and went to bed.

A day later William left Rose in the care of Mrs Lane to attend the funeral of his sons. It was a strange funeral. There were many dead. The service was not only for Paul and Phillip, but for others too, people William knew of, had heard of. All must be buried today, for tomorrow there would be more. The mourners were sparse: people were sick themselves, or nursing the sick, or afraid of contamination. The men who stood and sat and prayed – there was no singing, for there was no choir and no heart for song – mourned separately and apart, this one for his wife, that one for his brother, this other for his child. They offered each other no comfort, each needed what little he had for himself. Someone will be making a fortune out of black crape, he reflected, dismally.

William lost himself in complicated calculations. What was the measurement for bereavement? How to count, weigh, evaluate grief? He had enjoyed good luck in the past, he was the first to admit it. He had not known it, but there was a price to pay. He was paying it now. Somewhere, he calculated, a fair-minded spirit of justice, seeing that

122

things were now – what? equal? – would start sending good luck again. A dark calculation worked itself out on the abacus in his heart: Lucy was lost, his two sons were lost. That made three. He still had a wife and a daughter. It did not seem unreasonable to expect to keep them. A sixty–forty split. It was a generous deal to the other party. Sixty–forty. Too good to refuse. There was a solace in numbers.

In the graveyard, William was not at all surprised to see the man in black. For all the curious depth of his funeral garb, he did not look like someone bereaved. He did not look as though his wife were agonising at home. He lacked the haggard air of a man who has spent days at the bedside of a dying child. Why had he come, then? Was it for William he was there? The man met William's eyes with the intimacy of the very well acquainted. It was too much for William who today had no strength to resist the man's certainty. He nodded at him. The fellow returned his acknowledgement with an expression of intently sad so-licitude.

Sixty–forty?

Know your opponent, that is the secret of successful negotiation. What if his negotiations came to naught? William felt the ground suddenly unstable beneath his feet.

When one thing fails, try another. There is always a way.

He took a breath. Recovered himself.

He returned to the sickbed, to the wrapping of cool cloths around Rose's skull, the application of nitrate of silver, the spooning of broth, the warming foot baths, the mixing of aloes and salts with treacle . . . He was learning his way around this sickness. Observe. Understand. Intervene. He would find the way.

William did not go to bed during these times and he did not properly sleep. But sometimes at Rose's bedside, between one spell of con-vulsions and the next, he drowsed lightly in his chair. Something broke into his reverie and he looked about him for a clue. All was as it had been in the sickroom. There was no significant change.

Then he realised: the acrid smell was coming from the corridor. Elsewhere in the house someone was burning hair.

He rose in alarm and ran to Dora.

She stood in a white nightdress, by the fireside of her bedroom. A small, neat fire: she must have just lit it herself. She was slicing the blades through her long, dark hair and dropping the locks into the fire.

'Did it wake you?' she said. 'It makes such a ghastly smell. Shall I lie down in my own room? Or would the boys' room be more convenient? All the nursing things are there.'

He took the scissors from her hand. Her pretty face looked peculiar. Shorn on one side only, a red flush over her throat and neck. 'There's no need to cut it,' he said. 'I can't see that it makes any difference.'

'Oh. Well, I've started now. I may as well go on.'

He cut it for her, dropping the locks into the fire and weeping. When he moved from the back to the side and was in front of her again, her gaze was steady. She smiled at him, a small, apologetic smile.

28

On the day of Rose's funeral, William's state of mind was not improved by the presence of the stranger. He was annoyed when the man stepped back courteously as he approached the church, and again afterwards, on finding him outside, by the graveside. He was looking around, with all the pleasure of a satisfied picnicker on a summer afternoon.

As the vicar spoke the words that laid his wife to rest, the fellow made himself scarce, which was a relief, but then, when William was handed the trowel to cast the first earth onto the coffin, he caught sight of him again. Blow me if he hadn't sidled up, next to Ned on the opposite side of the grave. What nerve! There he stood, surveying the scene as if it were nothing but a play, put on for his own entertainment. Harassment, that's what it was!

William would have liked to confront the man, have it out with him, but today was not the day. He resolved to ignore it. But as if he knew what was in William's thoughts, the fellow turned to look directly at William. He even nodded, in a plain, how-d'you-do sort of way and with a jerk of the head towards the gate seemed to indicate that he'd like to catch William later, have a word. William lifted the trowel and prepared to hurl the earth straight over the mouth of the grave and into the despicably agreeable face of the man in black. But the man slipped swiftly sideways, ducked out of view, and there was only Ned, looking alarmed.

William flicked the earth into the grave and walked quickly away.

That was that. He had buried his wife. He had buried three of his children. His task now was to go home and help his fourth and last child to die.

'She knows no one now,' Mrs Lane told him at the door to the sickroom.

Nothing could surprise him now at the deathbed. All was as it had been before. He spoke to his child and observed that she appeared not to know him. Mrs Lane pressed a cool cloth to Dora's forehead from time to time; she no longer murmured the endearments that the girl could not hear. The minutes stretched out and he measured the empty length of every long second that filed past him. Mrs Lane prayed. He murmured amen.

Neither of them suffered the hope that had burdened them the first times. There was still the habit of protest inside him, though it was much weakened. The remnant of the father he had once been still raged at the taking of his child, but he felt it as an empty mansion feels the anger of a fly against a window. Death had him in harness. He lumbered in his servitude.

As for Dora, it was quite normal that Bellman did not recognise the figure in the bed. Hair shorn, pale skin stretched tightly over the sharp bridge of her nose, sunken eyes: this child in the bed seemed quite unrelated to his curly-haired and pink-cheeked girl of a fortnight ago. Her eyes rolled back in her head and her breathing was hoarse and painful. Already she more than half belonged to another realm.

Bellman was prepared. Each stage of this illness he recognised; each moment told him what the next would be. Minute by minute, hour after hour, he had stood like this, feet planted on the limewashed floors, watching his children die. He knew the process so well he could foresee each step of the descent. And now a great gasp, he predicted, and the moribund gave a great gasp. And now the start of the great convulsions, and the convulsions came. Death had him so well trained that he could have overseen the work in her place. He was himself a kind of conductor, knowing all the movements, all the rhythms, the arpeggios and the cadences of its melody.

Now, he assessed Dora and realised that the end was still a long way off. Ten hours. Twelve, more likely.

'Why don't you get some sleep?' Mrs Lane suggested. 'You look done in.'

He left the sickroom and went to his own bedroom. Rose's dress was at the end of the bed, where she had left it after taking it off to die. It was made of sturdy stuff that held a bosomy shape even when she was not in it. When he reached for it, the fabric collapsed and Rose's bosom exhaled its last breath. He turned his back. He could not sleep here. He could not sleep at all.

He went to the Red Lion.

Poll greeted him and poured a jug of cider without a reference to either the old days or the new one. He sat quietly and drank one glass after another. He drank methodically, expecting nothing from it. The cider obscured the sharper details of his grief, without denting the fearfulness of its bleakness.

At a certain point of drunkenness William understood a good many things that had evaded him previously. The world, the universe, God too, if there was one, were ranged against mankind. From this newly unveiled vantage point he saw that his old good fortune was a cruel joke: encourage a man to think he is lucky all the better to bring him down afterwards. He realised his essential smallness, the vanity of his efforts to control his fate. He, William Bellman, master of the mill, was nothing. All these years he had believed in his own power, not once recognising the presence of the vast rival who could crush him in a day, if it once chose to. His happiness and his success, that he had taken to be solid things, hewn out of his own effort and talent, had proved as fragile as the seed head of the dandelion; all it took was for this unsuspected competitor to release his breath and the clockhead disappeared. Why, he wondered, had he never known? He, who knew everything? What had kept him in ignorance all these years?

He drank. The clarity of his thinking on this new topic was dazzling to him, but his head dropped lower and lower until it rested on his arms on the table and eventually he snored.

Poll shook him awake. She heaved him to his feet and got him to the door. 'Home, William Bellman. It is not a good place but it is the only place. Go there.'

Outside it was dark. He did not know whether it was cold, because the alcohol had isolated his body and filled it with an artificial trembling warmth. Stumbling in the dark he went. He did not know where he was going, but put one foot in front of the other, because if he stayed still his agony would settle all the more heavily on him. All his adult life he had lived with a purpose. His every minute had been actively spent with some object in mind. Now he sought to know what his purpose was. There was nothing for him to do at home. All that could be done was being done. He was superfluous there. He was not wanted at the mill. His tragic presence cast a shadow over the hands. They feared him, because they feared what had happened to his family. Where then?

There was a part of Bellman's mind that functioned automatically to solve problems. Whether it was habit, self-training, or just a characteristic he had been born with, he couldn't say. It functioned so efficiently that he never needed to set it into action, for it was up and running the moment he wanted it. In fact, it was so fast that it often provided solutions before he'd even realised he had a problem. It ran like clockwork, ticking routinely in the back of his mind, while the front dealt with the immediate, the superficial, the mundane. This evening he observed that this engine in his mind was running through a number of options for dealing with a powerful rival.

Option one: agree terms. So much for you and so much for me, and we all get what we want . . . He'd tried that, and it hadn't worked. Option two: sell. But this is Dora. So even if this rival seemed willing to buy – and so far he had only destroyed and stolen – Bellman could not sell. No sale then. Option three: hide. Keep a low profile, stay small and hope the rival finds you too insignificant to worry about. Too late. He was already in the rival's sights. What does that leave? Option four: collaborate. But how on earth could that come about? It was impossible. Back to option one. Agree terms. But he'd tried that . . .

The mind machine worked on and on. Its proposals grew more and more desperate: he would sabotage the fellow's machinery! Slash prices to force him out of business! He would hire thugs to set fire to his premises, steal his best men, spread malicious rumours about his shoddy goods! Ludicrous notions, given the rival in question. The wilder his ideas grew, the stranger he grew to himself. He had never known he was capable of such devious and desperate measures. He was not the man he thought he was. He was too fatigued to stop the mechanism in his head and, in any case, he didn't know how to switch it off. He'd never needed to.

How could he live, with this in his head – this ceaseless effort to solve the unsolvable?

Agree terms, sell, hide, collaborate.

It would drive him mad. It was already driving him mad.

Why would his brain not learn that nothing could be done and he had lost?

And now, suddenly, he was here. Close to the old cottage where he had grown up. The fields were dark, but the cottage was a visible rectangle of darkness and the old oak reached its branches blackly across the sky. He began to make his way towards it.

Here was a new project: how to switch off his mind?

He came to the tree and stood beneath it. This was the right place to be. He felt it. His brain was clear and working smoothly.

This branch here was strong enough and the right height. He could climb up on the other side, make his way onto it, sit there to make ready and when all was done, let himself fall, plumb, to the end. He eyed it all up, ran through it in his mind to see where the flaws in the plan were, made some minor alterations . . . Perfect!

All he needed was some rope – and he knew where to get it! The coffins were lowered into the graves on ropes and because there were so many funerals at present – two or three every day – the ropes were not put away but left on a hook halfway down the steps to the vault. He'd seen them. There was no risk of theft. No thief wants a rope that has been lowering bodies into graves.

Bellman set off to the churchyard. An achievable goal! He was feeling better already.

Lit by a sliver of moon, the sky was less than black, and the yews of the churchyard were dark against it. He walked slowly, stumbling where he veered off the path onto the uneven grass. He found the rope and on his way back to the churchyard gate, Rose's new grave came into view.

His pace slowed and then he stopped.

He was not alone. A little way off the man in black was leaning against an old gravestone. He was doing nothing, only gazing patiently at the treeline, dark against the sky.

If there had been a breeze, it fell still now. The air did not move, but hung still.

The man gave the impression that he had been waiting a long time, yet he was not in a hurry. He appeared to have all the time in the world.

Turning to William, there was a kindly curiosity in his gaze.

'I'm sorry about this afternoon,' he said, and his voice was ordinary and benign. 'I could have handled things better, I admit.'

'Who the hell are you?' said William.

'A friend.' And he eyed William beadily, to see how this went down with him.

'A friend? We've not been introduced.'

The man in black put his head on one side and considered. 'True. And yet my intentions are friendly. I thought we might have a talk.'

William shifted the rope on his shoulder and made to move on.

'Might you feel better for a talk?' the man suggested.

'So that's how it goes! I stay for a chat with you now and in the morning my body is discovered here in this graveyard? Is that it?'

The stranger's eye lingered for a moment on the rope that William was carrying. Then his gaze, gentle and ironic, moved to William.

He knows, William thought.

But the man in black made a gesture as though to brush that idea right away.

'No, no, no. I can see you've got me all wrong. I've come to help you – or rather to ask you to help me. It amounts to the same thing. Why don't you put that down,' he nodded at the rope, 'and take a seat.'

Wearily, William dropped the rope and slumped on a tombstone on the far side of Rose's grave from the man in black.

'Look at this, Mr Bellman.' The man raised a cloaked arm and swept it to take in the entire graveyard. 'Tell me what you see.'

'What I see?'

Before them were graves. The older ones had their statues and their

130

tombstones, their angels and their crosses and their urns. The newer ones had bare earth still. Flowers gleamed white on Rose's grave. New graves waited empty, ready for tomorrow and the next day. One would be Dora's.

Anger fired up in William, through the drink. 'What do I see? I'll tell you what I see! I see my wife. I see three of my children. I see them dead. I see that grave there, cold and empty, waiting for my last child who is dying now. I see misery and suffering and despair. I see the futility of everything I have ever done and everything I may ever do! I see every reason to do away with myself right here and now, and be done with it! For ever!'

William collapsed onto the tomb. He shrank into a ball and pulled at his hair, face contorting so powerfully it was as if his skin wanted to come away from the bone. He waited for the pain to submerge him, to sweep him away and deposit him in some other place, but it did not happen. The agony remained, unaltering, unending, unendurable and here. He craved escape but the only thing that could escape was the cry from his lips, an expulsion of feeling, a howl, a bellow. It set up a welcome vibration in his head.

The ringing in his head died down. Perhaps the man was gone by now. Perhaps he had never been there in the first place? Could he go and do the thing he intended to do? Bellman raised his eyes.

Still there. Standing, hands clasped behind his back, chest out, imperturbable.

He glanced down at William. 'Good! Good!' he said, encouragingly.

William scowled. Was he talking to a madman?

'Well. It's early days.' He unclasped his hands, thought better of it and clasped them again. 'I see things differently, you know.'

'I suppose you would.' William's voice was weakened from the bellowing.

'Yes. What I see here, in front of me' – he took a deep breath, as though drawing on a particularly expensive and exotic cigar, and exhaled it with relish – 'is an opportunity.'

William stared. The fellow was unhinged. Then something rang a bell in his mind.

What was it?

Agree terms, sell, hide, collaborate.

Collaborate.

He thought of Dora.

He nodded once. 'You've got a deal.'

29

Chill morning air entered his nostrils. A pause. Warmer air, stalely scented with liquor emerged from his mouth.

Was he awake? This was like waking. He had been asleep, then.

With the slowness of Lazarus he gathered his senses to him. His head ached. His chest felt bruised as if his lungs had been in a battle all night. He was lying in a cold, hard place and something damp and coarse was scratching his cheek. He opened an eye. Ah! He was in the churchyard. A tombstone for a bed and a pillow of rope. A new grave was nearby. Rose's grave.

He closed the eye to think. It had been his wife's funeral. He had gone to the Red Lion. Drunk too much. And then? The feathered end of something stroked his consciousness . . .

. . . and was gone again.

Then a very clear and urgent thought barged into his mind.

Dora!

With clumsy urgency, he swung himself up, got to his feet.

He must go home.

Without a glance at the coil of rope behind him, he set off, his mind full of his child and the things that must be done to safeguard her life. For she would live. He was persuaded of that now. She would live! And – though he did not think of this – so would he.

When Bellman entered the sickroom, Mrs Lane did not comment on the rope furrows impressed in his cheek, nor the smell of drink and the grave upon him but only opened the door and ushered him in. All could be forgiven a man in his circumstances.

It appeared to be the final movement: Dora was gripped by the great convulsions. This time Bellman did not flinch nor clutch at his hair. His eyes did not roam the room in desperate search of salvation. He stood by, face unchanged, still as a tombstone.

The quiet period of ever-shallower breathing began. Mrs Lane folded the girl's hands over her breast, and knelt by the bed where she began to whisper the Lord's Prayer.

Bellman spoke it with her. His voice was steady and unwavering.

When they had finished the prayer, flickers of life danced about her lips, unextinguished. Mildly perturbed, Mrs Lane began the prayer again. 'Our Father . . .'

At amen the girl was breathing still.

A faint embarrassment took hold of Mrs Lane. She glanced uncertainly at Bellman, was struck by the calm of his expression.

'Does it seem to you, Mr Bellman, that her breathing is freer?' she asked.

'It does.'

They leant over the girl, peering into the white face. Mrs Lane lifted an eyelid with her gentle thumb then took the girl's hands, uncrossed them, and began to warm them in her own. 'Lord in thy mercy,' she began and, ambushed by her own astonishment, got no further.

Dora's breathing remained shallow but grew more regular. Degree by degree her hands thawed. Her pallor diminished fractionally. Mrs Lane shifted her ministrations away from the girl's soul and back to the body. An hour or so after the crisis, Dora seemed to stir. She did not wake, but resettled into something that appeared more like sleep than coma.

Bellman did not move. He appeared neither to see nor to hear Mrs Lane. He stared fixedly at his daughter, yet it was not certain that he saw her either.

After Sanderson had been and shaken his head in astonishment at the miracle, Bellman at last allowed himself to rest. He tossed Rose's dress to the floor, lay down fully dressed and sank instantly into a deep slumber.

*

Last night. A handshake – or as good as – over a grave, in the dark, with a man he could hardly see. Today. His daughter returned from the dead.

Into his sleep there crept not the faintest chink of light to illuminate the unmaking and the remaking of the mind of William Bellman.

Something had ended. Something was about to begin.

PART TWO

[Socrates] Let us suppose that every mind contains
a kind of aviary stocked with birds of every sort,
some in flocks apart from the rest, some in small groups
and some solitary, flying in any direction among them all.
[Theaetetus] Be it so. What follows?

Plato, The Theaetetus

1

At five to eleven, Bellman entered his daughter's room and Mrs Lane stood ready to leave it.

'The gong?' she asked.

'As you like.'

Downstairs she went to her daughter, Mary, in the kitchen.

'What is it to be today, Mother?'

'Whatever we choose.'

'Can we not let off the pistol out the kitchen window?'

Her mother frowned. 'Mary, this is not for your entertainment. What have we done lately? Pans yesterday and the gong on Tuesday. What did we do on Monday?'

'The piano?'

'He can't expect us always to think of new things. I'd throw the dessert plates down the stairs, if it would do any good but— Good heavens, it's time!'

They dashed to the reception room and lifted the lid of the grand piano. Mrs Lane sat down with an air of sad futility; her daughter beside her full of relish. They raised four hands, watched the clock, and on the stroke of eleven, brought twenty fingers heavily down on the keys.

'There!' Mary exclaimed, satisfied. 'If she can't hear that, she can't hear nothing!'

Upstairs, watch in hand, Bellman stood over Dora, scrutinising her face as the vibrations from the piano strings reverberated unmusically through the house.

He made a one-word note in his book. *Unresponsive.*

'Patience,' Sanderson counselled, when Bellman showed him the pages of his notebook, with the results of the daily tests. Dora's breathing was shallow and slow and constant. Her pulse was faint and slow and constant. She saw nothing, heard nothing, spent most of her time in what appeared to be deep sleep and when her eyes opened, she saw no more than a newborn kitten would. Her hair was not growing back and every day Mrs Lane or Mary brushed more fallen eyelashes from her white cheek. Suspended in a place of limbo, Dora had not died, nor did she live.

'She has been to the brink,' Sanderson said. 'Her condition is stable, we must be grateful for that.'

Bellman had had his miracle; it was unrealistic to expect another. The fever had ravaged the town and Bellman's family, it had come within a heartbeat of taking Dora and, moments from taking her life, it had receded. In the aftermath of the devastation Bellman did not ask himself why he had been granted this reprieve. He simply contemplated it, stunned.

Bellman spent all his time at the bedside of his daughter and did not go to the mill. After seven days a small boy knocked at the door with a message. All was well, but should the chief bookkeeper call to report to Mr Bellman?

That evening Ned was shown into the study by Mary. Crace was with him. The room struck cold; the fire lit by Mary had not yet cast off the chill of a month's emptiness. Crace had never been inside Mill House, Ned only rarely. They stood in silence, looking at floorboards and corners of cornices and other such insignificances, their curiosity and compassion at the ready. They were waiting so hard that when the door cracked and Bellman appeared, they jumped. Perhaps they had reason to, for he was changed though the alteration was not external. Their eyes puzzled over him, as the gaze returns to a spot where something used to be that is now absent.

They expressed their condolences in the usual terms. Ned knew their faces would say the rest: that sorry was only the smallest part of what they felt, that all in the town knew suffering, but few had suffered as extensively as Bellman had suffered. What had happened at Mill House was beyond measure . . . But Bellman seemed not to see him, hardly to hear him either. Ned glanced at Crace who was similarly perplexed.

'Sit down,' Bellman said, gesturing vaguely, and they did. He turned the desk chair into the room as if he meant to sit in it, but didn't. Had he forgotten to sit down? Were they to wait, or to start?

After a silence, Ned cleared his throat. 'Perhaps you would like us to report on the last month?'

Bellman raised a hand to his unshaven chin and rubbed his stubble. They took it as an invitation and began. The dramatic events in the town had had their impact on mill employees. Despite the turbulent events, over half the orders had been filled as planned. As for the rest, good relations with merchants had made it possible in almost every case to negotiate new delivery dates. There had been few cancellations. All in all, things were better than one might expect.

Bellman now lowered himself wearily into his chair, but there was no sign that he was listening.

Ned turned a raised eyebrow to Crace, and Crace picked up the narrative. 'As to technical and processing matters . . .' He described succinctly the few difficulties that had arisen, explained the action he had taken and why he had acted as he did.

Bellman stared at his hands, clasped in his lap.

'We've kept a written log that you can look over when . . .'

Ned offered the sheaf of notes, and when Bellman made no move to take it, he rose and placed it on the desk. Anxious to conclude the awkward meeting, Crace rose with him.

'And Dora?' Ned asked. One more attempt to reach the man he considered his friend as much as his employer. 'Her health improves, I hope?'

Then Bellman's eyes met his. The question had stirred something dark in them, but he made no answer.

Crace proposed that he and Ned would call twice a week to report on events. Absently Bellman nodded and the men took their leave.

On their way back to the mill the two men thought of the tragedy behind them and their own griefs. They passed the Red Lion where Crace had celebrated his marriage five months before, and the church where he had buried his wife. Each man followed his own thoughts, knew pretty well what the other was thinking. When the mill gate was in sight and their privacy was coming to an end, Ned said, 'He did not offer you condolences.'

Crace shrugged. 'There's not much help in condolences. He didn't offer you any either.'

'My mother was old. It was her time. She knew it and I knew it.' Ned could not apologise on behalf of Bellman but he could, and did, say, 'He's a broken man.'

Crace's stride did not alter and he did not look up. 'We're all broken, Ned,' he said grimly. And then, with a twitch of the mouth to take the sting out of his words, 'Come on. There's some can afford to be broken. We've got rent to pay.'

Bellman's days were taken up with the care of his child. Along with the balms and oils and medications at her bedside were numerous lists: pulse rate, the length of inhalation, temperature. Her father grew adept in comparing shades of pallor; he watched for the return of colour to her cheeks as intently as a sailor watches the horizon for the first sign of land. Bellman fretted over temperatures: was Dora too warm? Too chilly? Was she lying in a draught? He opened and closed windows, called for extra blankets and then had them folded away. Bedjackets and mittens and muffs were added to the invalid, then subtracted again. All through the day Mrs Lane and Mary were on hand, he shared some of this care. At night, he remained alone to nurse his child.

After the last counting of heartbeats and measuring of temperature at midnight, Bellman sat in the armchair in the corner of Dora's room and slumbered and dozed until he fell into profound unconsciousness. Later in the night, the totality of blackness receded and he found himself deposited on an unknown grey shore, a place between sleep and wakefulness. In this place, strange and fanciful ideas formed in his mind, and in the dark he reached for his notebook and pencil and turned to some future blank page to scribble, fluent and prolific words. Were his notes reasonable? Would they be legible even in the light of day? Questions such as these did not enter his head, they belonged to some other realm: distant, irrelevant, foreign. Then the tide changed; already half asleep, he put his notebook away and drifted away to oblivion. When he awoke in the morning, it was to be claimed immediately by his charts of figures, today's tests to be carried out, and behind it all a vague and unimportant sense of having dreamed. And perhaps the faintest recollection of his night in the graveyard, so faint that it escaped his attention.

For weeks Bellman sought patterns in his figures. He was anxious to detect an underlying upward trend, but his accountant's exactitude could not be outwitted by his fatherly wishful thinking: the best that could be said was that the average was stable. And then, one Thursday, there came an alteration. All at once, Dora's condition improved. Bellman fancied that her hand, when he touched it, felt less waxy, more like human skin. Mary agreed with him. Mrs Lane counselled caution, but she agreed that her pallor was a little diminished.

The next day Dora opened her eyes, and for the first time, it was clear that she recognised her father.

'Look,' Bellman told Sanderson, holding out his notebook, 'her pulse is stronger and more regular. Her breathing is deeper. She swallows more broth. Time to try her on something more sustaining, don't you think? She turns her gaze towards me.'

The doctor could not deny that there was a change. An improvement. The child was aware. Yet still, he could not look at the patient without feeling a profound malaise. Pallor, emaciation, loss of musculature, muteness, alopecia, absence of response to sound, touch, the human voice . . . She was an encyclopedia of symptoms, you could fill a textbook with Dora alone, she ought to be exhibited in the universities. All that to worry about, and the father rejoiced over his tables and the maid's great lament was that there was nothing a hairbrush could do to disguise the pink circles of smoothness on the girl's scalp. Her looks – though he dare not say it – were the least of their worries. The fever had done worse than ruin the girl's skin and make her bald. He very much feared it had reduced her mind to ashes.

In the town the fever had run its course and ebbed away.

Everyone had lost someone. Some had lost everyone.

People remembered. They wept and they grieved. In the spaces between, they were glad that the leeks and rhubarb were doing well this year, envied the bonnet of the neighbour's cousin, relished the fragrance of pork roasting in the kitchen on Sunday. There were those that registered the beauty of a pale moon suspended behind the branches of the elms on the ridge. Others took their pleasure in gossiping.

Being known to all in the town, Bellman and his tragedy were the focus of some of this gossip. Mary's tongue meant no harm, and she talked to any willing listener. Neighbours, employees, tradespeople, everyone added their ha'p'orth to the story: Dora Bellman was a skeleton. She lolled in her bed more dead than alive. She was blind, she was deaf, she was mute. Her body lived but her soul had passed over. She had lost her mind.

The joiner who had raised the level of the invalid's bed so that she could see out of the window, told of Dora Bellman sitting up in bed, her dark hair turned to tufts of down.

'You wouldn't hardly know she were a girl. A scarecrow maybe, or a puppet made to frighten the children.'

And had she lost her mind?

No. The joiner did not think so. That's not what he had heard from the girl who looked after her.

And they gossiped about Bellman. His frown and his sombre gaze; the absence of his old energy; if he was seen in the high street at all, he kept his head down, no more the nods and the tilts of the hat he had once broadcast with liberal geniality.

The Bellman family graves were not being tended, and Bellman was never in church these days.

'He is too occupied with his daughter,' people said, and for a time Bellman's neglect was forgiven.

'Has he still not gone to the mill?' they wanted to know.

He hadn't.

Nor did he go to the Red Lion.

'He does nothing but fret over his poor scarecrow,' the townspeople concluded. They pitied him for his losses. They admired his paternal devotion. Yet all the same, he was Mr Bellman of the mill. Surely the mill was where he should be? This state of affairs couldn't go on for ever. Could it?

2

Dora's hair did not grow and her eyelashes did not come back. But flesh softened the contours of her bones and a tinge of colour grew every day more marked in her cheeks. Her breathing deepened. Her pulse was firmer. There came a time when it was clear that her eyes were following movement with intelligence, and then one day Mary was astounded to hear a hoarse old man's voice asking for honey water: it was Dora. She kissed Dora and shouted at the top of her voice for Mr Bellman.

'You have come back!'

Bellman wept.

For three months Bellman had thought of nothing but his daughter. He had lain down the reins of his life to sustain Dora in hers. Now that she was out of danger and her health was stable, it was time to return to the world.

Mary cleaned the study window and left it open to air the room that had gone so long unused. She took the carpet out to beat, and rubbed wax into the furniture. She polished the brass fireguard, plumped the cushions of the armchair and refilled the inkwell.

At ten o'clock Bellman entered and sat at his desk. He exhaled a great sigh of old, stale breath and replaced it with fresh April air. He ran his fingers with satisfaction over his empty desk. There were days out there waiting for him to awake them. There was a future. It wanted only his touch to stir it into life.

From his pocket he took his leather notebook. He flicked past the lists of temperatures and times and pulse rates. He'd done that now. He tucked them under the loop of string that he used to separate yesterday's dead pages from today's and tomorrow's.

What about these other pages? A wild scrawl, written at speed, the lines sloping up or down, a second line sometimes superimposed over the earlier one. Oh, yes, he remembered. A father must do something to while away the dark hours while he keeps vigil over his child. Notions, that's all it was. Playthings for a fretful mind at midnight . . .

A word caught his attention and he peered more closely.

From the growing intentness of his reading an onlooker might have judged that he was finding more interest in his half-forgotten notes than he had expected. He turned the pages slowly, scrutinised the night-time writing with close attention so as not to miss a thing. Once or twice he flicked back to something he had read before. Here and there he made a few brief annotations.

The things a man does not think about can incubate in him without benefit of conscious attention. The idea, blithely indifferent to William's human troubles, had implanted itself, sucked sustenance from him, fed on his blood without his knowing it. Now that he was ready to turn his daytime mind to it, the incubus was ready to be born.

At the end of his reading he stared into space for a single minute, gathering his thoughts, then turned the page and wrote unhesitatingly, fluently for a full hour. Objectives, timetables, lists, costs, plans, obstacles, strategies. At the final word, he put down his pen and, waving his diary in the air for the ink to dry, smiled the smile of a man who has put his hand in his pocket for a farthing and drawn out a golden goose.

What a gem of an idea! he exclaimed. What a glorious opportunity!

The word made an echo in his mind. It evoked the raw earth smell of the graveyard. He knew he ought to track down the man in black and hammer out a proper contract. He wouldn't negotiate hard. That wouldn't be the right thing to do. The idea was such a good one, and the man had offered it with such an air of generosity that it would be churlish to argue too hard over terms. Find out what he wanted, a bit of argument for form's sake – business was business, you had to respect that – but at heart he meant to give the man what he asked for. He could afford to be generous; there was more than enough to go round.

There was the matter of finding him. That raised a difficulty or two. The man must have said his name was Black at some point in the conversation, even if Bellman couldn't remember it precisely. But his appearance was distinctive, wasn't it? One day when he had the leisure for it, he would sit down for a minute or two, that is all it would take, and the man's face would swim up to the surface of his mind easily enough. And then it would be enough to ask around. He had tried before to find out about Black, but that was different. Admittedly, he hadn't been methodical in his approach. He had asked the wrong people. His failure then meant nothing. When he applied himself, things would come right. Things always did, when he applied himself.

When the time was right.

Bellman took up his pen to add an addendum – *Find Black* – to his notes, but the nib had dried. Between the page and the ink pot, his pen hovered uncertainly. Was he missing something here? Was there something else he should be taking into account? He thought for ten seconds, fifteen. He found his thoughts entering unfamiliar, unsignposted territory. He frowned. It was a thing he had seen too often in others: people got lost in their own doubts. With a strong objective in mind, success well within reach, they hesitated and pondered, fretted over minutiae, and in the time they lost, the whole project was sunk. Essential to keep abreast of the whole. Details always sorted themselves out in the fullness of time.

Bellman didn't write it in his notebook. There was no need. It wasn't something he was likely to forget.

He rubbed his hands in anticipation at the thought of his new venture, and anticipated his lunch with an excellent appetite.

'Did you hear all the racket we made?' Mary asked Dora, when they were alone together. 'The piano and the gong and the pans?'

Dora shook her head. 'The only thing I heard was the rooks. I heard them for a long time. And then I woke up.' She thought for a moment. 'Don't tell my father.'

3

On a Tuesday at the beginning of May, William Bellman returned to the mill. He heard in the rhythm of the machinery that things were all right. There was some awkwardness: he saw in people's faces that they found him changed. Well, he found himself changed. He did the rounds with Crace, nodded and shook hands with the senior men, took in a hundred and one pieces of information and asked short, considered questions. He left early.

He spent the Wednesday in the office with Ned. Orders, invoicing, accounts. All was in order. He left early.

On Thursday he made a methodical and rigorous assessment of mill affairs and concluded that it was running perfectly well without him. He sent Mary over with a note and, fifteen minutes later, Ned and Crace were before him in his study. He set out what he wanted of them and they agreed that it was no more than they had been doing these last weeks. He asked them what aspects of the work they needed him for. They mentioned one or two things, and when he added one or two more they nodded. Otherwise they thought they could manage.

'Good,' he nodded.

What was this all about? Ned and Crace wondered. Just when Bellman had come back, sound as ever, troubles behind him, he appeared to be making plans for another absence.

'How long might this new arrangement be for?' Ned asked. 'If it is to be more than a month or two, is it worth training one of the junior clerks to take over some of my responsibilities?'

'Certainly,' said William. 'The new arrangement is to be permanent.'

This new future was too large to be grasped immediately.

Crace found his bearings sufficiently to ask a question: 'But who will manage the mill?' and immediately lost them again, when Bellman answered, 'You two.'

Ned was stunned. The mill without Bellman? He and Crace to run it? It was unthinkable! He took a deep breath in shock, but as the air entered him, he felt himself expand. Was it unthinkable? It took Bellman to think of it, but now that he had . . .

Ned breathed out.

It could be done.

For a week William was quite busy at the mill. He sat in the office while foremen and clerks were called in to talk about their changed futures, changed fortunes. Bellman insisted that it must be Ned and Crace who took charge of these interviews. He was just overseeing, there for his new managers to refer a question to, to offer an opinion when asked. At first they hung back, expecting to take the lead from him; very quickly they understood what he intended: they were the decision makers now. They interviewed, conferred, made their choice and then glanced at William. A nod was all that was required. They knew as well as he.

During the following weeks, Bellman gradually reduced his hours at the mill. His presence was enough to stabilise confidence during the handover. What was already clear to Bellman now became clear to everyone else: the Bellman touch was there in the system, the routine, the habits. Like a clockmaker who has weighed and cleaned and balanced every cog and spring in a mechanism, he could leave it to others to wind it every day. There was no need for him to be there in person, and little by little he withdrew.

Six months after the fever left the town, the mill was running all by itself.

When all was still in the house, when the candles were all blown out and the last steps had sounded creakily in the landing, Dora heaved herself to a sitting position in her bed and arranged the pillows around her like companions. Fussing was over for the day. Mary and her mother were asleep. At last there was no one to take her temperature,

150

ask about her appetite, weigh her or measure her or otherwise scrutin-ise her well-being. Only now was she free to remember.

As she gazed into the blackness of her room, she could conjure the past. The noise, colour and movement of remembered scenes from the life she had lost reproduced themselves on the darkness, and the more she gave herself to this practice the more vibrant it became. It was effortless, this casting off of the present, this reunion with what had gone before.

She began where she always began: Thursday evening, father arriv-ing with the red felt bags and her brothers cheering. She saw and heard the pennies tumble into the bowl, felt the weight of the pitcher, smelled the vinegar as it splashed onto the coins. The tang of vinegar on Phil's little hands all night long, no matter how many times he scrubbed them.

From the coins, any number of other scenes might come to mind, all as bright and as vivid as the day they happened. One day and another and another, days and days of living there had been, and she remem-bered every one with such freshness and vigour that it was scarcely less true and real than life itself. Her eye lingered on faces and expressions, she received again her mother's loving looks, she made her brothers laugh, she sniffed the sweet and musty baby smell of her sister. Her remembering nights were vividly alive to her though they passed in a flash. It was the days she lived now that were dreary and long.

The lightening of the sky, discernible through the curtains, drew her out of her reverie. She wriggled back into a sleeping position and closed her eyes. When Mary brought the tea, not long after, she put her head on one side to study her.

'Hm,' she said, unimpressed. 'You don't look very rested.'

'Open the curtains, would you?' Dora asked her. 'The rooks will be coming soon.'

&

Rooks are not fussy eaters. They like insects, mammals (dead is best), acorns, crustaceans, fruit, eggs. If the rook has a preference, it is for earthworms and juicy white leatherjackets. But really he is pleased to gorge himself on almost anything he can find or steal.

The poor blue tit loses heat so quickly that he must spend almost every waking moment looking for food. Equally the guillemot, whose wings are so inefficient out of water that he must think of nothing but eating all day long if he is to stockpile enough energy to get airborne. In contrast, the rook, supreme creature that he is, can find all the food he needs in a couple of hours a day and consider the rest of his time leisure.

What does the rook do with this leisure time?

1. he tells jokes and gossips
2. he engineers handy, throw-away tools
3. he learns to speak foreign languages. The rook can imitate the human voice, a logger's crane, the crash of broken glass. And if he wants to really make fun, he can call your dog to him – with your own whistle.
4. he enjoys poetry and philosophy
5. he is expert in rook history
6. he knows more geology than you do – but since it is knowledge passed down through the generations from his ancestors, he calls it family anecdote.
7. he has a good grounding in mythology, magic and witchcraft
8. he has a keen passion for ritual

In essence, the benefits of having the key to the world's larder are that rooks have the time to think, the brain power to remember – and the wisdom to laugh.

In Latin the rook is called *corvus frugilegus* which means the food-gatherer, because of the extraordinary efficiency with which he meets his nutritional needs.

4

In a large house in the Oxfordshire countryside, a wealthy haberdasher named Critchlow sat in his high-backed armchair by the fire
and opened a letter with a silver blade. He had not been born to
comfortable firesides and silver blades; the pleasure he took in them
was greater than any earl's or prince's.

The letter was from a man he knew only by reputation: William
Bellman. It was not a long letter: from the opening salutation it went
straight to the point. That was in keeping with what he knew of the
man. William Bellman, a man of great drive, acted with purpose and
didn't waste time.

'What do you know of William Bellman?' he asked his wife.

'The clothier from Whittingford?' She put her head on one side.
'He lost his child in that outbreak of fever, didn't he? Unless it was his
wife . . . What does he want?'

'Money.'

'Hasn't he plenty of his own? Besides, we've never met him.'

'Fact that a man prefers working to standing about chatting in other
people's reception rooms isn't a reason not to invest in him. On the
contrary.'

Critchlow's interest was piqued. He wrote a reply inviting Bellman
to his house.

By the same log fire, twenty-four hours later, William revealed the
scheme to the haberdasher. He set out the idea, the costs (building,
stock, labour costs, warehousing), the time scale, the product range,
the demand, the supply chain.

'All very sound,' the haberdasher said. 'The profit?'

Bellman passed a leaf of paper to him, containing a table of figures.
'The first three years.'

In private Bellman had higher expectations than were shown on the paper. These private figures looked well founded to him. Still, he was businessman enough to know that a canny investor is likely to be put off by promises of gains that look too great. Safer all round to promise something less ambitious, enticing but attainable. So he had reined the figures in.

Critchlow drew the paper towards him and looked. He raised a rapid eyebrow at Bellman. 'You're sure of these figures?'

'No sensible man of business is ever sure of anything. An estimate is a guess. A conservative estimate is a conservative guess. But death doesn't go out of fashion.'

The man rubbed his mouth with his hand, looked back at the page. The guess of a man like William Bellman had to be worth something.

'How much do you need?'

Bellman named a figure. 'I'm putting up a quarter of that myself. I need three others.'

'Who have you spoken to?'

William mentioned the names of the other investors with whom he had made appointments. Critchlow nodded. He knew them and they were solid people.

'I like the idea. Give me some time to think it over.'

'Tomorrow?'

'You don't waste time, do you? Tomorrow it shall be.'

William picked up his table of figures and left. The man sat back down in his chair by the fire and looked into the flames.

Death doesn't go out of fashion, he thought.

This interview was repeated twice. William was offered brandy or whisky; he sat by a roaring fire; he set out his idea; he passed across a sheet of figures. None of the meetings lasted more than an hour.

William went home believing he had not long to wait and he was right.

None of the haberdashers had ever invested so much money in a single project. None had ever made his mind up about a deal so rapidly, nor with such a surge of confidence. William Bellman was putting up a full quarter of the money himself, was he? Well, well, well.

Three men by three fires poured themselves another brandy – or whisky – and leant back in three chairs with three satisfied smiles. They were rich men and they were about to be made richer.

The morning brought William three letters. Yes, yes and yes.

Good.

He could see the future. He could make it happen. He set about things.

5

First the land. No simple matter, that. Then lawyers to see off the small tradesmen scratching a living there. Meanwhile, architects and draftsmen to work on designs.

'Five storeys,' Bellman told them, 'and the essence of it to be light. The centre of the roof to be an octagonal glass window to the sky, and the entire building to be pierced through the middle, so that light will fall through the centre of the shop and not only through the windows.'

'Hmm,' the architect said and stroked his beard. 'Alternatively—'

'An atrium,' said William. 'Exactly as I have described. How else can my seamstresses see to stitch? How else can my customers see the black detail on a pair of black gloves at four o'clock on a November afternoon?'

The architect presented plans for the building: there was no atrium. 'It is hardly practical,' he pleaded. 'It will be too hot in summer. Think of the maintenance costs! And is it safe?'

William sketched out the atrium himself in his calfskin notebook, tore it out and handed it to the man. 'Go to Chance in Birmingham for the plate glass. You must get these men,' another scribble and torn-out page, 'for the installation. They are familiar with the ridge-and-furrow system. There is a system that will raise the entire glazed ceiling to let the hot air escape in summer. And if you don't know how to do it, I'll subcontract the entire roof to one of Paxton's men.'

The architect produced new plans in accordance with Bellman's wishes.

A manager of works was needed. Bellman's architect knew just the man.

'Come with me, I'll take you to him now.'

The man's office was as comfortable as any reception room. He was plump and jovial, the buttons of his waistcoat shone, and he shook

Bellman's hand with confidence. Bellman suppressed a grimace at the handshake: it was the man's clean nails, the soaped and scented softness of his skin. He stayed ten minutes with him then took his leave.

'He is not the one,' he said. 'He has not the voice for speaking to labourers. If a thing is to be done well, it cannot be done from the fireside. You have to be there yourself.'

'With respect, sir,' the architect said, 'Bensen has a very experienced team of intermediaries and he has vast experience. You need a man who is your equal in talent and experience, someone who can take the responsibility of the construction off your shoulders leaving you free for the rest of the enterprise.'

Bellman shook his head. It was not his way.

Someone younger, he thought. *Callused. Closer to the men. Closer to the work.* He asked around, and his enquiries led him to a man called Fox.

They met in a small park, round the corner from a noisy construction site. Fox wore heavy boots, had dirt under his nails and when he spoke to his men, sounded like one of them. Fox reminded him a little of himself when young: talented, hungry for a big project. Bellman set out his terms plainly. He meant to pay Fox less than the fat man with the soft hands had wanted – a lot less – but the young man stood to gain not only a lengthy and lucrative contract but something far more valuable: a reputation.

'Night and day, I'll work,' he promised, and Bellman believed him. The project would be the making of Fox, they both knew it. They shook hands, both satisfied.

Together Bellman and Fox visited stonemasons, builders and carpenters. Fox spoke their language – 'My father was a builder in Exeter' – and Bellman watched and listened. Then he asked questions and Fox fell silent, listening to Bellman ask about materials, the raw costs, the transport costs. He watched Bellman scribble sums in the notebook he always carried in his deep pockets, work out reductions, take it upon himself to draft letters to quarriers and timber merchants. Sometimes coming away from a potential tradesman and shaking their heads together over a man's perilously weak grasp of his own business, Fox would say, 'Ah, but he's got a good lad working for him. Did you see the work he was doing? Very nice. Now the lad would be an asset . . .'

'Steal him away,' Bellman directed, and Fox set about the theft of the apprentice.

The enterprise was not only a building to be constructed out of stone, but a legal entity that had to be made secure and watertight with pages of impenetrable jargon. Bellman spent long hours in lawyers' offices poring over paperwork, puzzling out contracts of labyrinthine complexity. He arrived at these meetings with a series of common-sense questions and listened to the answers with a quite uncommon intelligence. The instructions he gave were decisive, and framed in the lawyers' own language. If there was any aspect of ownership, responsibilities and entitlements he was in doubt about, it did not appear so to the lawyers who were impressed by his decisiveness and acuity.

The third aspect of the venture was financial. The grand entrance hall of the Westminster & City Bank was an impressive place. Half a mountain of Italian marble sliced into slabs for the floor and walls, hammered, chiselled and pumiced into columns, expensive, hard, intimidating. Few entered here without an inner tremor: respectable ladies felt their voices tremble like schoolgirls as they asked for their balances, and baronets adopted an exaggerated swagger as they made a withdrawal. Even the blameless vicar suppressed a nervous cough. It was impossible to escape the awareness that somewhere in this place dozens of suited clerks laboured like angels over their ledgers, entering in black copperplate the sage economies and financial imprudencies of every customer, keeping account of every transaction in guineas, shillings and pence, until the day of reckoning. No, the grand hall of the Westminster & City was not a comfortable place. No matter how stain-free one's balance, it caused the souls of even the most prudent to quail.

Quailing was quite unknown to William Bellman. He took the steps three at a time and entered the hall with as much awe as a bee that flies into Westminster's other great cathedral and comes to rest on the altar there. Quite by chance, Mr Anson, a senior manager at the bank, was passing through the hall as Bellman strode in, and had noticed his indifference to the grandeur. A strong, dark man, possessed of great energy and force, he entirely bypassed the clerk at the desk where an ordinary customer would have made an appointment, preferring to cast an observant eye over everyone in the hall. When it alighted on Mr Anson he stepped purposefully towards him and introduced himself and his requirements in a few words. 'Are you the man to help?'

Anson was not used to being accosted in this informal fashion but something in Bellman's manner and demeanour told him it would be worth his while giving him a few moments, and a few moments were enough to persuade him to give the man a longer hearing.

In a private room Bellman set out his financial projections. It was a large loan that Bellman wanted. The construction of the shop was being paid for out of capital, but a loan was wanted in order to stock it. Anson considered the figures Bellman had prepared.

'So you are in need of a loan and will be holding the shop account here too. A personal account as well, perhaps?'

'Two.'

'Two personal accounts? Both for yourself?'

Bellman nodded without explanation.

Well, that was unusual, but he could see no administrative or legal impediment. Anson looked at the proposed turnover figures. Over-optimistic, he thought, but if Bellman achieved even half of what he intended he would be doing well enough to cover the repayments. The outlook was rosy. There was nothing to stop him agreeing a deal today, and besides, he had the feeling that if Bellman didn't get the answer he wanted here and now he would take his figures and his business to another bank.

'Glad to be able to help,' he said, and offered a hand. Bellman took it and gave it a firm, single shake by the end of which he was already on his feet and ready to leave.

Anson accompanied Bellman back to the hall. They shook hands again and the banker watched his new customer cross the marble floor towards the exit with the same assured and purposeful gait he had entered with, undaunted by the great vault above his head, undiminished by the expanses of marble around him. *How unusual,* he reflected. *This is a man to whom a bank is just a place to put money. If money were raindrops then the Westminster & City is no more than a water butt. Large, expensive and made of marble, but a water butt nonetheless.*

Turning into the corridor leading to his colleague's office in search of the paper he had left there this morning, he congratulated himself. If Bellman's venture did as well as he thought it might, then he, Anson, had just done the best day's business in his life – and in less than three-quarters of an hour.

6

One wet February day, Bellman stood under a cloud-thick sky surveying his site. The ramshackle buildings of yesterday were gone, razed
to the ground, and London's earth had been broken by a hundred
shovels to expose this vast crater. There were no shovels today:
impossible to work in weather like this. Inches of rain lay in the
bottom of the pit and the new raindrops fell so heavily and insistently
into it that there was a continual splashing and flying of water. Rain
slicked Bellman's hair to his scalp and darkened his coat to an
indistinct colour. Puddles were seeping through the stitchwork of his
shoes. Every man and beast that had shelter had withdrawn to it so
that Bellman was alone in his contemplation – except for a solitary
rook on a rooftop, indifferent to the rain, who eyed both man and site
with an air of faint interest.

It was a day to inspire gloom, but not in Bellman. Another man,
more poetic or fanciful, might have seen a violent gash in the surface
of the earth, a giant's grave, a burial pit for a thousand dead, but
Bellman's eyes were attuned differently. It was the future that he was
gazing at: he saw not a pit, but a palace. London's new and greatest
emporium of mourning goods.

He knew the building to come better than any man, for it was the
child of his own mind. The wet air solidified before his eyes into a
massive block, five storeys high and twice as long. The strict ranks of
symmetrical windows borrowed their glimmer from the rain, and
between them the mistiness coalesced obediently into pilasters
topped with Corinthian capitals. Bellman's eye coaxed cornices and
corbels and lintels and mullions out of thin air and he studied these
details with an attentiveness as great as if the building had been
materially present. His glance swept the length of the full-height

ground-floor windows with their mirrored black and silver fascia and paused at the grand entrance in the middle of the frontage. A few steps, the oak double door with brass footplates and ornamental knocker. When open, the doors would be high enough to permit two men to pass through, one on the shoulders of the other. Over this door was to be a projecting platform. It would provide a porch, shelter from bad weather, somewhere to stop and shake out an umbrella or, for the nervous or hesitant, simply gather oneself before entering.

Bellman's eyes rose to the platform and squinted. On top of it was to be mounted a large insignia, elaborately carved and expensively gilded. It would represent the name of the shop. He peered and puzzled, but this spot, twenty feet above the ground and in the dead centre of his project, refused to be anything but mistily blurred and wet air.

What was the shop to be called?

Bellman did not know.

He had not neglected the matter, far from it. In fact, he had consulted Critchlow and the other haberdashers on this very question in the early days, but none had wished to lend the shop his name. Having launched their daughters into marriage with respectable, impoverished gentlemen, they now waited to marry their granddaughters to greater status. For the success of such an endeavour, the wealth they had accumulated from retail needed to hide its origins, for it is well known that the purity of gold increases the further removed it is from labour. The impression must be given that a man's riches spring from his noble nature as naturally and spontaneously as water springs from the earth.

'No,' they had said. 'Let the shop be called Bellman's.'

Why did he hesitate? Bellman had no qualms about giving his shop his name. The notion of a grand marriage for Dora did not enter his head. Nor was it modesty that held him back. There was something unfinished in his thinking about the name and today, when the rain had dissolved all busyness and activity around him and left only this misty haze, was as good a day as any to complete it.

Standing alone before the mirage of his shop, Bellman's thoughts turned to the man in black.

Was it any wonder that he had let the question of Black lapse for so long? For over a year, Bellman had worked on the project. He had developed it from an idea to a financial reality, then nursed it into legal existence. The legal side of things had required lengthy and delicate negotiations that had consumed him for months; the land purchase had not gone smoothly; the architects had stubbornly refused to understand what he wanted – good lord, he had ended up practically drawing the plans himself; there had been contractors to engage, more negotiations, more contracts . . . Night after night he had sat by candlelight, working out solutions to problems that others deemed insoluble. In all that time he had not thought too closely or too often of Black and frankly, what could be more natural? Bellman's diary was very full. Every hour from morning till night was accounted for, days and weeks ahead. He moved from meeting to meeting, from decision to decision with scarcely a pause to draw breath. He never ate a meal without either company or his papers and notebook beside him at the table. He reserved little difficulties to be thought about while he brushed his teeth and dressed in the morning. Bathtime was the occasion to lock himself away with knotty problems that could be unravelled while the steam rose off the water.

When problems arose that did not lend themselves to being broken down into components, tabulated and calculated in order to afford a neat solution, Bellman's habit was to put them aside in a category marked 'waste of time'. One of the first keys to success, he considered, was to recognise the difference between problems you could do something about and problems you could do nothing about. A great many people, he had noticed, spent large parts of their time worrying about things they were powerless to alter. Had they concentrated all this energy on things they could influence, think how different their lives

164

would be. He advocated concentrating on those things where you had some guarantee of an outcome. Every minute of Bellman's day was spent actively pursuing some benefit or other, and for months now it had not been clear that there was any benefit to be had from thinking about Black, so in he went to the category of 'unprofitable' and there he stayed.

Now Black's idea was about to become material. As soon as this weather cleared up, construction would start. Naturally the problem of Black was starting to appear to Bellman in a more pressing light. It bothered him that his recollection of his meeting with Black was so unclear. Clarity was everything in a business relationship. What did Black expect of him? And what could he expect of Black? He felt anew the sense of indebtedness that haunted him. Black had been the one to recognise the magnitude of the opportunity, he had wanted to share it with Bellman; it was essential that the man should be adequately recompensed. What had they agreed?

He closed his eyes and thought.

'Percentages . . .' he muttered. 'Division of responsibilities . . . Dividends . . .'

He strained to hear an echo from the past, an indication of the conversation they might have had, the deal they might have struck. Nothing came to his ear.

Well, there was only one thing for it. He would do something that would make plain to Black that he had not been overlooked. It would be an invitation to him – wherever he was – to come forward and claim his due. It would be evidence – not that it would come before a court of law, of course not, there would be nothing so extreme – that he, Bellman, had no intention of claiming as his own that portion of the business that was rightly Black's.

He would call the shop Bellman & Black.

Opening his eyes onto the misty mirage of his emporium, he found the point where the platform projected over the front entrance and his imagination placed a grand double 'B' on it.

That would do it!

165

'Hoy!'

A loud cry broke into Bellman's reverie. He discovered himself somewhat adrift in his own mind, and it took him a long moment to recover himself. He was a long way from reality, the four floors of stone and glass before him had to dissolve into rain and it was with mild astonishment that he found himself in front of a great gash in the ground. When a creature crawled out of it, slick with rain and mud, Bellman took a step back and almost let out a cry of alarm.

'Look at this!' the creature exclaimed, demonstrating itself thus to be a living thing and human. He stood up and held out to Bellman what looked like a stone. His voice was cultivated, expensively schooled, but his appearance and behaviour was more than strange. Bellman wondered whether it was a madman. Then, seeing that the man stood straight and held himself still, and that the light in the man's eyes was enthusiastic, not wild, Bellman felt a little reassured. He glanced at what the man was holding.

'It's a stone.'

'Ah! That's where you're wrong!'

The man rubbed some of the mud away. 'See the tool marks? They are man-made.'

There were indeed abrasion marks that William had taken for striations in the stone.

'And?'

'It's not carved as such. The stone already had a form that called the shape to mind, and these marks are just to emphasise it. See the knot in the stone that gives the idea of the eye?'

The man began to talk. He had been in Egypt lately, was what he called an archaeologist – 'I dig up the past,' he explained – and was now home in London for a few months. He would go back to Egypt. 'But when I saw this site I thought it looked just like an excavation and I couldn't resist coming to have a look. There have been men crawling all over it, but today, thanks to the rain, I have my chance.'

'I am glad that somebody profits from the rain. Every day that the construction is not finished costs me. Is it worth something, your stone?'

'Worth?'

'Money. What would a museum give you for it? A collector?'

'A museum! Why nothing! This is London, not Egypt! I don't know why the past of Egypt is worth something when the past of London is worth nothing, but there it is.'

'I can tell you the reason for that easily enough. In London it is the future that matters.'

'And what is it to be, in the future, this site of yours?'

'It will be Bellman & Black. An emporium of mourning goods.'

'You are Mr Black?'

Bellman felt a lurch in his chest. 'I am Mr Bellman.'

'Well, Mr Bellman, you should do nicely with your mourning goods. Death comes to us all. The future, eh? Mine. Yours. Everyone's.'

The young man's eyes followed the curving flight of the rook that turned and swooped, brilliant with rain, through the air that was to be Bellman's Emporium.

'They used to put the dead out on stone platforms for their bones to be picked clean by the rooks. Did you know that? Long time ago. Before our crosses and spires and prayerbooks. Before' – he swept his hand in a broad, vague gesture, taking in the pit, Regent Street, London, who knows what else – 'before all this. Perhaps the ancient ancestor of that rook there' – it swooped and flapped and dropped with exactitude onto a piece of rock waiting to be tipped into the foundations – 'feasted on an ancient ancestor of mine. Or yours, come to that.' Through the downpour he caught a glimpse of Bellman's disgust. 'Every era its own ways, eh? Who knows what will come next, eh? They burn the dead in Italy, I hear.' He shook his head and smiled at Bellman. 'Must be going. The old man will be wondering where I've got to.'

He went.

Had Bellman just had an encounter with a half-wit? Had he really spoken the words Bellman thought he had heard? It seemed scarcely

167

credible. Man crawls out of the mud, talking a lot of nonsense about rooks . . . An eccentric, at the very least.

The cloth of Bellman's coat was sodden over his shoulders. The rain had crept fibre by fibre through his overcoat, jacket, shirt and underclothes. His skin was clammy.

Bellman turned the stone over in his hand. Was that the eye the fellow meant? A round indentation in the stone, revealing in the centre a dot of the shining core. It looked for all the world like a little eye gleaming at him. Curious, he rubbed the last of the mud off. These must be the tool marks . . . Feathers? Yes, here was a wing and turning it over, another. The still-falling rain brought out the iridescence in the stone. Flashes of purple, kingfisher blue and green came to life in the black as he held it.

Horrible thing!

With a shudder, William tossed it away from him and into the pit. It traced a curve in the air, a graceful parabola that recalled a feeling of something from long ago.

It disturbed a bird where it fell. Like a black rag the creature rose up into the wetness, the first powerful flap of its wings lifted it through deliveries and as far as ground-floor umbrellas, with the second it ascended to coats and hats on the first floor. Up it rose through the offices, into the seamstresses' atelier and out of the building through the atrium's glass ceiling.

Bellman turned away, sick at heart, longing for a fire and his work.

'Bellman & Black,' he announced that night at Russell's, his club in Mayfair where he met at regular intervals with his haberdashers.

'Excellent!' said Critchlow. 'It never hurts to indicate two owners in a company name. Gives a sense of solidity. Security. Two heads are better than one, that kind of thing.'

The second haberdasher nodded. 'And a clever choice of name too. What is the first thing people think of when they need mourning goods? They think of black. And having thought it, they will already be halfway to thinking of our company!'

The third haberdasher smiled. 'It sounds right, don't you think?

Musical. As if the two names were meant to go together. I'm all for it. Gentlemen,' he raised a glass, 'to the success of Bellman & Black!'

Bellman raised his glass and sipped, but he didn't stay long enough to finish the glass. His feet were damp and he had work to do.

7

It would take fifteen months to complete the shop: twelve for the construction work and three for the fitting out. Bellman had seen Fox at work long enough to know that he could be left to oversee the construction of the building for weeks at a time. That was good. It meant Bellman could get on with the rest.

Bellman had expanded his own mill, but even so large a mill as his own could not supply all the cloth needs of a shop the size of Bellman & Black. So in bumpy carriages and on horseback he covered hundreds of miles.

In Scotland he inspected peat-black tweeds and cashmeres. On the quayside at Portsmouth and Southampton he opened crates of foreign silk, rubbed the slippery folds between his fingers, shook out a length to judge the weight, drape, opacity. He went to Spitalfields and further, to Norwich, in search of the flattest, most light-draining crape that could be had. He visited mills in Wales, Lancashire and Yorkshire, criss-crossed the country, tirelessly, looking for bombazine and parramatta and mourning silk and merino and woollen barège and grenadine and barathea.

'Show me your black,' he announced on arrival. Bellman always looked at the black first. It emptied the eye and the mind of passing impressions, cleared the visual palate, as it were. His eye was expert, he could spot a touch of green in this one, a blue tendency in another, a purplish tint here. Nothing to be concerned about from a commercial point of view: there had to be a black for every complexion, one black for fair hair and another for brunettes, red-heads needed blacks all their own . . . Once in a while he found what he termed a true black. These were hard to come by. Most people couldn't tell the difference, but Bellman would lose himself for a minute in the depths before ordering as many yards as could be produced.

If he was pleased with the blacks, he would go on to see what the clothier might do to supply him in semi-mourning and quarter-mourning. So every visit saw him plunged into deepest mourning before moving on through shades of grey from the darkest to the palest emerging at last into the mauves and puces of quarter-mourning.

Bellman grew to be a stranger to colour. When he looked out of the carriage window en route from one mill to the next, he found himself thinking that the bold green of the grass was verging on the indecent and the azure sky on a summer day struck him as vulgar. On the other hand, he saw endless degrees of gravity and tenderness of feeling in an overcast November landscape, and as for a midnight sky, now there was beauty no fabric could match – though he searched high and low for one that came close.

Bellman sent home to Mrs Lane endless parcels of fabric samples with detailed instructions. 'These dozen squares to be cut in half and one half hung in a south-facing window, the other half left in a closed drawer; after one month the two halves to be reunited to test for light-fastness.' Or else, 'One half to be washed, dried and ironed fifty times, then compared with its twin for fade.' Mrs Lane grumbled and wrote a letter of complaint. Did he not think she had enough to do, what with Dora and a house to keep? So Bellman took on a girl who thought it a great lark to be paid to scrub squares of cloth against a board with soap as hard as she could, and start all over again as soon as the pieces were dry.

There was an old dyer in the north whose reputation for black was unequalled. He was soon to retire, and had no sons to pass his secrets to. Bellman offered him a large incentive to talk about black. The dyer agreed, but when Bellman presented himself to learn the secrets, the man's lifelong reticence got the better of him, and he was reluctant to speak.

Bellman showed him his purse, to jog his memory, but the man shook his head.

'What good is money to me now, eh? Old as I am, I'll not have the time to spend it.'

So much for nothing! But a thought struck Bellman.

'A funeral then. Six horses, two mutes, and an angel over your grave.'

The man told him everything he wanted to know: '*Haematoxylum campechianum*, otherwise known as bloodwood. You can buy it anywhere, but in my experience the best comes from a man in Mexico . . .'

From there, Bellman rode to the south coast and met with the captain of a ship heading for South America.

'There is a man in Yucatan,' he explained. 'I want to buy all the bloodwood he has. He is to supply no one else. I want you to bring it to me and on no account to let it be mixed with bloodwood from other sources.' He pointed to some figures on a paper. 'This is what I will pay you. This is what I will pay him.'

The man looked at the paper. 'He will be a rich man.'

'We will all be rich men.'

It was not all cloth and bloodwood. In Whitby Bellman watched young men being lowered on ropes down the perilous cliffs of shale to the stripe of black. Suspended over the waves, the men hammered and tapped to extract the jet. From the shore he went into the town, where he visited a number of carvers, selected the best of them, instructed them to take on assistants and apprentices and placed orders for rings, brooches, lockets and necklets, earrings, hair decorations. He ordered beads by the thousand: plain and faceted, carved and polished, beads of every shape and size to be stitched to gowns and hats and cuffs and bags where they would catch the light and gleam and glitter darkly. Fathomless black for the first phase of mourning, certainly, but after that, why should black not be as brilliant as any colour?

In the course of weeks and months, Bellman discovered a great diversity of workplaces. There was the milliner's studio, the cordwainer's atelier, the low-ceilinged premises of the umbrella makers. At bookbinders across London he negotiated prices for books and diaries bound in all grades of black and grey skin and linen, in which the bereaved might record for all posterity the last days, pious words and divine visions of their lost ones. He climbed stairs to a damp-free room where paper of various weights and qualities and sizes was laid out for his inspection, all with black borders, ranging from half an inch to one-eighth of an inch thick. He placed the largest single order the company had ever received, so that countless widows and children, as yet unbereaved, would be able to inform their circle of the deaths that were yet to happen. In a reek of oil and ink he got his fingers dirty poking into the mechanisms of a printing press. 'Productivity?' he wanted to know. 'Maintenance?' What it boiled down to was this: would he be able to deliver headed notepaper within London within four hours of notification? When he got the answer he wanted, he ordered a press.

'Seven months wait? Too long.'

He bribed the manufacturer to jump the queue.

Coffins, of course. Bellman ran his finger along smooth finished pieces of work in a dozen different joinery workshops. How much oak do you have in stock? What about elm? Mahogany? Where do you season your timber? For how long? In warehouses he followed the grain in the wood, looked for knots and warping and other flaws. When he had found the best in the hundred miles around London, he drew up contracts. 'I pay the best prices, but you sell to no one else. No one, mind.'

Bellman turned his attention to his catalogue. He advertised at the art school for artists to produce drawings for his catalogues and a series of young men presented themselves at his office with portfolios. He looked through sketches of antique ruins, classical statues with naked breasts and missing arms, architectural fragments. He was looking for the ability to convey a lot of information in a small space, accurately and with clarity. After that it was a matter of judging who could work fast and reliably.

Bellman employed a trio of such artists. The students spent their evenings and Sunday afternoons drawing detailed pictures of over two hundred different styles of coffin and funerary ornament. Coffins would be lead lined or unlined or metallic lined; with handles and escutcheons in brass or silvered, plain or with many degrees of ornamentation; lined in silk or velvet or satin, embroidered or plain; the lid embellished with plaques engraved with lilies or ivy or the eternal serpent.

Two greying sisters with long fingers and mysterious smiles wrote lavish descriptions of these funerary items to accompany the drawings. In a separate section of the catalogue, certain of the designs were repeated with delicate adjustments and additions making them suitable for children's coffins. The grey sisters excelled themselves here; their smiles when they delivered the copy were even more enigmatic. All these drawings, all this text, Bellman had printed on best quality paper and bound into catalogues that were a marvel of gravity and beauty in themselves.

The prices he put on a separate sheet, slipped into a quarter pocket inside the back cover, like an afterthought.

Bellman surprised himself sometimes.

But I can sleep anywhere! he thought as he turned over yet again and rearranged the sheets that had enshrouded him.

It was true. On his long journeys he stayed at roadside inns where he laid his bones down on a rough straw bed and slept as sweetly as a lapdog on a silk pillow. At his London lodgings the revels in the street never disturbed him. Even in a coach being driven along a pitted and stony country road, he could close his eyes and nod off, giving his overworked brain a rest.

Only in Whittingford, in his own bed, was he sleepless.

His habit was to lie on his left side. In the old days that had meant Rose was behind him. He would hear her breathing in the night. Sometimes, as she edged close to him for warmth, her hand would gently stir his sleep. Now that she was dead, the space at his back was ·
alive with her absence.

He had tried sleeping on his right side and on his back. He tried sleeping on the other side of the bed altogether. He moved the bed into another room and brought in a new one. He changed rooms. Nothing worked. The bed stroked his back with its fingers, the sheet embraced him, every draught was her sigh.

It was no good. He got up and went to the window to look outside. The sky was almost dark but a sliver of moon highlighted the church spire. On just such a night he had found himself in the churchyard, talking to Black with the dark shapes of the yews around them and freshly dug graves waiting. One of those graves should have been Dora's, he reflected.

Criss-crossing the country by road and rail, in London one day and a hundred miles away the next, it was easy to keep his thoughts in careful order, but in Whittingford, with that spire piercing the moon, thoughts he preferred to keep separate had a tendency to find each other.

He had entered into a deal with Black and Dora had survived.

The possibility that these two events were connected troubled Bellman. At the time of Dora's recovery he had been in a state of great distress, and the activity of his mind could not be accurately described as rational. He recognised that. Later, the relief he felt left little room for thought. Then there had been Bellman & Black to think about.

On nights like this, things he should perhaps have thought about before came back to torment him. He had made a deal with Black and his daughter, on the very brink of death, had been returned to him. Now that his association with death was professional, he liked to think he benefited from certain related advantages, and in the middle of the night, his mind proposed to him that his child's survival was one. Yet he had only to see her – her frailty, her halting progress from room to room, leaning on her stick, the lace mantle she wore to cover her white scalp – to suspect that death had not retreated but was only biding his time.

What was the deal? He had tried more than once to remember what had been agreed, but it was possible, wasn't it, that his failure to remember was because he had agreed nothing? What if this opportunity had been given and the boon had been conferred and nothing had been agreed? Presumably the boon could be removed at any moment. The opportunity could be withdrawn at no notice. Without a contract, there was no knowing what he was to do to meet requirements . . .

Bellman turned his face from the window and drew the curtains closed. He did not like the moon peering into this house, pointing out what he held dear and showing where his treasure was. Rather hide his love for his child, rather cloak it in darkness than advertise it.

Perhaps it was better for all concerned if he just kept away. Like the bird that lures predators away from the nest by making a display of itself far off, he would protect his daughter by keeping his distance. The greater the success of Bellman & Black, the safer she would be.

8

Bellman did not lose sight of the construction of his shop. Between visits north, south, east and west, he came to London to check the progress of his emporium.

He kept an office in London, close enough to the building site so that from his window he could see the shop rise, stone by stone, from the ground. He held interviews here for the senior staff. He had found an excellent fellow to be his right-hand man, Verney by name. He had the same soft, white hands as the chief of works his architect had suggested and whom Bellman had refused. When he performed mental arithmetic, the fleshy fingers performed a kind of high-speed ballet, fingertips bouncing off each other in a spellbinding display of prestidigitation until, arriving at the solution, he rubbed both hands together and noted the answer fastidiously. No, there was nothing wrong with fastidiousness in a numbers man and Bellman offered him the job and was paying him already though there was only half a job there at present.

Today it was Fox he was meeting with. He saw him frequently when he was in London to go over forthcoming work, timetables, problems. The main business at present was doors.

A minute before their meeting was due to start, Bellman saw Fox come away from the site. He strode towards the office with an energetic gait he had copied without realising it from Bellman.

'Come in! How is it all coming along? Will you be ready by the fifteenth of May?'

Bellman always began like this.

'All will be ready on the fifteenth of May. Rest assured. The design for the oak entrance doors are with Mr Deakin. He is giving the job to his very best man. The side and back doors are in hand with his team.'

Bellman nodded. 'It's the internal doors I want to instruct on today.

I want you to think of the emporium as a theatre. The customers must not be distracted by any sense of what is happening offstage. You have already noted the cork lining to the corridors?'

'It is in the warehouse now. The doors to be lined on the other side with cork too? We left that undecided.'

'It will be quieter than baize. Do it. There is more to be considered than noise though. Stock is to be replenished as invisibly as possible. Staff must be allowed to enter and exit the shop floor with the utmost discretion. The doors between the staff passageways and the shop floor are not to appear as doors at all, but must seem to the naked eye as part of the panelling. The way I see it, the edges of each door will be concealed in the shadowed part of the relief, so that the wall will appear unbroken.'

'Handles?'

Bellman shook his head. 'A ball latch that will answer to pressure from either side. A member of staff must come and go noiselessly and invisibly.'

Fox nodded as he noted these instructions in a calfskin book he had got from the same supplier as Bellman's. The pencil he wrote with was one that Bellman had given him.

'Consider it done.'

'You will be sure to have the building complete for the fifteenth of May?'

Fox smiled. 'I will have it done for the fourteenth if you wish it.'

Bellman stared. 'Can you?'

Fox had spoken lightly. It was only a joke. He had forgotten that Bellman had no sense of humour. But being young and ambitious and liking a challenge, he couldn't help answering, 'Of course.'

After lunch they spent half an hour in a brougham before arriving at a courtyard, then a room fragrant with cedar and pine, and carpeted with curls cut from the heads of babies, that were crisp underfoot. On the wall, a rack of gouges and chisels, meticulously arranged. The carver, with bone-white hair shorn to his skull, bent over his work with intent concentration.

'Best in London,' Fox murmured and then, louder, as the man

looked up to greet them, 'Mr Geoffroys. This is Mr Bellman. Come to see how things are progressing.'

Mr Geoffroys returned the gouge to its place.

'Two of the large elements are complete.' He invited them with a gesture to walk to the back of the workshop, where two forms rested against the wall. Taller than a man, the elaborate 'B' shapes were exact twins.

Bellman and Fox ran fingers along the curves of the Bs, admiring the smoothness of the carving, the grace of the flourishes, the closeness of the joints.

'Once it's plated these joins will be quite invisible,' Mr Geoffroys told Bellman. 'And see here' – carved trains of ivy leaves and fine wooden lilies – 'these will fit together like so to make the garland.'

Bellman could not have been more satisfied. It was fine workmanship, the letters had grandeur, once silvered they would be even more impressive; the floral garland would be exquisite.

'It looks nearly finished . . . What is it that remains to be done?'

'The and.'

'The end?' Bellman was puzzled.

'And. Ampersand, I believe you call it. Come and see.'

They moved back to the work area. The block of wood that Mr Geoffroys was working on was clamped. Roughly hewn at the edges and the base, marked out lightly in pencil, it was starting to take shape at the top. The carver selected a gouge and applied it to the wood. Standing on a platform to be at the right height, he shifted his weight to one foot, leant into the tool with meticulous control. The movement came not from his arm, but his whole body, it seemed, and a shaving of wood pared away like a curl of butter. He repeated the movement with tiny modifications, over and over and the curve took shape.

Ampersand. The sign that denoted a commercial relationship. The figure that bound B to B. The connection. The tie.

A sudden and unexpected thread of doubt wormed into Bellman's thoughts. He put his head on one side and looked again. Was that really right?

'You don't think that's going to be too . . .'

Fox looked alarmed. 'Too . . . ?'

Mr Geoffroys stopped his carving and both he and Fox watched Bellman.

What was it? Bellman's chest constricted and his mouth was dry. Was he too hot?

Because his employer didn't speak, Fox broke in. 'If it's wrong it can be redone. Let's see . . .' He had the original design with him. He unfolded it and spread it flat. He compared it with the sketches and measurements given to the carver. 'All is as planned – the ampersand equivalent in height to the initials – of course if, seeing it in reality, it seems out of proportion . . . At present it is incomplete, so it gives an impression of solidity that will be alleviated once it is finished. And the gilding will lighten the effect again. It will be less – er – wooden.'

'Yes. Less . . . Yes.'

There was a moment of uncertainty. Mr Geoffroys looked at Fox, who looked at Bellman, who looked at the ampersand appearing out of a block of oak.

Complete, it would be less solid. Gilded, it would appear lighter.

Bellman pulled at his collar and swallowed uncomfortably.

'Of course, if it troubles you, it can be redone. It might even be possible to reuse some of the completed—'

'No. Go ahead. It's all right.'

They turned to leave.

'Ready middle of next week, then?' Fox asked Mr Geoffroys.

Mr Geoffroys nodded as they took their leave and said something Bellman didn't quite catch.

'An inn,' Bellman instructed their driver.

'It's the wood dust,' Fox agreed. 'It does make the throat unbearably dry. You didn't catch what Geoffroys said, I think?'

'What? No.'

'He said, "Goodbye, Mr Black." Funny, eh? Suppose that happens all the time.'

Fox found Bellman unusually silent over their drink at the inn and on the way back to Regent Street. He appeared to be brooding over some intractable problem. It was quite unlike him to be abstracted or indecisive or at a loss. His characteristic resolve and energy had melted from his face and the expression revealed was almost unrecognisable as Bellman's. What was it? Fear? Anguish? Despair?

'All right?' he asked, uncertainly.

Bellman did not respond. Eyes fixed in the middle distance, he gave every impression of being miles away, so Fox was taken aback when all of a sudden Bellman started to speak.

'Fell into conversation with a fellow. Couple of years back, now. Barely knew the man, never been introduced. He's the one that put me onto it. The mourning-goods business. Spotted the opportunity, as it were.'

He locked eyes with Fox, who said, 'And?'

Bellman frowned and scratched his head. 'It raises questions. Doesn't it? If he should turn up, wanting . . .'

'A share of the business?'

'For instance.'

Fox thought about it. He was no lawyer but he'd signed a few contracts in his time. 'Just a conversation, you say? You hadn't met with a view to talking business?'

'No! No! Pure chance we even met.'

'He didn't set out his terms and conditions? Ask you to sign any-thing?'

Bellman shook his head.

'Well then, he hasn't got a leg to stand on, has he?'

'You think so?'

'Of course! Having ideas is one thing, but putting them into action is quite another. What's he done since for you?'

'Nothing. Haven't seen him.'

'Well, then. A lawyer would laugh it out of court. Who's to say it wasn't your idea anyway? You were in the production business already. Had the contacts. The investment. You're the one who's been putting the hours in.'

Bellman grimaced. 'If it was his idea, though . . .'

'Ideas! I have a hundred every day. Worth nothing till someone puts

181

a bit of time and effort into it.' Something struck him. 'Any witnesses to this conversation?'

'Not a soul there but us.'

'Don't give it another thought, then. If he turns up with his begging bowl you can either give him a slap-up dinner and a bottle of brandy or send him off with a flea in his ear, depending on how amenable he seems. If he wants to fight you in court, let him. What's to stop you denying the conversation ever happened?'

Bellman seemed half convinced. 'I've told you though.'

Fox winked at him. 'I haven't heard a word you've said this last ten minutes.'

Back at Regent Street, the slowing of the carriage and the opening of the door onto the clamour of the construction site roused Bellman. He jumped from the carriage with all his old vigour and brought his hands together in a booming clap.

'So. How many joiners do we have on site today? Twenty? Let's see how that mahogany is looking.'

Well, thought Fox. *He's forgotten about it now. On to the next thing.*

9

That night, at three in the morning, an ampersand coiled rope-like round Bellman's neck, knotting itself tightly and squeezing the breath out of him. When his eyes opened to the bedroom of the London house where he habitually slept, he was gasping and his heart was beating as if it was really his dying minute.

Send him off with a flea in his ear . . . Deny the conversation ever happened . . . God in heaven, had he really allowed himself to entertain thoughts like this? What if Black were to overhear a discussion of that sort? What if he found out that Bellman was thinking about ways of breaking their partnership?

What kind of partnership was it he had entered into? Black was on his side, surely? Otherwise he would have chosen some other person to share his idea with. They had an understanding, he was certain of it. Bellman was the active partner: it was he who went out into the world, wrote the letters, held the meetings, engaged contractors, negotiated terms, paid the invoices; later, it would be he who engaged seam-stresses and shop girls, recruited clerks, set up the systems, dealt with the haberdashers, took charge of the day-to-day running of the busi-ness.

Black was – how to describe it? Black had done none of the work, Fox was right about that. He had not put up the money. He seemed content to let Bellman get on with things. When you studied the thing objectively, it was hard to see what Black's role in the venture was at all, he admitted to himself. Except that it *had* been his idea in the first place, and a damned fine one too. The haberdashers had not hesitated to come in with him. The bank needed no persuasion to lend large sums.

He frowned. His memory of the night in the churchyard refused obstinately to come into focus, yet he retained from it the acute sense that Black was not a man to be fobbed off with a bottle of whisky. Merely picturing the scene – You've done me a great service my friend! Here, let me offer you this bottle as an expression of my gratitude! – made him feel uncomfortable. As for the idea of court, denying Black his rights . . . He seemed to see Black's eye, bearing witness against him, staring at him implacably from the dock. It cut through time and space and the wall of the room he slept in, pinned him to his mattress in fear. He was amiable and jovial all right, but at the same time, wasn't he powerful? Menacing, even?

But what did Black want?

Bellman got out of bed. He would draft a contract here, now, tonight. Whenever the man appeared – for he would appear – he could open a drawer, pull out the paper and say to him, 'Where have you been, Black, my good fellow? Better late than never, eh? This contract has been waiting for you all along, and I have made you a wealthy man.' That should do it.

He sat at his desk in a nightshirt and started to write. It was a fairly standard contract and goodness knows he had drafted and signed enough of them in his time to know what he was doing. He could leave a space to fill in the exact percentage later once he'd done some calculations, the main thing was to get the terms and conditions clearly set out.

For some reason, when he was a few lines in, he found the whole thing rather unsatisfactory. On paper the words seemed inadequate, beside the point. They lacked their usual solidity.

Perhaps he should get a lawyer to look it over . . .

The thought of setting out the difficulty before a lawyer drew him up short. It had been peculiar, the way it had all come about, certainly. The whole situation was unorthodox. When he'd put the thing before Fox he had been able to leave certain things vague, unexplained. That wouldn't do for a lawyer. It would be – Bellman winced – awkward.

He read through what he had written, then tore the paper to pieces and dropped it in the wastepaper basket. There would be a better way of wording it. He'd do it tomorrow, when he was fresh.

10

For more than twelve months up to a hundred men a day had been kept busy in the construction of Bellman's great monster. The skeleton had risen gigantically from the ground, stone by stone. Glaziers, tensely handling vast sheets of glass, fitted eyes in the creature's gaping sockets. Along the bones of the building ran arteries designed to carry the very life blood of the enterprise: money. Canisters containing money could be placed at any sales point into a niche in the wall. Once the door to the niche was closed a pneumatic system would whip the payment swiftly to the accountant's office at the heart, where a cashier would make out a receipt for the payment, this receipt being returned to the customer the same way. Meanwhile the shop staff would be able to continue their business of sympathy and consolation, activities which did not sit naturally, Bellman considered, with the handling of cash. A second network of veins delivered the gas to illuminate all this. Over the bones and arteries, covering them, joiners applied a skin of fielded mahogany panelling.

Bellman saw all this. He was pleased.

The day came when the shopfitters went in. Theirs was the job of giving the monster the character of a shop: the provision to the retail floors of counters, shelves, cupboards, drawers, display cabinets and racks; on the second floor the offices with their desks and filing cabinets; on the third floor, the seamstresses' work stations; in the attics, tiny bedrooms for the seamstresses; in the basement the shelving and work stations for dispatch, the reception area and storage for incoming stock together with related offices.

This same day there was activity outside the building. A small crowd of passers-by had gathered for the spectacle. All eyes were on the platform over the main entrance. There was an air of expectation, as if it were a sculpture or a monument ready for unveiling – not that

186

there was really any surprise in store, for the top edge of the shop windows already bore the names Bellman & Black.

Eighteen feet up in the air, three men stood on the dais. One was gesturing firmly to his fellows on the ground and calling out. 'Up! Up! Up! Steady! To me! Steady!' while a weighty form, padded, wrapped and trussed so that its true shape could only be guessed at, was raised on a hoist. Calmly it swung on its ropes, careless of the height and the nearness of the window glass. Below, men laboured at the pulley; above, arms stretched out to steady the weight and guide it onto the projecting ledge. A second padded shape was hoisted into the air, then a third. Next there was a certain amount of business on the platform. Ropes to be untied, sacking covers stripped, packing removed.

Bellman's neck was aching from looking up. Wishing for something to settle his stomach, he brushed his coat free of the bits of straw that had come to rest on it.

Next to him, Fox was now doing the calling: 'Left! Again. Stop!'

And now Fox nudged him: 'What do you say? About right?'

Bellman looked. The workmen, dwarfed by the scale of the centre-piece, stepped to the edge of the dais to give them a clear view, and there it was. His initial and Black's, linked by the sinuous handcuff loop of the ampersand. The silver glittered in the sun and the crowd burst into applause.

Lighter, they had told him. Less solid.

He was prepared this time.

'Yes,' he said curtly to Fox. 'Good.'

Some in the crowd had turned their attention away from the shop front and towards him.

'Mr Bellman, that is,' he heard someone say. 'The man himself.'

And another voice came from the crowd. 'And Mr Black? Where is he?'

Bellman waved an abrupt thank you in the direction of the men on the dais and strode rapidly in the direction of the entrance.

'You don't want to oversee the positioning of the garland?' Fox chased after him. At the back of the platform were a number of crates awaiting attention. He had checked them this morning. They were filled with a botanical tangle of silversmith's lilies and garlands of gilded ivy leaves.

'You see to it. I'll come back when it's done.'

But the day was a busy one and he didn't find the time. He couldn't be everywhere at once. Not that it mattered. The men knew what they were doing and Fox was there. In any case, there was always to-morrow.

11

Men balanced on ladders to fit the gaslights. They hammered nails with not a shred of pity for the ears. They sanded and retouched paintwork, where a poorly fitted window had leaked. They heaved mattresses from the basement to the very top of the building so that the seamstresses would have somewhere to sleep. They crouched on the stairs marking the positions for the brackets for carpet rods. Tools and men and materials were everywhere, and no man could find his chisel when he wanted it. Fox was in all places at once, nodding, checking, ticking things off.

Only two weeks remained before the grand opening of Bellman & Black. There were a thousand things to be done before that day and they were all being done at once.

To add to the chaos, there were girls in the shop. Today was the day of the interviews for the seamstresses. Arriving by the side door, they came into a hall of hammering, banging, measuring, carrying, shouting and cursing. The smell of paint and varnish were in the air. The girls held their skirts carefully out of the sawdust and away from the paint. A surprising number of obstacles contrived to be in the path of the women – rolled carpet, planks, lengths of architrave – but the men were endlessly willing to grasp them by the waist and lift them over. The mattress carriers winked promises to one girl after another – the softest mattress for you, my lovely – but most were too intent on getting a job to flirt.

One of the girls, as pretty and as well made as any of the others, was pale and hesitant. The noise and the boisterousness of the work seemed to inflict itself on her painfully and she flinched. Seeing that she had to cross an entire floor of workmen the girl seemed ready to turn tail and leave, but a joiner, paternal and kind-hearted, spoke.

'That's the way, miss. That door over there.'

She thanked the man, but was secretly sorry for his kindness: it obliged her to go on.

'They won't eat you!' he told her, and she thanked him with the ghost of a smile.

In the midst of all this busyness and flirting was Bellman. He strode about the shop, a dark figure in his black suit, and where he went, the circle of his influence moved with him. Men within the reach of his aura laboured seriously, with none of the chat and teasing that was going on elsewhere. Even the girls picked up the altered atmosphere that surrounded him. They could not prevent themselves from staring and their eyes had both admiration and alarm in them.

When he had passed through the first floor and disappeared – through a solid mahogany wall, or so it seemed – the pale girl turned to the man who had helped her.

'Is that Mr Black?'

'Mr Bellman that is, sweetheart. We don't see hide nor hair of Mr Black here.'

The girl found her way to the suite of offices where the interviews were to be held. The junior clerks' shared room – still without its desks – had been designated a waiting room. There were no men here, only a tight-lipped woman who asked the name of each newcomer, and checked it on a list. The seamstresses collected themselves. Deft fingers tucked strands of hair under hats. This was serious. Bellman & Black was offering good money.

But then a door opened at the near end of the room, and the whispers ceased as a middle-aged woman with the plainest of hairstyles appeared. She was dressed with immaculate plainness, in deep black, unadorned by anything except her neatness, and all the seamstresses understood instantly what would be expected of them.

Her counterpart handed her the sheet of names and she called the first on the list. One of the girls raised a hand.

'Would you come in?'

The door closed behind them, and it had begun.

*

Bellman took the staff staircase to the second floor. The corridor smelled of fresh paint, he took care not to brush against the walls. Like the rest of the shop, it was not finished: his desk was there and he had already used it, but it had not found its permanent position; boxes of stationery were piled in a corner; a vast cork noticeboard was propped against a wall; rectangular objects wrapped in paper and tied with string – prints for the walls? – were marked with the word FRAGILE.

The shutters had been fixed in a hurry yesterday evening. Bellman three-quarter closed them. In the semi-darkness, he shifted the notice-board a foot to one side. He ran his fingers over the mahogany panelling behind, located the picture hook and tugged. The plug of mahogany came away with no difficulty.

Bellman applied his eye to the spyhole. The table had been angled so that he saw the excellent Miss Chalcraft, his senior seamstress, sideways on and the seamstresses almost full face.

'Where have you worked before?' Miss Chalcraft asked. 'How long have you been there? What examples of your work can you show me?'

As the interview was progressing, Bellman took his notebook from his pocket. *Girl No. 1*, he wrote. He listened to her answers, studied her manner and her appearance and gave her *7* to indicate her general aptitude for the job. The third column – for technical ability – he left blank. Miss Chalcraft would be the judge of that. The fourth column was the one that gave him pause for thought. The figure he entered here was to reflect a more elusive quality. His seamstresses would not always work out of sight upstairs. Sometimes they would be called on to go out to customers' homes, to measure up and make dresses in situ, to dress a whole family and the servants in mourning-wear in just a few days. To properly enter a house of mourning where they would represent the company, some of the girls at least had to have some-thing special, something he already thought of as a particularly Bellman & Black quality. Not every girl would be right to hold a tape measure to bosoms heaving with sorrow, and pinning distressed ladies into crape required a special kind of tender invisibility. It was hard to define, but Bellman thought he would recognise it when he saw it.

Miss Chalcraft had been instructed to ask certain more personal questions, in order to elicit evidence of this vital factor. This is what the last column was to indicate, and Girl No. 1 did not have it. He wrote a plain zero.

Bellman was quick in making his assessments. He did not hesitate. Girl followed girl, and he jotted down his numbers in columns. As he watched and listened the rest of his mind turned over other difficulties: the glazier that Fox had turned off the site after an expensive breakage had stolen another man's tools away – or so the man said. And the fellow they'd taken on to manage dispatch hadn't turned up today. What was the matter there? Yes, the building was pretty much under control, it was the people now . . .

Something captured his attention in the interview room.

Girl No. 9 was speaking.

'. . . so sudden. I wasn't expecting it. Everything was all right, and then—'

She raised her hand, a beseeching gesture, as though to call someone back, or retain something that was drifting out of reach. Although she couldn't know about the spyhole, it was in that direction that her hand moved, and Bellman had the curious impression that the girl was reaching for him. Her face was naked with yearning, as though even now the person lost might be restored to her. Her fingertips closed on thin air. There was a moment of silence. Then she drew her hand back and placed it in her lap, closed her eyes and when she opened them again her sad gaze was reconciled to her loss.

The excellent Miss Chalcraft allowed a perfectly judged pause to convey her kind sympathy before asking, 'And what can you show me of your work?'

The two women bent their heads over the items that Girl No. 9 had brought with her.

Bellman made his notes and decided to speak directly to the man whose tools might have been stolen. He would not persist in a lie if Bellman himself was present. When he bent his eye to the spyhole again, Girl no. 10 was sitting down.

After the first dozen interviews were completed, Bellman entered the interview room via the connecting door as arranged. He conferred with Miss Chalcraft and found that they thought alike. They went through the girls in the order they had been seen. Some were quickly rejected; Miss Chalcraft crossed their names through with a firm line. Others were as quickly in. 'Yes?' he asked, 'Yes,' she answered; a big tick went against the name on the master list and the decision was made. Sometimes there was discussion. Miss Chalcraft had seen the work, he had not. They deliberated, evaluated, compared and contrasted and within the space of half a minute the girl was erased or ticked.

'Number nine,' Miss Chalcraft announced. 'Now, I gave her a five generally. She has no experience in a large enterprise like Bellman & Black.'

Bellman had also given her a five.

'And her work?'

'Very neat. But whether she can work at the speed we need . . .'

Miss Chalcraft's pen hovered ready to delete her.

Bellman noticed that he had failed to give the girl a grade for that elusive quality that would make her right to send into a house of mourning. Someone who would wordlessly emanate the right kind of sympathy. Someone whose presence would comfort – but at least not distress – the recently bereaved. He tried to picture her – chubby girl? Brown curls perhaps? – and couldn't.

What he did remember were the half-raised hand, anguish and her ability to soothe herself.

'I think we'll try her out,' he said.

The excellent Miss Chalcraft did not show her surprise. He was the boss. Her pencil moved to the right-hand side of the page and entered a tick.

12

He blamed Fox. He had wanted a shop for the fifteenth and Fox, unable to resist a challenge, had promised it for the fourteenth. Hence this useless, empty day.

Bellman was out of sorts. He had felt it, even before he was awake. Now he stood before his mirror, lathering soap with his shaving brush, and studying the black points protruding darkly over his face. He applied a beard of white snow to his chin and took up the razor. What was the matter?

The preparations were complete. Bellman & Black was ready to meet its staff tomorrow. Bellman's role as constructor-in-chief of a great emporium was over – and his life as manager of a working enterprise had not yet begun. His life was poised between the one thing and the other, and this in-between state was uncomfortable to him. He wished it were tomorrow, when before eight o'clock the side door would open and clerks and shop girls and department heads and seamstresses and maintenance men and doormen and a coachman and packers and handlers and messengers would come pouring in. Tomorrow he would be at the heart of things, all day long he would be answering queries, smoothing out unforeseen difficulties in the life of the shop. He would be entirely absorbed in it. But that was tomorrow.

It was today that was the problem.

No difficulty waited to be smoothed out. All was straight and ready and in order. Every floorboard was hammered down, every lock oiled, every uniform ironed.

It was all right for Fox. What would he be doing today? Celebrating the end of the job, no doubt. He would be with friends. Family perhaps. Bellman supposed Fox must have some family.

Bellman met his eyes in the mirror and saw something troubling look back at him out of his own eyes. Quickly he averted his gaze.

Had he forgotten something? The uneasiness that was disturbing him had that kind of weight and density. But he was not prone to forgetfulness.

A crimson flower blossomed on the white lather by his nose. He had caught that little mole. Damn.

Bellman breakfasted. He wrote some unnecessary letters.

Dora had arrived for a brief London visit but he did not wish to disturb her: she would be tired after yesterday's journey.

He leafed through his notebook. All his lists of recent weeks. Every item with a tick against it. It almost reassured him. But he was restless: it wasn't a day to sit at a desk.

When he had word that Dora was up, he went to the drawing room. 'I am sorry I have been so busy of late.'

'You have been busy ever since I was born, Father. I am perfectly used to it.'

'I will be busy in the coming days too. More than ever.'

'Naturally.'

She was occupied with her binoculars, looking into the treetops in the square opposite. It would have been pleasant to stay and talk for a while, but he did not know what to say to his daughter. He had forgotten how to talk of normal things now that the business of death kept him so busy.

Under a cloudy August sky he walked to a restaurant for lunch. He read a newspaper. Leisure! What did people see in it? It only put him out of sorts.

At five o'clock he could resist no longer. He walked to Bellman & Black, inserted the heavy key and turned it. The smooth function of key in lock satisfied him and went a little way to soothing his irritation. The door opened with a weighty swing, and under the curious eye of the passers-by, Bellman let himself in.

All was still. All was hushed. The ground-floor windows were masked, casting an early dusk, and Bellman walked to the atrium in the centre where the light fell from the upper floors. He had been inside the building a hundred times before, to oversee, to discuss, to sign off, to solve problems and resolve disputes. Always there had been the noise of tools, voices, equipment. Always he had had some specific objective in mind that caused him to perceive the shop piecemeal. Today, alone and in silence, he took possession of his domain.

He ascended the staircase. He had already assessed the smoothness of the handrail, already checked the colour of the carpet against the sample. Tonight he had only to take delight in these details and marvel at how exactly they matched his intention.

Bellman continued his tour. Every now and again he nodded, satisfied. Here were display cabinets for the jewellery; here the drawers for gloves; here the mannequin busts, naked, but soon to display mantles and collars and tippets; here the wall racks where fabrics could be compared; here the counters, with a niche in the wall for cash payments and a book in the drawer for orders . . . Here would be the umbrellas and here the shoes . . . Everything was in a perfect state of readiness – all the more strange then, this feeling of having forgotten something.

Upstairs again. Now he left the public arena behind him. Gone was the mahogany panelling. Gone the high ceilings and grand windows. This was backstage. The realm of paper and ink and of money. One room was the heart of the pneumatic payment system. At each hatch a desk; on each desk ink and blank receipts and blotters.

The clerks' room that Bellman had seen almost empty when Miss Chalcraft interviewed the seamstresses was now filled with rows of desks. He sat down at one of them. His eye was drawn to the spot in the panelling where the spyhole was. Nothing was visible.

Sitting in her place, Bellman raised his hand in the direction of the invisible spot, as the seamstress had done, and studied his fingers, his arm. A reaching out in order to capture – what? The fingers closing on nothing. The hand falling dispirited to his lap. He shook his head in puzzlement, and repeated the action, as though it were a mechanism he had not yet got the measure of. After a couple of attempts he shook his head clear, and left the room.

His own office awaited only him. It was larger than it needed to be. To impress, according to the architect. Bellman had shrugged. He had never relied on room dimensions to impress people; he had never been impressed by room dimensions. He might yet divide it. From his office he looked into the antechamber, where his secretary would work and control access to Bellman. The last room making up the suite of offices contained nothing but a safe, taking up one-third of the space. The size of a safe did not impress Bellman either, not while it was empty. He entered the code, opened the door, relocked it.

Upstairs again. Further and further away from the public. Deeper and deeper into the private realm of Bellman & Black. On the third floor was the seamstresses' workplace. The architect had tried to dissuade him – waste such a view of the city on seamstresses? – but Bellman had insisted. The girls who made the dresses needed every last ray of sunlight to stitch by. Every degree of elevation was worth good money. 'A corner of the second floor is all I need,' he'd told the man. 'You can count money well enough by gaslight.'

Bellman was delighted with the seamstresses' work space. He smiled to himself, remembering the day six months ago when he had interrogated Miss Chalcraft on every aspect of couture. She had taken him to watch seamstresses at work. He had handled needles, thimbles, scissors and thread himself. He had learned to thread a needle and, having finally succeeded – it was a hundred times more difficult than he had anticipated – had driven it in and out of a few offcuts of cloth, first by the window, then in shadow. The excellent Miss Chalcraft had failed to hide her astonishment.

'How else can I know what your girls will need, Miss Chalcraft?' he had asked. 'I will give them large windows, because black cloth is harder to stitch than coloured when the light starts to fade. And I will give them time to stand and move about and a space to do it in, so that they don't have to pretend to have run out of thread or lost their needle when their neck hurts from being hunched over their work. And that way, they will want to work for Bellman & Black because we understand what makes their work easy and what hard, and there will be less time wasted and fewer needles lost.'

Bellman imagined one of the seamstresses – though he did not attend particularly to the fact, it was Girl No. 9 he imagined – arriving for the first time tomorrow in the seamstresses' workplace and marvelling at the precise and practical way in which everything was arranged. Light falling copiously onto the long workbench which was divided by sloping wooden ridges into individual sewing stations. Each workplace had its own hooks for scissors and pigeon holes for needles and thread and thimbles and drawers for braid and ribbon.

Yes. He nodded and smiled.

It was soothing to see how closely the realisation of his plans matched the image of it he had carried in his mind for so many months. All the thoughts that had once existed only in his imagination now had material reality. Here was evidence that he was not forgetful. He tried to draw reassurance from it. He tried to put the uncomfortable feeling behind him.

Up again. Around the light well were arranged the seamstresses' bedrooms. He turned into one at random; they were all the same. It was a narrow room with sloping walls under the eaves and a tiny window. A bed with a thin mattress was built against the wall. A hook behind the door for a black dress. A chest. A pitcher and a bowl. Was it big enough?

He pictured a seamstress in the room. Like an obedient marionette, Girl No. 9 stood at the basin and washed her face. She unpinned her hair. Was her hair brown and curly? It was brown and curly now. She sat on the bed to take her shoes off, then lay down.

Yes, the room was adequate, he judged.

Girl No. 9 continued to lie on the bed, as if waiting to see whether he required her to stand and undress and hang her black dress on the hook behind the door. She watched his face, attentively. She had – or his mind supplied her with – an attractive shape under her black dress. Her eyes looked tenderly at him. Her lips parted as though she were about to speak, invite him to—

And now, abruptly altering, she raised her hand and reached towards him hopelessly, as if to grasp something lost, something forever out of reach. Tears welled in her eyes and her pretty face was disfigured by grief.

Bellman stepped back and closed the door on Girl No. 9.

Through an unobtrusive door on the third-floor landing were the very last steps. Rough and wooden, they rose steeply to a space that contained only two things: the hydraulic lever to raise the glass domed ceiling and a hatch to access the roof for maintenance. Bellman climbed, unlocked the padlock and pushed open the hatch. A scattering of raindrops fell on his upturned face as he stepped out onto the roof. In the centre of the roof was the broad octagon of plate glass. He crouched at the edge of it to admire the neat setting of the plates into the ridge-and-furrow grid. It had been very nicely done. This rain could patter as long as it liked, it would not get through. Beneath the glass was a vertical drop of hundreds of feet, but in the dark his atrium was not transparent but reflective. No hint of the depths beneath was visible, only the mercurial glitter of raindrops showed against the mirror image of the evening sky.

Bellman stood, turned and stared upwards at the rain, and beyond that, the stars that were beginning to show between the clouds. He took in a deep, contented breath and released it again.

On a clear day, Fox had told him, you could see as far as Greenwich to the east and Richmond to the west. Bellman could only make out Clerkenwell and Kensington. He squinted, puzzled, and took out his watch. Eight o'clock already! No wonder. What had happened to the time? Still, he could see Primrose Hill rise in the north and to the south he could make out the outline of the new House of Lords. Beyond it, he knew the city continued its sprawl.

How vast London was. How great the extent of its housing and commerce and population. There was not a living soul in this city, not so far as the eye could see, that would not at some point have need of the goods and services provided by Bellman & Black. He looked out, turning slowly, in all directions. Birds were swooping and diving in the darkening sky and beneath them, streets of houses stretched in all directions, grand and modest and impoverished. In one of those houses, in Richmond say, a fellow would be sneezing, right at this very moment. Just as in Mayfair someone was shivering. In Spitalfields, a tainted oyster was slipping down someone's throat, and in Bloomsbury someone was pouring the glass that would prove one glass too many and . . .

oh, it was endless. They would come all right. Sick today, dead to-morrow and on Thursday Bellman & Black would open its doors to the bereaved. It was an enterprise that could not fail.

He, William Bellman, had created this great engine. It was his, and tomorrow the staff would be coal to its stoves, water to its wheel, and when the customers came thronging, his machine would start to extract the money from them and disgorge them changed, lighter in the pocket and lighter at heart, as the process took their guineas and replaced them with consolation. He had made it. It was his emporium, Bellman &—

His hands were shaking. He had forgotten something. Never in his life had he been more certain! A feather stir in his abdomen, a turbulence in his chest: he was on the brink of remembering . . .

The rain beat harder against his back. As he felt the damp chill bloom across his shoulders, a scene seeped into his mind: there was a spot, down there, opposite the building where he had stood one day a year ago in the rain. He had made architecture out of air and water.

There had been a stone, was that it?

A bird? Shimmering purple and green and blue?

Buried! In the foundations of his emporium!

A rook had flown up from the foundations, risen on rain-heavy wings through the floors of his shop; he had seen it, that day.

The construction beneath his feet seemed suddenly insubstantial as mist. The notion came to him that he was suspended high above the ground with only rain and air to hold him up.

London dived and veered around him. Bellman's hands flew to his head as the city broke like a mirror and the shards flew apart, the roof line sheered off, the roof itself plummeted and him with it, in a breathtaking plunge. Afraid of the building's edge, afraid of the glass grid, Bellman fell helplessly to his knees. Desperate for a hand to hold, his fingers slithered over the wet flat lead as the building tilted viol-ently. He squeezed his eyes shut, but it was no help: a great fall was coming. There was no up and no down, only falling, and he vomited as he fell, and the world spun and tipped wildly around him. He fell and he fell and there was no end to the falling.

The sky was black.

It was still raining.

Bellman could hear whimpering and understood it was himself.

There was a bird, an ancient black bird buried in the foundations of his emporium.

His fingers ached from holding on and he wept.

At some point in the night, Bellman discovered that this would not do. He was ill. He would have to resign. He must go to the haber-dashers and tell them that a new manager must be found.

Tentatively he moved a hand. A foot. He crawled along the roof to the hatch. Descending the wooden steps, trembling and weeping, he was overcome by waves of heat and chill. He thought longingly of the beds in the seamstresses rooms, but no, first he had to hand in his resignation. Planes of blackness assailed him on the stairs and brought on the vertigo again. More than once he slumped and collapsed, clinging to the banisters before persuading himself back onto his feet and forwards. Getting to the ground was as arduous as coming down a mountain, and when he unlocked the door to step out into Regent Street no one would have recognised him as the man who had gone in.

13

A few souls were about in Regent Street, even at this dead hour of the night. They were on their way to work early, or on their way home after a long night, or else one of those who have no work and no home and for whom all hours of the day or night are equally comfortless. Passers-by took Bellman for one of the latter. Hatless, soaked to the skin, smelling sour, he walked as though he didn't trust the pavement beneath his feet, and once in a while he stopped to lean against a wall and close his eyes. People sped up to pass him, took wide detours, avoided looking him in the eye.

For an hour Bellman walked unsteadily in a city he did not know. He was aware that strangers were casting sideways looks at him as they passed, knew that with his erratic breathing and his drenched clothes he must look eccentric, alarming even, yet such was his altered state that he felt no embarrassment. No! For he was a man at a great turning point! He was the man who had everything! Everything and more! And he was going to throw it away!

Why this compulsion to escape from everything he had worked so hard to achieve? He could not precisely say. But he was resolved to do it, and he would do it, and the reason was powerful enough even if it wasn't particularly clear.

At the turn of a corner he saw, alighting from a cab, a familiar figure. Black!

Bellman halted.

He was not in the least surprised. It was in the nature of the man to appear at strange moments. At ordinary times he kept his distance, and then, when crisis struck, there was Black. Peculiar, but then that was Black for you.

Why not tell him now? It was as good a time as any. At the thought of unburdening himself of the emporium and all it entailed, he felt a profound relief.

Black turned into the side street and Bellman headed after him. He had to follow at a great pace for Black seemed able to walk at an unnaturally fast speed. More than once he thought he had lost him in a maze of alleys and passages, but each time he caught sight of him again: a tailcoat disappearing round a corner, the jaunty tilt of his hat half concealed in the shadows.

For all his great efforts Bellman never seemed to gain ground on Black, the man always stayed out of reach. After ten minutes of this chase, Bellman began to doubt himself. Was it really Black he had seen? Surely he should have caught up with him by now?

Staring down an empty street, Bellman took out his handkerchief to wipe his brow. He was shivering. He realised that he didn't know where he was. The streets were narrow and rough-looking and it was darker now. There were dark doors to the dwellings on each side of him, some half open, and it was not difficult to imagine what kind of ruffians might be hiding behind them. He was suddenly aware of how he would appear to any ne'er-do-well loitering in the dark. A middle-aged man, out of breath and trembling in a part of town he was clearly unfamiliar with. He had heard the stories: men like him, either lost or lured into dark side streets, emerging later with a bump on the head the size of an egg and missing their pocket watch, their purse, their shoes. Or worse. And Black? He was nowhere to be seen.

Resigned to the worst, Bellman heaved a sigh and forced himself to put one foot in front of the other, slowly making his way to the next turning. And there, to his amazement, he saw Black. How could he mistake a profile like that! He was in conversation with someone, a girl or a young woman.

'Black!'

The man appeared not to hear him.

'Black! Hoy!'

But then the next moment Black was gone – he must have nipped into that door just behind him, Bellman thought – and the woman was making her way along the street in his direction.

She has tried it on with him and now it will be my turn! he thought, and he prepared himself to put her off. But as they drew nearer she did not speak, nor even glance at him, until they were close enough to have to step sideways to avoid each other in the narrowness of the passage. Then her eyes briefly met his and a startled look crossed her face.

It was the seamstress. Girl No. 9.

Bellman made an effort to win control of himself, to straighten the desperation that had fixed itself upon his face.

'Black!' he heard himself say. 'I know that man!' But his voice came to his ears as though from far away and after some delay. He felt himself sway.

The young woman peered at him. 'Mr Bellman?'

He did not know how to answer. How to explain this feeling that something inside him had come undone, that some small but essential element was adrift in him where it had once been connected and until he could locate it he would never be himself again?

He tried to speak then, unable to help himself, he had to put his hand heavily on her shoulder to keep from falling.

He was aware of contact – despite his leather glove, despite her serge jacket – contact and a transfer of weight from himself to her. For a moment she supported him and they knew a precarious moment of balance; then there came a sinking, a giving way, and with something inevitable about it the flagstones beneath his feet, the shoulder on which he leant, his own bones, seemed to dissolve and he knew nothing but black.

When he came to himself he was in a low-ceilinged room, sitting in the only chair. There was no fire in the grate, no logs either. A cup of liquid appeared before him and he drank it: honey water.

'That man. Black . . .' he began.

'I don't know who you mean. Who is it you're looking for?'

'Black.' He frowned. How to explain. His business partner? A stranger? A friend?

'Black? Of Bellman & Black?' She looked nervously at him, puzzled. 'And you think he is here?'

'I saw him. He spoke to you.'

She embarked on a shake of the head, repressed it, reluctant to contradict her employer.

'There,' he insisted, 'just now, in the street . . .'

The point of a white tooth caught her lip and her eyes rose uncertainly to his.

A fit of trembling overtook Bellman.

'Your coat is wet,' she murmured. 'You are cold. I can walk with you to the main road, there will be a hackney carriage.'

He nodded, rose, the room swum around him and he sank back to his chair.

'There is nothing for it then,' she said to herself. 'You must sleep here.'

She peeled his rain-sodden coat off his arms and opened a door in the wall. A bed was concealed, cupboard-style, behind it. He sank, his face was for a moment against her breast, then on a pillow, then he was asleep.

An hour later he was awake. There was the beginning of light in the room. He sat up. The bed was firm beneath him. He put his feet on the floor and the floor felt solid. He took a few steps. No wall reared or tipped or sheered away.

Girl No. 9 was sleeping in the chair. He tiptoed past, returned to put some coins on the table, and she didn't stir. Her skin had traces of salt on it: tear trails, and her brown curls were damp where she had been weeping.

To get out Bellman had to edge past an infant's crib. Empty.

In his own bedroom, Bellman took off his wet clothes and hung them over the back of a chair. They would take a long time to dry. His slow, dull brain mechanically unearthed a fact and presented it to him.

He had no second black suit.

His face pulled into a grin or grimace. He had meant to get another two black suits made up for himself. That was what he'd forgotten! That was what had been troubling him all day yesterday!

Thank goodness!

The sob that escaped from his lungs might have been laughter.

Bellman had never been more grateful to clamber into bed and he sank instantly into a deep sleep.

Waking for the second time that morning, William leapt out of bed and ordered a bath.

He did not pause to think about his anxiety of the day before, his collapse on the roof, his mad chase after Black through the streets of London, his decision to renounce the shop. He merely recollected that he'd had a bit of a dizzy spell, a touch of fatigue and now, finding himself so extraordinarily well again, congratulated himself on his sturdy constitution.

In between the hundred and one other things he meant to do today, he would find time to be measured for a new suit. With thirty-five seamstresses on the premises it would hardly be a problem.

&

On a warm day in summer, pairs of rooks will ride the warm upward current, soaring with leisurely ease to a very great height, where they are – to earthbound humans – mere dots of black in the sky. There, they allow themselves deliberately to slip off the edge of the airwave, and plummet Icarus-like to earth, tumbling and twisting as they go. Then, when your heart is in your mouth and they are a short mortal second from the ground, they extend their wings, gain a featherhold on the rising air, climb aboard the breeze, and rise aloft – whereupon they do it all over again.

There is no purpose to this. They are teasing gravity, showing off, pretending for the sheer hilarity of it to be human.

To judge by the merriment of the sky laughter, there can be little in the world more pleasurable than to be a rook pretending not to know how to fly.

There are numerous collective nouns for rooks. In some parts people say a *parliament* of rooks.

14

Regent Street was alive. Nannies went about with their charges in smart, black perambulators. Young women trotted along listening to their mothers, while their eyes roamed the window displays, avid for bonnets, shoes, gloves. Men of all ages made their way busily here, there and everywhere, dashing across the street between the carriages. Street hawkers shouted their wares, assessing the passing trade with a professional eye. Children clung on the hands of adults far above them, but even they looked up at certain windows and dragged their feet: there were sugar canes the size of walking sticks and at the tobacconist's a mechanical monkey smoked a cigar and exhaled real smoke. People ambled or sauntered or strode, they wove in and out of each other, absently or impatiently. They were in a hurry or they had all the time in the world. Someone stepped into the street, carriages swerved, drivers cursed and shouted warnings . . .

In one place only there was a stillness and a hush: it was the pavement alongside the new shop, Bellman & Black. Curiously, the crowd was thicker here than anywhere else.

The shop was not yet open, but the day before, behind drapes, the windows had been dressed, and this morning at eight o'clock the black shrouds had come down to display the temptations of Bellman & Black to the world.

Each window was framed by theatrical sweeps of grey silk and contained an artistic still life. One composition was of gloves and fans, another urns and angels. One elaborate arrangement presented stationery, a dozen ebony inkpots. There were hats stabbed through with jet hatpins and there were veils. Everywhere were swathes of fabric, in every material and weave imaginable: cottons and linens and woollens and silks; baratheas and worsteds and crapes, each bringing its own individual note to the chord which was black. One window much studied had tombstones and memorial plaques, registering the passing of a number of generic colonels, beloved wives and sisters and dear children. But the most admired window was perhaps the simplest: a starburst of ribbons passing from white to black through off-white and dove grey and pigeon grey and French grey and donkey grey and slate grey and charcoal grey, more shades of grey in fact than there were names for. The message was understood by all: every gradation of grief would find its match at Bellman & Black.

At the very front of every window, dead centre, just the other side of the glass, was a six by eight white card, edged with black, and printed like an invitation to a ball:

Bellman & Black
Thursday 15th May
11 a.m. to 7 p.m.

It was only nine o'clock. The pavement was thick with people staring open-mouthed at the displays of funerary and mourning goods. Far from being drab, the black and grey was so artfully composed that the effect was mesmerising. Newcomers to the crowd looked first to see what everyone else was looking at, then fell into the same state of rapture that had ensnared the others. All were under a spell, conversations were whispered, then halted altogether as a thoughtful hush came over the viewers. Death, grief and memory offered so exquisitely for sale set the most robust heart throbbing and set the mind thinking.

Impossible to see it without thinking of the time when they would want the services of such a place. How soon? they wondered. And for whom? Some already suspected the answer to these questions; they considered their choices in advance of the event, and calculated the cost.

The windows of Bellman & Black reminded their viewers of what they most feared and at one and the same time showed them where to find consolation. Grief and sorrow come to all, but all the while you can honour your loved ones by saying farewell in a hat secured with a jet hatpin, there is consolation . . .

209

Some there were who leant more heavily on their sticks or felt again the pain that had been troubling them. These knew that they would not be customers of Bellman & Black in person, but that their contribution to the success of the store would be made before too long. They considered the tombstones and rewrote them with their own names.

The clatter of hooves, then shuffling in the crowd to make way for the carriage that drew up at the main entrance. A fine carriage it was too, and a stir of curiosity broke the rapturous disquiet of the crowd. A uniformed driver jumped down to open the door, and a woman emerged, neatly collared and cuffed in her grey dress. Together they went to great pains to extract the second passenger: a tiny, hunched figure swathed in black silk. Was it a child? She had the size of a child, but she was slow and twisted like an old woman. Her veil was so dense she must have been all but blind inside it, but she looked up, nonetheless, at the silver insignia announcing the name of the shop, before being guided step by painful step to the entrance.

The crowd parted to let the curious pair through. Neither woman appeared to notice the eyes that followed their progress, and they did not utter a word. All onlookers were thinking the same thing, but all held their tongues, waiting for someone else to speak.

It was a child that said it.

'It's not open yet. Eleven o'clock, look.'

He pointed to the card.

But there was the sound of a key turning, the door opened just enough, and the two ladies were swallowed up by the shop.

The key turned again.

In the crowd strangers murmured and turned astounded faces upon each other.

The little lad who had spoken pressed his face to the crack between the double doors, but he could see nothing.

'Eleven o'clock,' he repeated. 'That's what it says on the invitation.'

Inside there was a feverish circulation of people and goods. Swift feet ran messages; strong arms carried; tidy minds counted and noted; deft hands arranged and displayed. Crates were opened, the contents spilled out. Then, faster than you could believe, all was neatly stacked and ranged, the crate itself disappearing as if by magic, and the same trick was being repeated over and over again in every department.

Among all these black goods being carried about in all directions was one distinctive cargo. Sedate and slow, Dora was carried through the shop in a sedan chair. Bellman meant to show her the entire shop. She was introduced to department managers, shook hands, and although she did not speak, said with a look and a smile something that in words would have gone like this: *Yes, I know I am peculiar. Think nothing of it.*

Everywhere was something her father wished to point out to her: the uniforms of the various staff, the goods arriving, the fittings of the shop, every last detail was something he had imagined, brought into being, and he laid it all before her: the Italian gloves, the Chinese silk, the Whitby jet, the Parisian collars. She admired, complimented and approved.

Bellman led the procession of Dora, sedan, carriers, Mary, from floor to floor. When he had shown all the departments in the sales floors, they visited the offices, the clerks, the cashiers, Bellman's own office. Next they went up to see the seamstresses' area. Here again Dora felt herself being spied upon from the corner of eyes, understood that glances were being exchanged behind her back. Again she admired what she was called upon to admire, approved what was to be approved. *Don't mind me,* her eyes said to the seamstresses who could not help staring. *Be glad of your curls and your limbs and the curves beneath your clothes. Enjoy your good fortune.*

The staircase was too narrow to admit the sedan chair to the top floor. Might one of the porters carry her up? She was relieved when the decision went against. But Dora was not to be released yet. Oh no! For there was the basement still to be seen. She was shown the dispatch room, and the canteen and the kitchens at the side of the store where the windows opened into a narrow pit which permitted the smell of cooking to escape through a grill at ground level above. 'My!' Dora exclaimed.

'And it's not over yet!' Bellman exclaimed.

211

At floor level, at the back of the shop, next to the goods entrance, were wide double doors that opened onto a coach house. The Bellman & Black brougham was a sight to behold. A graceful black carriage, the B&B insignia in silver on the doors. Black horses were stabled nearby so that two seamstresses and a coachman could travel at a moment's notice anywhere within eighty miles of the capital.

Bellman opened the door to show the interior. With the air of a conjuror, he opened a compartment under the seat. In the dark it looked empty, and she was bewildered till she realised it was filled with fabric, crape, the blackest fabric available, so absorbent of light it seemed to be made of darkness itself.

'And this!' her father exclaimed, opening one of the portable cases with a flourish. Inside were a hundred little compartments and each one filled: scissors and tape measures and needles and spools of thread and a silver thimble.

'It's a miniature Bellman & Black!' she marvelled.

'In just two days our travelling seamstresses can provide essential mourning wear for a family; in four days, evening wear too. Give them a week and the servants of the house will be in black, down to the little girl who lights the fire in the mornings.'

She had run out of words and nodded her weary approbation.

'And what is more, as it goes through the streets of London our brougham will make a very fine impression. Everyone will turn to see it. When it races through the streets, when it arrives at the finest houses, it will be noticed. When the Earl of This and the Marquess of That call in Bellman & Black everyone will know. It will bring in more business than a hundred – a thousand – advertisements. So, what do you think, eh?'

He was tense with expectation, rushed through his words, awaited her verdict with obsessive intent. His eyes glittered, his pale face glittered. She hardly recognised her taciturn, frowning father. Bellman & Black had him in its grip.

Dora was astounded by her father's creation. Troubled too. It was beautiful, she supposed, in a powerful, uncomfortable way. 'A cathedral', someone had called it in the newspaper. She understood what they meant. But she had seen something beneath the feverish activity, the agitation and the rush. The sense of something silent, biding its time. What was it waiting for? The idea of a mausoleum knocked at her mind and she turned it away.

Her eyes returned to the seamstresses' bags. She picked out a silver thimble and held it up to the light. Even this was engraved with the double B motif.

'It is quite astonishing. You forget nothing, Father. Not even a thimble!'

They lifted the sedan and carried Dora back to the ground floor. Bellman led the way. He kept turning to tell her one more thing and then another about his grand project. She half listened, drifting in her own musing, until a thought struck her, idle but curious enough to make it worth interrupting her father.

'Father, you have never told me. Who is Black?'

That name on her lips! He should have thought of that.

'No one!' he told her, wide-eyed, a fraction too fast. 'No one at all.'

One minute to eleven.

The doormen stood like sentries at the gates of heaven. Mr Dent and Mr Heywood smoothed their impeccable grey lapels and positioned themselves behind their counters. Sales girls stood in orderly fashion, backs straight, hands clasped, meek as children at Sunday school. Upstairs every pencil lay straight and every needle was in its place. Smiles, coughs and other fidgets were suppressed. Everywhere was solemnity and composure.

Behind a column on the first floor, three-quarters concealed, Bellman stood and looked over the railings to watch the door below. As the clock hand moved to eleven and Pentworth opened the door, a heart a hundred times greater than his own jolted to life in his chest. It was the heart of Bellman & Black.

They came. Curious, fearful, longing, astonished, awestruck, pious, acquisitive, they poured in; and the first, whether they intended it or not, were swept deep into the shop by the sheer pressure of those behind. There was much dazed milling about as, overwhelmed by the scale and the beauty of it, people lost sight of whatever it was they had come in for – for most had invented some reasonable little need in order not to appear to themselves as mere tourists. They could not help it: on seeing the majestic glory of it all, they fell into passive, voluptuous rapture. Women and men, young and old, the bereaved and the unbereaved, all thronged, staring and marvelling and whispering.

For all their awe, it was not long before one soul, hardier than the rest, resolved upon a purchase. One yard of one-inch grosgrain to edge the fraying sleeves of a winter coat.

It was not the cheapest thing to be had at Bellman & Black, but it was certainly modest. No matter.

On the second floor a cashier tweaking his cuffs almost jumped out of his skin as the first canister of pennies rattled to a stop in his niche and his hand trembled as he wrote out the ticket, counted out the change and activated the system to return the canister to the shop floor. Then instantly another!

It had begun!

Now the canisters were flying, the coins were rattling into the cashboxes, goods were measured and counted out, items were wrapped and tied with string, orders were listed in elegant cursive script and – yes! – tears were shed, consolation offered and received.

Bellman & Black was teeming with life and money and death.

It was a success.

William Bellman took a deep breath. He did not smile – on the shop floor of Bellman & Black? Whatever next! – but he felt a smile. His fingers tingled with confident power and the floor was solid beneath his feet.

Unobtrusively he stepped from his vantage point, slipped between the crowds and melted into the panelling.

In his private office one wall had been lined with cork. On it was tacked a large sheet of paper. At present it was mostly blank, with only two lines on it, one vertical and one horizontal, joining in the bottom left-hand corner. Along the horizontal line the names of the months were marked against notches. Figures in pounds were indicated by the notches on the vertical line.

Bellman remembered his early jottings in the black notebook. Calculations of turnover, predictions of profit. It had looked very promising, though he had arrived at it in a somewhat rough and ready fashion, obviously. Then there were the figures – reined in a little – that he had dangled in front of Critchlow and the others to tempt them into investing. All that was a long time ago. Today he knew infinitely more about the business. He could tell you how many yards of black merino was sold annually in the nation, the city of London, the tiny shop two streets from here. He knew why coffins cost what they did and how they could be made cheaper yet be just the same. He had an idea of how much Bellman & Black would make this first month, and it was founded on fact. It was also, he congratulated himself, the same figure that he had come up with two years ago.

His plan on this chart was to plot predicted takings in blue at the beginning of every month, and the actual takings, in black, once the figures were in. He took up his blue pen and found the spot. At the last minute his hand rose slightly and he inked his blue dot a fraction higher.

Was it a sixth sense that nudged his hand? Instinct? Call it what you will. Bellman just knew.

15

Dora's nights of remembering grew less profitable as the years passed. She still did it sometimes, but the practice gradually lost its ability to comfort. In part, she told herself, it was because she had worn the memories thin from overuse. Like some of the coins they used to clean, the relief had been worn away.

There were other reasons. She was changing. The things that had pleased her when she was a girl were not the things that pleased her now. When she thought about her mother these days, it was new conversations she craved. She took to talking to Mrs Lane about her mother, and these memories, second-hand though they might be, were as precious as her own for they were adult.

And then there came another reason for spending less time rehearsing the past.

Rummaging under the bed for something else entirely, Mary emerged, hair all askew, with a painting.

'What on earth is this?'

Dora rubbed the dust off. 'My rook!'

The afternoon sketching in the garden was not part of her repertoire of habitual memories, for it did not involve her mother and brothers and sister. Now it returned to her with a fresh vividness.

'He taught me how to hold a pencil properly.'

Mary and Dora went through all the cupboards in the house until they found the old sketchbooks. Then for an entire afternoon the young women sat together turning the pages. One particular image made them pause. A few weeks before the fever Dora had made her first proper attempt at a self-portrait.

'Is that really what I looked like, then?' she asked.

'It is a likeness. That can't be denied. But you were even prettier.'

Dora judged differently. The portrait was less than confident. The lines were stiff. But she supposed the eyes were good. She recognised herself in them.

'I look as if I am thinking very hard about something.'

'You still look like that. Always did.'

That night Dora sacrificed a night of remembering in order to sit at the mirror. She unpinned the lace that covered her scalp and by candlelight she studied her new face. What a scarecrow she was. Her features seemed squashed into the lower part of her face, like a baby's. Her ears jutted out, flaring at the upper curve in an ugly simulacrum of the curls that were missing. The narrowness of her forehead was improved – was that the right word? – by the absence of hair, and her eyes were made striking by the lack of lash and brow, but they were not, for all that, what anyone would call attractive. It was an interesting face though. The skin of her scalp was smooth to the touch but the bones beneath had a landscape that her hair had hidden from sight. Her eye studied its lines, found crevices, shallows, ridges, a whole landscape of bone. She turned her head this way and that. A blue vein ran river-like over one ear. She raised her hands to read the back of her scalp with her fingers.

A powerful excitement took possession of her as she held her pencil. She traced a few lines, abandoned them, started again elsewhere on the page, abandoned again. From every disappointment she moved straight away onto the next attempt. She turned her head from side to side, captured a shape, then tilted her neck and made another rapid sketch. She replaced the candle and carried on drawing till dawn: her scalp, her bones, lines of nose and chin and lip, curls of cartilage, nostrils, cheekbones, temples, planes and angles and light and shade. She drew with as little personal emotion as if she had been drawing a landscape, something as remote from herself as the bones of the planet she lived on.

Eventually Dora produced something she was satisfied with. It was raw, as ugly and grotesque as she knew herself to be, and it reminded

217

her more than anything of a newly hatched bird, unfeathered, skin as thin as paper, all bone and hunger.

With a last pencil stroke, she extended the line of her nose into a little beak and was happy.

16

The launch of Bellman & Black created a momentum that carried Bellman with it. He worked eighteen hours a day, seven days a week, yet he never tired. His schedule was energetic, he toured the shop at 10 o'clock, 2 o'clock and 6 o'clock, from basement to the atelier at the top: a word in someone's ear, encouragement there, even lending a hand where the workload was excessive. Daily meetings (his senior retail men and with Verney from finance), bi-weekly meetings (Edmonds from dispatch, Stallybrook from deliveries and Miss Chalcraft). Three hundred and thirty-seven people worked at Bellman & Black and before the month was out he knew the name of everyone, from Henderson, his secretary and right-hand man to Molly who washed up for the canteen. The name of Girl No. 9 was Lizzie, and he noted it along with all the others. With prodigious energy he filled every moment with activity, with purpose, with achievement.

There were appointments with outsiders: Anson from the Westminster & City needed to see him once in a while, sometimes it was a lawyer or a haberdasher who came for an hour in the afternoon to talk business. He purchased a pair of deep-buttoned leather armchairs for these occasions and placed them one each side of the fireplace in his office. He resented their comfort, it led sitters to relax and after the main business was complete they continued to sit talking of one thing and another while cigar smoke rose lazily to the ceiling. He discouraged it politely.

After the shop closed and on Sundays he sat down to his paperwork. Letters, reports, accounts, lists. He processed everything with rapid, flawless method, made lists in his calfskin notebook and drew a firm line through each item as soon as it was done. He now ordered his notebooks in quantities of half a dozen at a time; when one was finished, he dropped it into the bottom drawer of his desk and took the next from the shelf and pressed the front cover back to continue without a pause.

How did he do it? By watching the clock. Washing, dressing and breakfasting might take an ordinary man an hour, but Bellman did it in thirty-five minutes. The manager of London's other large shop spent an hour every day with his secretary, but Bellman got through the agenda in fifteen minutes. He said 'Good morning,' and 'How are you?' but during these profitless seconds his mind was noting, thinking, planning.

When the shop closed and Bellman could at last settle down to his paperwork, he glanced at the clock. The workload he had resolved to accomplish would be half a day's worth to another man, but he glanced at the clock before he started and again at the end, and only an hour had passed. Those that knew this facility of his wondered at it.

'Never let time be your master,' Bellman told Verney when he asked about it. 'If you want to do something, take it on. Time will always make itself.'

But what he really felt about the matter was that he had discovered – or been given – the key to chronometry. He could open up the case of time when he chose, apply weight to the pendulum and slow its movement. He could take the hours apart, find the extra minutes that were going to waste in them, make them his own.

Years ago at the mill someone had once suggested that Bellman might one day work out how to make the sun shine all day and all night. Those that knew him at the emporium would have agreed: it was not so impossible as it might seem.

Verney tried to emulate his boss. By his watch though a minute was only ever a minute; he could never get a second more out of it.

When Bellman lost time – by someone else's miscalculation or mishap as a rule – he spent the afternoons in an intensity of effort to catch up. If necessary he would sit up late, stealing from sleep to finish what he had set out to do. Always he went to bed the victor. He never felt tired, though he must have been, for sometimes he fell asleep at his desk. When this happened for the third and fourth time he took action.

Fox was in Scotland, but when he received the letter he returned directly to London. He found the same vigorous handshake, the same brevity of greeting.

'You are well? Good, good,' Bellman said, leaving him no time for a reply, no time to say how fine the houses were in Edinburgh, how surprisingly mild the weather. Immediately they were straight to the matter at hand.

'Divide the space.' Bellman knew what he wanted. 'As far as here, see, and put in a wall.'

'It can be done.' Fox frowned. 'It will be a tight fit. You could borrow some space from your secretary's office. It makes it a bigger job, but you'd have greater comfort . . .'

Fox was aware of speaking fast, leaving no pauses between his sentences. The old ways came back to him instantly. To think he had lived every day for two years at this Bellman pace!

When Fox had first left Bellman's employ, he spent a fortnight astonished at the slowness of the rest of the world. Twenty, thirty times a day, you understood someone's meaning after the first sentence, but had to stand and wait while they meandered through until they had exhausted the stock of words and seconds they had put aside for it. He answered in a few taut words, and people stared at him. The meaning had come at them all at once, bullet-fast; stunned by the detonation his listener had to ask him to repeat himself. It exhausted his patience, he thought he would never get used to it, but quite soon he adjusted himself to the slower pace and before long he actually liked it. He had rediscovered the spaces in between words and tasks and thoughts, and they were surprisingly fruitful. He had met a young woman. He thought he might marry her.

'Space?' Bellman was saying. 'For what? All I need is a bed here, against the wall, and a cupboard here for a few things.'

'A wardrobe?'

'A hook behind the door will do.'

Fox thought of the bedroom he had made for his client at the white stucco house, its grand scale, the majestic bed, the art, furniture, mirrors . . .

'It will be far from spacious. In fact . . .' He paced out the area

Bellman had indicated. 'Yes. It's more or less the dimensions of the seamstresses' rooms we put in upstairs.'

It seemed to him then that Bellman did pause, for the briefest instant. Then, 'When can it be done?'

'If you're really satisfied to have something so modest, it can be done in a day.'

'Overnight?'

'I don't see why not.'

'Tonight?'

How did I do it? Fox marvelled at himself. For two whole years he had lived at this speed. It had seemed natural to him then. The way to get on. The way to make himself. He had all sorts of projects lined up now, work enough for years, a lifetime. Bellman & Black had done that for him.

He smiled. 'I'll see to it.'

The next day Bellman came in to find his office a little smaller, and behind the new wall, a seamstress's bedroom with tongue-and-groove walls, a narrow bed against the wall and a cupboard. He stood in it and an emotion stirred in him, but he didn't stop to put a name to it. He had things to do.

'Come in!' he called, without lifting his eyes from the letter he was drafting.

'Sir, Miss Chalcraft sent me . . .' The voice was hesitant, female, familiar.

He looked up. It was her.

'. . . with your suit.'

'It's Lizzie, yes?'

'Yes, sir. Should I hang it somewhere?' She looked round, but there was nowhere in his office to put it.

She blushed. Was she thinking of the night in the back streets? The night they had met so surprisingly, when he had slept in her bed and crept away at first light, tied his tongue. It had happened only three weeks ago, but he had forgotten it as wholly as if it were an event in the distant past. Now it filled the room.

'Behind that door, there. You'll find a hook.'

If she was surprised at seeing how like his bedroom was to her own, nothing in her face gave it away. The blood still high in her cheeks, she murmured a goodbye and exited the room as quietly as she had come.

Bellman's hand returned to his page and for a second or two he failed to remember what it was he had meant to write. He hadn't got to the bottom of that Black business. Next time he saw her, he would ask her about it again. Then he picked up the thread and applied his pen to the paper as before.

It was the end of the first month. He and Verney had double-counted the day's takings, separating the coins into stacks of like with like, and putting them into red felt bags. Every penny was accounted for. The figures were in. When Verney left he locked the money in the safe and then, smiling to himself, took his pen and dipped it in the black ink. At a point well above the target he had marked on his graph four weeks ago, he touched his nib to the paper at the level of sales actually achieved. The wet ink shone at him, like a beady black eye, and Bellman smiled contentedly at it.

Now, what about this coming month? Ordinarily in retail you might expect novelty to inflate the first month's takings artificially. Your second month's takings would conceivably be less than the first. But mourning goods had their own laws and in this, as in so much else, they were the exception to the rule. Quite naturally people felt a repugnance at the idea of having mourning wear ready and waiting in the home. Why, it was the equivalent of opening your front door to death, inviting him in and lining up your family for him to eye over. Certainly some of the people milling about the shop on opening day had had no reason other than curiosity to be there, but they had not purchased. Every sale this first month was authentic. The figures could be counted on as an accurate reflection of real deaths that had occurred in the world beyond the walls of Bellman & Black. They were a reliable indicator of future expectations. So what should next month's target be?

The bead of black ink was dry and besides, now Bellman had drawn from it all the information he needed, it was no longer important. He dipped a clean pen into the blue ink and prepared to mark the coming month's target. The nib neared the paper, rose a little and touched a dot a little higher than he meant.

That again! He considered the ink. It winked at him. Well, why not?

Having fixed his target he must make it happen. Bellman took his notebook from his pocket and opened it up. The Spanish gloves weren't selling: he must see Drewer about reducing the price and reorder from the Italians; he must get to the bottom of the reason why the gunpowder velvet was doing so well; he must . . .

His eye fell on a task he had listed yesterday. *Paintbrushes.*

Dora!

He was supposed to go to Whittingford tomorrow. Once a month, he had promised. An overnight visit. She had written and asked him to bring particular paintbrushes, narrow ones that she couldn't get in Oxford.

Bellman thought of everything he had to do. It wasn't the best time to be away, not even for a single night. He would write and explain. A messenger would run out tomorrow and get the brushes for him, dispatch would wrap them. They might even be sending the brougham that way in the next few days, you never knew, otherwise he would get someone to deliver them. He would go when he could afford the time, and stay for longer. *Write to Dora*, he added to his list.

Once, a long time ago, he had opened a book like this one and found in it, in childish handwriting, *Kiss Dora*. How he would like it if she was here to be kissed now!

But this was wasting time. All these things to do!

He selected half a dozen pen and paper tasks and settled at his desk. It was twenty to eight. Let's see if he couldn't complete these things by . . . nine? No: he wouldn't need that long. A quarter to nine. That would do it.

He set to.

*

At the top of the shop the atrium glass gazed blankly up at the black sky and down into the well of the shop. Looking either way could make you feel dizzy, so the seamstresses avoided glancing up or down as they scurried along the walkway to the room where they were allowed to congregate in the evenings and heat milk or water on the little stove.

'Who is Mr Black?' Lily was saying. 'Does no one ever see him?'

She was a skinny thing, all knuckles and elbows, but what really distinguished her was that she was the new girl. Of course, in a way they were all new girls, but Lily was the newest of the new, brought in to replace a seamstress who had not turned up. Her arrival was significant because the others, in telling her the hundred and one things she didn't know and they did, began to feel established.

'See him? Whatever do you mean? Have you not seen Mr Black, then?' her neighbour, Sally, began to tease.

'Never.'

Sally laughed. 'Of course you've seen him. You saw him only today!'

Lily frowned. 'I never did.'

'But he spoke to you!'

Lily shook her head. 'That was Mr Bellman.'

'It was Mr Black.' Some of the girls giggled, but others nodded their heads gravely at Lily in support of Sally's words. Lily looked from one face to the next, trying to decide what was true.

A girl leant forwards. 'Mr Bellman and Mr Black are as like as the two pins that you keep in your cuff.'

'Twins?' Lily was amazed.

Susan, an older girl who enjoyed a reputation for knowledge that extended beyond the fact, shook her head. 'Don't tease her. Lily, think about it. How could two men be twins and yet have different names? Only brothers can be twins. No, Mr Black is a sleeping partner.'

The girls exchanged uncertain glances. A sleeping partner? What on earth was that?

When Susan had enjoyed her knowledge in private long enough she enlightened them. 'It means he has invested in the shop, put some money in to get it going, and now leaves the running of it to Mr Bellman but takes his share of the profit.'

'Well,' said Lily. 'You learn something new every day.'

Leaning in the doorway, Lizzie listened sleepily to the conversation while she looked out of the room and up to the glass ceiling.

Sleeping partner. What a peculiar expression. An image rose in her mind: Mr Bellman and Mr Black tucked up, one at each end of a narrow bed just like hers, in matching nightcaps, as like as two pins. It made her smile.

She had thought Mr Bellman was Mr Black the first time she had seen him.

And now she remembered that Mr Bellman had spoken of Mr Black the night she had met him in Back Lane . . . As if he thought she knew him! But he had been unwell, and people said strange things when they were ill.

Beyond the glass ceiling, high in the night sky, a star disappeared momentarily then came back. A bird probably, passing over the shop in the dark.

17

Dora opened the parcel first because she already knew what the letter would say. Her father was not coming home, he was too busy.

The brushes were exactly what she wanted. The artists' supplies shop in Broad Street in Oxford had most things she wanted, but these finest brushes, a sparse half-dozen goat hairs in each, were hard to come by and for the detailing of feathers, no broader brush would do. She had tried to improvise. Rob Armstrong, the son of Fred from the dairy, generally came to collect the milk churns after the mill break-fasts and he had the strongest, straightest hair of anyone she knew. He had agreed – abashedly – to sacrifice a lock to her experiment. She had glued a few hairs to the end of an old brush, wound them round with string, trimmed them to length, then attempted to paint. The result was laughable. Human hairs did not pick up colour adequately, they had not the right flexibility and neither glue nor string were enough to hold them in place. Gradually they fell away, into the paint or the water; one dried into the picture itself. Dora gave the painting – a thrush, she was actually quite pleased with it, all but the feathers – to Rob as a thank you gift for his contribution to the experiment. He ran his finger over the wing that concealed his own hair, felt it with his fingertip and laughed.

Now she had the new brushes she could do better. She rose to go to her studio, then remembered the letter.

She read.

It was just as she thought. He wasn't coming.

She could not honestly say she was disappointed. She had not been expecting him to come and, in truth, they had little to say to each other. In the old days, when her mother, brothers and sister were alive, the house had been filled with talk, but now that they were the only ones left, she had little to say to her father, and he had little to say to her. In his presence she could not speak what was on her mind – he did not like to be reminded of the old days, discouraged brooding – nor do the things that interested her. Her binoculars and her paint had to be put aside, along with the distraction and comfort they brought her. All in all – she looked the fact full in the face – she was not sorry he was not coming.

Gathering her paints together she looked forward to losing herself for a few hours in the pleasure of painting. It removed you from yourself. She could forget all about grief and sorrow while she was intent on reproducing a certain visual effect on paper. Remembering was all very well – and there had been years when it was all she wanted to do – but these days it was a relief to forget. Forget sorrow, forget the past, forget what was lost . . . It took something engrossing to enable her to do that, and painting was the one thing she could rely on.

When did her father's mind ever fall still? He never read a book. Not for pleasure, not a novel or verse. He was not particularly fond of music, despite his fine voice. Did he never daydream? she asked herself. Never allow his mind to roam at will, surprising him with what it came up with?

She supposed that he must find respite from himself in his work. And so, since he was always at work, did this mean that he was never quite himself?

It was a terrible thought and most young women would have turned away from it, but Dora was used to terrible thoughts. When your mother is dead and your brothers and sisters are dead and your pretty hair has fallen out so no one will ever marry you, dread loses its power over you. Dora thought dreadful things all the time and had quite lost her fear of them. She turned this one over, examined it carefully, curiously, from all angles. It was clear to her that a person might lose his sense of himself in his concentration on graphs and lists and calculations. You could lose your bearings if you spent excessively long periods engaged on a single project at the expense of rest and friendship and the peaceful contemplation of life's mysteries. Was it feasible that a man might do this for so long that he slipped his moorings altogether? Was lost to himself for good? Could this be what was happening to her father?

Perhaps it was so and her father had mislaid himself permanently.

Dora's list of sorrows was so long already that, relatively speaking, the addition of this new one was no great burden.

She saw a time coming when she would be polite to her father and as kindly as ever, but would expect less of him. Their relations would be more superficial and simpler. There need be no disappointment.

Everything was ready. Dora took up her binoculars and settled in her garden chair. A dunnock was flitting from tree to earth, where Mary had scattered stale breadcrumbs. Her hand moved quickly over the page, capturing the balance of the bird's head, the set of its body, the angle of its legs. She worked rapidly, happily, with concentration.

By the time the picture was finished the afternoon was drawing to its end. Before long the rooks would be going over.

She waited to see them pass, a long skein of them, cawing and laughing in their habitual friendly fashion. She got up close to them with her binoculars, admired the purposeful ease of their flight. Twisting her body, she followed their passage overhead, until they became blurred grey specks and at last disappeared into an indeterminate whiteness beyond the edge of her vision. Even then, she watched a little longer.

'Where is it that you are going?' she murmured aloud.

She gathered her drawing things together and put them in her bag with her binoculars. The bag across her body on its strap, the folding chair under one arm and her walking stick in the other hand, she jerked and hobbled over the grass and back to the house.

18

'My wife says she sees more of Mr Black than she does of Mr Bellman. She's beginning to wonder whether Mr Bellman exists at all and taxes me with having invented him.'

Bellman stared at the haberdasher – it was Critchlow – who had one of Bellman's cigars in one hand and a glass of Bellman's whisky in the other.

'It's a little joke of hers,' the man explained mildly, seeing Bellman's face.

It was true that Bellman didn't go out much. Opportunities were numerous: every day the post brought invitations to this ball and that dinner and grand events here, there and everywhere, but Bellman was a busy man. It was tiresome enough getting round the shop thrice a day without being ambushed into conversation. With an air of sorrowful amiability he saw what he wanted to see, checked what he wanted to check, while avoiding eye contact. In a manner befitting the manager of the shop he bestowed his condolences with a look left and right that encompassed all and singled out no one.

Socialising was impossible to avoid altogether. Often it was the only way to do business so, inefficient though it was, he had more than once made business deals in a box at the theatre. The first half of the play he barely attended to: there was generally a great deal of sentiment, outbursts of feeling, and he watched the audience who looked on with stricken faces. In the interval he and the fellow came to an agreement and shook hands. When the second half started, Bellman made his excuses and left.

Once a month Bellman met with his haberdashers in Russell's on Piccadilly. He would arrive to find them waiting for him, on their second drink already. He reported the business side of things, they asked questions and commented, and at a point when all were satisfied with Bellman & Black and the talk drifted into more general matters he would rise and ask for his coat, ready to come away.

'Time for another?' someone would ask, but once the business was over he didn't even finish the drink he had.

'Work to do!' he said, and they weren't exactly unhappy about it. Sooner have their business assets managed by a man like Bellman than one who lingered over a whisky by the fireside. The profits spoke for themselves.

These business sorties were the only social events Bellman could be induced to attend. He was a wealthy widower though, handsome and in his prime, and it was only natural that women should be interested in him. The fact that he was known to shun all invitations only increased his value in their eyes. There were daughters and younger sisters in need of husbands and if Bellman was not snared quickly it stood to reason that some pretty widow going into half-mourning would snatch him up.

The haberdashers were better placed than any to apply pressure.

'You know what women are,' Critchlow said, with a grimace. 'Sometimes they just won't take no for an answer.' He sat in Bellman's chair, making no indication of leaving, and Bellman understood that, painful though it was to both of them, he meant to stay until Bellman had accepted.

'It's nothing grand. Family and a few close friends. You'll be home by eleven.'

Bellman thought he could draw him away from the topic by asking about Woking. The Queen's surgeon had purchased a plot of land there with a view to opening a crematorium, and had induced a few men of means to form a society with him for the promotion of cremation.

'It will never happen,' the haberdasher said. 'You take my word for it. How is the good Lord to raise us on the day of judgement if we are burnt to ashes? That's how people think. They never think to ask how he will raise them when they have been eaten by worms and their bones are dust, but that's by the by. No, take my word for it, Bellman. It'll take more than a few overcrowded cemeteries to bring the English mind round to the idea of burning the dead. We're not heathens in this country.'

But Bellman's strategy was ineffective. As the haberdasher rose to go, hand on door handle, he turned back into the room.

'I'll tell Emily to expect you then,' he said, as if the invitation had been accepted, and before Bellman could protest, Critchlow was gone and it was too late to do anything about it.

At the party – for party it was, despite the promises of a small, family meal – Bellman was stunned by the colour of it all. From the Prussian yellow hall to the emerald curtains of the dining room, from the sapphire dress of his hostess to the red glass at the table, the colour dazzled him. Within ten minutes he felt the beginning of a headache. He was amiable though. He still knew how, though what had once come naturally now cost him a degree of effort. The food was elegant and elaborate and interminable: it killed his appetite as soon as he set eyes on it, but he smiled and listened to the conversation that went on around him. When he spoke he said just the right kinds of thing. He made himself agreeable in a hundred small ways, and reserved enough of himself for it to be noticed.

'I have a daughter of twenty,' he said, and when he received invitations for Dora to a dance, to tea, to a play – the ladies were conscious that they had sons to marry as well as daughters – he graciously shook his head. 'She has not the stamina for London life. She lives quietly in the country.'

'Do tell us, Mr Bellman – it is the reason we have all been so keen to meet you, and the answer to the mystery all London is talking about – who is the mysterious Mr Black?'

The young woman down the table smiled at him, pink lips and white teeth, and her blue eyes gleamed with a teasing happiness. Her colouring was different, yet he was reminded of Dora, the way she used to be and it was a shock to realise that his daughter must be the same age as this girl now, this laughing young woman, happy to have found a husband and wear cornflower-blue silk to a dinner and be merry with friends.

'Yes,' others chorused in the room, 'who is Black? We are all so anxious to know!'

All the smiling faces turned expectantly towards him.

'Black? Black is only a word that sounds well with Bellman.'

The ladies were as delighted as if he had said something witty or graceful.

'Only a word!' Mrs Critchlow exclaimed. 'I am glad to know at last!'

'An assonance!' somebody suggested further down the table.

'An alliteration!'

'A poem!'

They laughed. Bellman laughed. The conversation changed to something else.

At the end of the evening, brushing out her hair, Mrs Critchlow could not persuade herself that the dinner had been a success. It should have been the beginning of a friendship. She had wanted Bellman to become a regular at their house. She wished to be instrumental in finding him a wife, and for that wife to be related to her or at least someone who could be useful . . . The evening should have been a prelude to something, but as her guest left, at the moment when she had intended to say, 'Will we see you again before long, Mr Bellman?' she had been unable to utter a word – and a glance from him had thanked her for not saying it.

'Is he in mourning?' she asked her husband. 'I didn't feel I could ask.'

'I don't know.'

'It is four years, surely, since his wife died?'

'Something like that, yes.'

'Perhaps he is mourning for another relative?'

'He is always in black when I see him, dear. He wears it at Bellman & Black and since he is always at the shop or on his way to or from the shop, I have never had the occasion to see him in anything else.'

She plaited her hair. 'He didn't like it when we were joking about the shop name, did he?'

She received no answer other than a snore.

233

Mrs Critchlow accepted the compliments from her competitors on having caught Bellman at last, but the victory was hollow. She gave the report on her party a hundred times to those who had not been there. What the man had said, what he had done, what he had eaten.

'Charm itself,' she heard herself repeat.

The more she told her story, the more she felt she was describing a phantom, a chimera, a figure from a dream. He had the outward appearance of a man, the weight and the solidity of a man, but there was something exasperatingly insubstantial about him. She couldn't escape the feeling that the essence of him was elsewhere.

'So – is there a woman, do you suppose?' one of her friends daringly wondered aloud.

Was that it? Did some secret lover hold the key to Bellman's heart? Was he engaged in a passionate liaison with a woman who was not free to marry? Perhaps his heart was already committed but his love went unrequited? Along with the rest of London she wondered. Might it be that the deceased Mrs Bellman still lived in her husband's heart and saw off all newcomers?

The haberdasher's wife considered these theories, expecting her intuition to alight upon some remembered gesture, comment or expression of his and illuminate it, giving the key to the puzzle. Her intuition was silent.

Bellman's staff wondered too. The seamstresses exchanged whispers out of the hearing of Miss Chalcraft, invented more and more unlikely tales about their employer and his women. The shop girls sat over their mutton stew in the canteen dissecting his attractiveness. There was gossip about a widow who lingered over her purchases and kept a sharp eye open for the manager. It was said that Bellman sent a boy to spy out the land in advance of his daily tours, and if she was in the shop he waited till she was gone. A good many other things were said too, silly stories mostly. His looks were universally agreed to be virile and impressive; it was understandable that girls found romantic interest in his dark brow and his intense gaze. But others preferred a fairer man and all agreed that a few smiles and a bit of laughter went a long way with a woman. Whatever their romantic preferences, in the light of day and faced with the man in the flesh, flirting seemed out of the question and the fantasy of romance evaporated.

And Girl No. 9? When Lizzie hung up her dress at night on the hook behind her door, she thought of the hook behind Mr Bellman's door, and when she got into her bed, she thought of Mr Bellman getting into his bed in the little bedroom behind the wall of his office. She had reasons of her own for wanting to bury the night of his sudden appearance in her old neighbourhood in forgetfulness. Mr Bellman himself had given no indication that he remembered it; were it not for the money he had left behind – too late for her to take her child to a doctor, and besides it could not have made a difference, not for long – she could almost believe it to be a dream. He behaved as if it had never been, and she was glad. They were a teasing lot, the seamstresses, and she preferred not to draw their attention. Beyond this, she had no other thoughts about Mr Bellman. Her night-time thoughts took her elsewhere: to the young man who had abandoned her, and the child she had lost. Sometimes the memories that came to her were happy ones, sometimes not. Both made her cry, but not for long: it was a tiring job and she couldn't help falling asleep.

19

The end of the working day followed a pattern. Upstairs the seamstresses worked for as long as they had the light: longer hours in summer, shorter in winter. The sales floor closed at seven o'clock sharp. Given the abundance of grief, a sentiment that recognised no clock, this was no easy matter and required close and careful management. From half past six the consolers – girls who were employed for the delicacy of their sympathy and their understanding expressions – were gradually withdrawn from the floor, leaving the business to be concluded by those who were supreme at selling. At a quarter to seven, without any discernible alteration in their manner, these girls deferentially placed a distinct choice before the indecisive. In cases where grief still hesitated at five to seven, Mr Heywood himself would intervene.

'Take your time, madam,' he said, and 'A wise decision is always better than a hasty one.' After all – he implied this with a delicate gesture of the fingertips – an hour here or there counts as nothing when compared with the eternity which attends us all one day. Mr Dixon would not allow anyone to be rushed, he would wait until the end of time for their decision – yet by a minute to seven the decision was invariably made and generally in favour of the more expensive item.

At seven o'clock Pentworth closed the door on the last customer with a gravity that expressed his personal condolences in a most heartfelt way, before turning the great key in the lock.

Now the consolers and the sympathisers puffed their cheeks out in relief at the departure of the customers. They rubbed their aching feet, closed their eyes in exhaustion and, hands on hips, stretched their backs, tired from reaching and fetching and carrying. Tongues remained guarded. The rules of no laughter and no gossip still held after hours, as they held within five hundred yards of the shop, so any exchanges of a more personal nature could be made only by glances or in whispers out of the hearing of the floor managers. This moment of relaxation only lasted a few moments in any case, for then came what was perhaps the busiest hour of the day.

Brooms and wax polish and dusters were produced from concealed cupboards, and there was the flurry and bustle of cleaning. Counters were polished, bolts of fabric and reels of ribbon straightened, stairs were swept, floorboards scrubbed, mirrors and windows polished . . . It was not finished till the girls themselves were ready for inspection as they queued to leave by the side door. 'Not a hair out of place,' they heard, over and over. So they took turns at the mirrors and pinned stray strands of hair for each other, and when the shop was in perfect order and when they were in perfect order, the side door was opened and they stepped out.

Counting the paces, one, two, three . . . and five hundred yards from Bellman & Black (it was the tobacconist on Regent Street west or the little restaurant on Regent Street east, and on Oxford Street it was either Marcham's or Greenway's depending on your direction), they came to the spot where they were entitled to live again. Zest and relish and delight were let out from where they had been contained all day, laughter was permitted to tweak the mouth, hands that had been meekly folded since eight in the morning were allowed to gesture and articulate. No customer of the angelically compassionate Susannah would have recognised her as she bent double with laughter, almost weeping with mirth at a vulgar tale told her by the man from the warehouse. Even the lugubrious Mr Pentworth – in practice, you'd have thought, to be doorman at the gates of heaven itself – was transformed into an averagely jolly chap when he met his sons at the King William. Going home from work: it was glorious!

William Bellman did not go home. He had spent so little time there in the first year of Bellman & Black that he had resolved in the end to let it. When the house adjoining it had come up for sale he had bought and let that one too; he owned four London houses now, but he continued to live out of preference at the shop, sleeping in the little narrow bed in the tongue-and-groove panelled room behind his office and standing in an iron tub he filled with a jug to wash. It was less fuss than going home. It was home.

Tonight he just wanted to look over the contract with Reynolds of Gloucester: he had an idea the man was making savings on his raw materials that were not being passed on. And a few minutes perusing jet sales would be time well spent. He was sending his representative up to Whitby again next week, and it wouldn't hurt to know how the different designs were doing. He spent half an hour pleasantly enough on these and other similar tasks; thought of another little job that was easier done now than tomorrow, which reminded him that . . .

When he looked at his clock he realised with familiar surprise that it was after nine o'clock.

At night, Bellman & Black had an allure all its own. It was a great beast, asleep. Now, as he leant back in his chair, he felt a pulse and it seemed to him it was the pulse of Bellman & Black, though he knew it was the pulse of his own blood in his own veins. Yet Bellman & Black was like an extension of his own body. With his hand he signed an order and his warehouse was filled with goods; with his voice he ordered that something should be done and it was; he commanded workshops and studios and factories and mills just as he commanded his legs and his hands. He was the very heart and brain of this enterprise. It belonged to him. And he to it.

He gave in to temptation, lit a lantern and stepped into the shadows of the shop. His creation was inactive but he inhabited it like the dream self that breathes in a sleeping body. From counter to counter he went, opening drawers and leafing through order books. He verified stock, centred a mannequin here, tidied a shelf there. In the cavernous darkness of dispatch his lamp illuminated long empty tables. He placed an approving hand on the brown paper and string and labels, replenished in readiness for tomorrow's work. A single parcel was unsent. He frowned and made a note of the address. Something to follow up tomorrow.

Upstairs, at the clerks' desks, he pored over the day's calculations like a headmaster over homework, paid attention to ink blots and hand-writing. Upstairs again, in the seamstresses' workroom, he counted the

238

pairs of scissors, shone his lantern on the stitchwork of the garments waiting to go out, counted the stitches per inch to the new girl's hemming.

His nocturnal supervision of the work of the shop was interrupted then by a sound.

Voices. Upstairs, the seamstresses in their rooms were singing.

Bellman smiled as he listened.

He shone his lamp onto his watch: nearly eleven o'clock. They had been out listening to some café singer, perhaps, and just come back.

He strained his ears to hear the song. Sweet voices conveyed the tune to him, melodic it was, and tender, but he could not catch the words. It was a song from long ago, he thought. He seemed to half know it . . .

How did it go, now?

He caught a thread of something . . . *Plashing fountains*, wasn't it? Ta-dah, te-dee, and *Happy hours*, something something, *Calling voices* . . .

It was a song for girls. Men liked the more robust numbers that could be accompanied by fists banging on the table and where the chorus came in as a great communal roar. A night in an inn began with the popular numbers and got bawdier as the night went on. Sometimes though, a long night could take hard-drinking men, young and old, beyond lust to sentimentality. Then, at the end of the evening, in husky and wavering voices, they sang songs like this one: tender and yearning. He had known this song once, but it was no good pretending: he didn't know the words now. But he hummed as he continued his rounds and when the girls reached the end of the song and began it again he lingered in the workroom. Their beds were a few feet above his head. He remembered – with some surprise – that he too had been something of a singer once, a long time ago.

The singing came to an end. There was a faint murmur of conversation, then silence.

Everything was just so in the workroom. Bellman left a note of congratulations for Miss Chalcraft and his rounds were complete.

The song, evidently, was not to be repeated.

He wished . . .

What did he wish for?

He did not know. Unless it was his bed.

Washing his face and undressing, Bellman hummed the tune again. He climbed into bed, blew out the candle and settled his back securely against the tongue-and-groove panelling. In the second between being awake and being asleep he longed intensely for soft arms around his neck and the breathing of a woman in the crook of his neck. Lizzie's face, on the edge of his thoughts. And then he was overcome by blackness.

The plashing fountains and the happy hours found Bellman's brain a congenial place and made a permanent encampment there. At times of deep concentration or contentment or tiredness, a few bars of the song would escape his lips and he filled in the gaps with 'ta dees' and 'ta dums' and other fillers of his own devising. Through the months that followed, it became the pleasant, undemanding companion of his solitary hours. Once or twice he imagined another life for himself in which he was a singer. He stood on the first-floor gallery as if on a stage, and projected his song so that his voice echoed through the empty theatre of his shop. The headless mannequins and half dummies listened with the appearance of rapt attention, but as the final notes died away they did not applaud.

In the silence that followed he wondered how far his voice carried. Had he woken the seamstresses two floors up? He allowed himself to imagine a midnight choir: himself and his seamstresses, their voices raised together in song, then he told himself it was ludicrous and put the thought away.

20

In a narrow back street, in a cold and dingy bedroom in Holborn, an innkeeper turned over in bed one morning to find his wife had died in the night. His neighbours heard the weeping and came running to find him ashen-faced, his eight children standing dazed around him. 'What must I do?' he asked his neighbour's wife. 'Go to Bellman & Black,' she told him. 'They'll know everything.'

A mother and father in Richmond received news of a riding accident and minutes later the body of their son was brought into the house. Later they would weep and pray together, but in this first moment their minds responded differently. The father's mind was stilled by shock. He neither heard nor saw anything. His wife was afforded the distraction of domestic organisation. *Someone will have to cancel the dinner*, she thought. Someone will have to find out whether the horse is found. But before she did either of those things, before the pain possessed her completely, she reached for her ink and writing paper. 'I suppose that I had better send for Bellman & Black,' she said.

A young Clapham widow opened her closet and ran her finger over the crape dresses inside. Two years to the day, since her husband had died. A good man. A handsome one. Two years . . . though some nights it felt like yesterday. She wouldn't be sorry to see the end of this black though. Grey was decorous. Dignified. There was a particular shade of it, she remembered, that brought out the blue of her eyes and flattered her fair curls. They would be bound to have it at Bellman & Black.

The mighty and the meek, the rich and the poor, were equal when faced with death: all dabbed their eyes and thought of Bellman & Black. The safe in the little room behind Bellman's office grew fuller and the accounts at the Westminster & City grew richer. The haberdashers married their daughters and granddaughters and the guests at the weddings ate and drank lavishly thanks to the spendthrift grief of the bereaved. All was well.

Bellman was a contented man. His wages bill grew every month as he took on more and more staff to cope with the demand. His kitchen cooked more and more lunches to fuel the staff who made the sales. There was a constant flow of deliveries coming in at the back of the shop to replace the goods that were carried out the front door. You could measure the success in any number of ways, right down to the bills for string and brown paper with which to wrap the customers' orders and the shoe repair bills for the porters who wore down their soles running up and downstairs between customers and dispatch with purchases piled high in their arms. It all came together at the end of every month, when Bellman read his monthly reports, checked the monthly figures and entered the month's actual sales on his graph. Over the years the curve had never ceased to rise. Those predictions he had made in his calfskin notebook at the very beginning, and that he had reined in so as not to look overconfident in front of the haberdashers . . . Well, look now! The profits were seven times greater than he had imagined! Seven times!

Bellman chuckled. He had every reason to be pleased.

He had not forgotten Black. There was a time, he remembered, when he had been anxious about him. No longer. Unorthodox their arrangement might be, but it worked. Black's money was piling up in the second account, it could be withdrawn at a day's notice whenever the man wanted it. And what a sum! Was Black aware of the success of Bellman & Black? Bellman wondered. Did he keep an eye on it from afar, biding his time, satisfied at his nice little nest egg? Perhaps sometimes he might walk past, assessing the window display? Perhaps he came in and browsed once in a while, passing himself off as an ordinary customer?

Bellman relished the thought of one of his shop girls serving Black, all the while in the dark as to his identity.

And yet, somehow he thought not. More likely the man was away. Travelling, probably. Perhaps he was in Europe, or America. Who knows what life the fellow was leading? Intrepid adventure of some kind, exploration into the furthest corners of the globe . . . It wouldn't surprise him, for Black wasn't a man to accept limitations. And in this case, it would come as a great surprise to him, the day after he docked, to discover on a walk through London that the idea he had sown a few years ago had grown into this huge emporium. With what joy he would come bounding in, asking for Bellman.

What a day that would be! Bellman looked forward to it with intense longing. There would be a knock at the door, Verney saying, 'Someone to see you, sir,' and then in would come Black, large as life.

Like long-lost friends they would embrace, Black's arms would envelop him, he would feel his hands slap his back and they would be instantly at ease – like brothers! He would put his work aside, no matter how important, and say to Verney – he could picture his astonishment! – 'No interruptions! Not even for Critchlow himself!' Then the pair of them would sit, one each side of the fire, a glass of best brandy in their hand, and Black would talk about all manner of things. What he had been doing, where he had been. A great number of things that had mystified Bellman would become clear. 'I expect you've been wondering about all this!' Black would say and, lighting a cigar, Bellman would tell him, 'I knew you would turn up sooner or later, old fellow. I never doubted it!'

Bellman would tell his friend all about the business, everything he had done on his side to make it the success it was today, and Black would approve it all. 'I could tell you were the one, Bellman, my friend.' Yes. He would point to the graph, turn through the pages of the ledger, show him the statements for the bank account he had opened for him. Then what satisfaction there would be.

Two men, their fortunes made, talking business by the fire until – yes, this is how it would be! – their talk would drift away from commerce, rise above it, and they would speak of loftier matters, philosophical questions and universal issues . . . There were aspects of life that Bellman had no names for, they were off the edges of the pages of the dictionary, but Black was bound to know a great deal about them. He was clearly a man of unusual influence. Working alongside him had already conferred protection of a kind that went well beyond the financial, on Bellman and his daughter. He had a hundred questions he would like to ask and Black would answer patiently, in simple words – words that would say a good deal – and Bellman, listening, would learn marvellous and miraculous things, things undreamt of, things of the gravest importance.

What a conversation! By the time they came to the end of it all the moon would be high in the sky and the stars would be out. All London would be asleep while the two great men of commerce sat here in this office and fathomed the mysteries of the world . . . Camaraderie. Understanding. Companionship to cherish. How he was looking forward to meeting Black again.

The day would come. It was all in Black's hands; there was nothing he, Bellman, could do about it, no matter how heartfelt his longing.

In the meantime, there was Bellman & Black. Work to be done. Sentimentality wouldn't put money in the bank.

Bellman turned his thoughts from his fantasy and back to his calculations. While he occupied his conscious thoughts with meticulous adding, subtracting and multiplying, he was heartened at the knowledge that there was a good deal to be said for having a fellow like Black on your side.

&

The rook has few predators. He is too large, too strong, too well organised and above all too clever to be more than a rare supper for owls and eagles. Humans are occasionally a threat though – and not only boys with catapults.

There is an old ditty that English mothers sing to the babies they bounce on their knees. It goes like this:

Sing a song of sixpence, a pocketful of rye,
Four and twenty black birds baked in a pie,
When the pie was opened, the birds began to sing,
Now wasn't that a dainty dish to set before a king?

The black birds in question are rooks, and you may well be thinking that a pie containing two dozen rooks would be a very large pie indeed, but that is far from the truth. The meat of an adult rook is bitter. You would not like it. The only palatable rook (if you're not too fussy) is a branchling. These are the young birds that cannot yet fly, but spend their days on branches outside the nest, watching the world that is to be theirs. These flightless birds of June are the only ones worth eating, and each one has only two slivers of meat – a morsel on each breast the size of the pad of your fingertip – to recompense the effort of hunting and plucking and preparing. Hence the king in the rhyme, for whom the novelty pie might just be worth it since he has a retinue of gamekeepers with guns, and white-aproned cooks to provide it for him.

Still, hunger is a great motivator and your ancestors had to eat. It stands to reason that in times of hardship there will have been some patient enough to aim a bow and arrow into an oak and bring down a branchling.

You might well turn up your nose at the prospect of eating rook pie. But the rook would not turn up his nose at the prospect of eating you. If the chance came his way – at the roadside or on the battlefield or where the tide pulls back – he would happily redden his beak in your flesh. Go back before churches and crosses and coffins and it was ritual practice to lay out the dead on a stone platform for the bones to be picked clean in this manner.

What I am getting at is this: some time ago, a rook ate the flesh of your ancestor and some time ago your ancestor ate rook pie. Man eats rook: rook eats man. Bodies mingle. Thanks to this mutual ingestion, protein from human flesh becomes blue-black feather and protein from rook flesh becomes human skin.

There is a cousinly intimacy between rooks and men. Humans, with their unmatched ability for forgetting, are surprised at learning the closeness between the species. The rook, with his better memory, knows perfectly well that he is your flighted, feathered kin.

There are numerous collective nouns for rooks. In some parts people say a *building* of rooks.

21

Bellman & Black was the main but not the only part of Bellman's business empire. For a start, he still owned Bellman's Mill. Every week he received Ned's report from Whittingford and wrote a letter in return – some twelve or fifteen pages – instructing, advising, querying. There was a second mill too: half a year ago he had bought it at a very good price after the original owner came a cropper. The owner had made the mistake of coming to rely overmuch on a single large customer; that customer then defaulted on a payment. It was a rudimentary error, and Bellman – who had had the foresight many years earlier to offer the miller a long-term loan on good terms, and thus was first to know of his financial predicament – took advantage. He moved Ned's right-hand man in to align the mill with the practices at Bellman's, and after an initial period of turbulence – no one likes change – things had settled down and the mill was already starting to be profitable.

Bellman also owned a dozen London houses in the very best areas: they made a good return for him in rents as well as holding their value. They didn't run themselves though. There were tenants to find, rents to collect, roofs to mend . . . He had people in place to act for him but still, being Bellman, he liked to know just what was being done on his behalf.

Furthermore, Bellman kept a very close eye on his investments. Many a young entrepreneur had sought and been given capital by Bellman for some innovation in the area of mourning goods production. With capital came scrutiny. If there was a flaw in the business thinking, Bellman would find it. He familiarised himself with areas of business far removed from his own, saw the fundamental, universal factors that influenced success and failure, evaluated the specificities of each venture and never invested capital without the understanding that his money came with the expectation of a hand in the guidance of the business as well. He had a light touch, yet it was the touch that made all the difference. At the Westminster & City, Anson came to see him as a kind of bellwether. If Bellman invested, you could be sure the endeavour was a sound one, and where Bellman's money was, so was Bellman's acumen and overseeing eye. Where he could, the banker shifted his own capital, nested it in alongside Bellman's and benefited from the gains.

One evening at Russell's Bellman met with his banker and his haberdashers to discuss an ambition that was close to his heart. It had been planned for some time to extend Bellman & Black by opening new shops in Bath, York and Manchester: sites for these shops had been found and between the haberdashers and the bank, funds had been found to purchase land and engage architects. Anxious to press on with the programme of national expansion, Bellman had hit upon the idea of – this was how it appeared to the other four – hiring out the name Bellman & Black to independent retailers in the mourning goods trade, and supplying them from Bellman & Black's established supply chain, in return for creaming off a percentage of their profit. It was an idea that struck all of them as bizarre.

'But why should a retailer who has always been his own man wish to do such a thing?' one of the haberdashers asked, perplexed.

'How can we know when a shop in Manchester is running low on size six Italian leather gloves?' another objected.

Bellman had answers for everything. For every obstacle, he had a solution. For every doubt, he supplied certainty. He plugged gaps in their knowledge with firm facts and figures. He had looked into every aspect so thoroughly and he explained it with such clarity of vision that the strange idea came, little by little, to seem so obviously sensible that they all found themselves wondering why no one had ever thought of it before.

'Where on earth do you find the time for all this?' Anson asked him in a gap in proceedings as a waiter was delivering new drinks to their table. 'What is your secret?'

Bellman shrugged. 'Time passes more quickly for the man who lies abed than for the busy man. The more I have to do, the more time I have to do it. I discovered that a long time ago.'

They sipped the brandy and went on with their talk. The consensus was turning towards yes. Anson would not have a say in the decision – he was only the banker – but his views were nonetheless listened to and considered with respect. 'What are we to make of Thompson and his crematorium campaign?' he asked. 'He is right about the grave-yards. They are unhygienic and something will have to be done. With change in the air, is it the moment to be expanding so radically?'

There was a quick outburst of feeling within the group.

'It is ungodly!'

'Quite so. The English will never stand for it!'

'It is only because he is the Queen's physician that people give him the time of day. The idea is nonsensical.'

Bellman was the only one to relate the issue to the business. 'In my view a funeral is a funeral whatever the method. The desire for ritual will never change. A coffin is a large piece, but most often made in wood which is relatively inexpensive; moreover, being destined to be buried in the ground, there is a natural limit on what people are prepared to pay for it. A casket destined to contain ashes and which people may desire to keep in their home, may be made of all kinds of expensive stuff, even silver and gold, and permits of a great many decorative finishes and artistic additions. Were Thompson to be successful, I see no reason to fear for the health of the business. I myself would be inclined to see it as an opportunity rather than as something to be feared.'

'You would press ahead immediately with the expansion plans rather than wait for the outcome of this case in Wales?'

'The druid doctor, burning his child's corpse on a hillside!' Heads were shaken and lips curled disparagingly around the table.

'It is a wicked thing. The man is a heathen.'

'He is making trouble for himself more than for anyone else. He is to be pitied, surely.'

'You think he is mad?'

And the haberdashers fell into debate about the case that was so exercising public opinion.

249

'There may be one good thing to come out of it,' Critchlow suggested. 'Placing the matter before a Christian judge will clarify the law once and for all, and thus put an end to Thompson's Society.'

The others nodded their heads sagely.

'I hope you are right,' said Anson.

'So we press ahead?' Bellman put the question to them, though the way he said it was more like a statement.

The haberdashers nodded. Agreement reached, Bellman rose and a moment later was gone.

'He's gone back to work,' one of the haberdashers told Anson. 'Devoted to it. Got to admire the man.'

Walking home later that evening, Anson thought back over the conversation. Got to admire the man? Yes and no. He had the utmost respect for Bellman's commercial instincts and his financial acumen, but his admiration left room to wonder whether his single-mindedness was an entirely good thing.

Anson considered himself hard-working. Ten till four, Monday to Friday at the bank; evenings entertaining clients and doing more business at his club; paperwork at weekends when he had to. But most days, for a few hours, he was free to live his life.

Anson was enormously fond of the company of his children, both the grown ones from his first marriage, and the little ones from his second. His Saturday morning walk around the garden was something to which he attached importance. What is more, on those days when he could not spend half an hour in the company of a good book he felt deprived. And then there were women. His wife, of course, whom he loved dearly and treated with great tolerance and kindness, and also one or two others: cheerful souls, discreet and affectionate. Yes, he had always liked women. All this, he considered, was the stuff life was made of. It was what he worked for. When he spent his earnings – on hydrangeas, a piano for his daughters or adornments for one pretty woman or another – it seemed the justification for his time at the bank, the natural end of a cycle that began with his labour. He could not for

250

the life of him see what it was that held a parallel position in Bellman's life.

There was a daughter, or so they said, but he didn't seem to spend much time with her. She didn't live in London and Bellman was never away from the shop for more than twenty-four hours. There were not known to be any women. The top floor of the shop housed a harem of seamstresses adequate in number to satisfy any number of sultans, yet an instinct – more insightful than Mrs Critchlow's feminine one – told Anson that Bellman left them unmolested. Nor were his appetites gastronomic or alcoholic. The bottles he kept in his office were only opened for business acquaintances, so far as he could see. If Bellman ever came to him at home, as he had once or twice when a matter was urgent, he accepted a cup of tea or a glass of brandy indifferently and left it unfinished as often as not. He had no hobbies. He hadn't even a home that merited the name. The man simply worked, seemingly without fatigue, and never needing the respite, the restoration of repose, of comfort, of company. It was impressive. But was it natural?

We are not made of the same material as him, Anson thought. *And yet he is human. How long can a man go on in such a fashion?*

22

Bellman's waistcoat pocket had developed a hole where his watch weighed it down, and the fabric had bagged. 'You had better send a girl down to measure me up for a new one,' he told Miss Chalcraft, and she sent Lizzie.

He took off his jacket and placed it over the back of a chair.

'It is made of English merino, I think?' Lizzie asked. 'It is soft to wear but less resistant than the Spanish.'

'Yet it is the same yarn. It is only the weaving that is done in the one place or the other.'

He took it off and stood in his shirt sleeves to be measured. She took her tape measure from the pocket attached to her belt and he felt the lightness of her touch, nape to waist, collar bone to shoulder, chest dimension, waist. In between each measurement she distanced herself to write it down. She went away and came close, once, twice, thrice . . . She did not look at him all the while, not his face, and he did not look at her, except out the corner of his eyes.

He found that he was not singing, nor even quite humming, but merely breathing a tune. His ribcage must have jerked to do it, for he felt her fingers on his shoulders to still him, and then he heard her voice.

'They are saying, upstairs, that Mr Black haunts the shop.'

He tried to distinguish her breath in the air at the back of his neck, but could not.

'What makes them say that?'

'They hear him singing.'

'Ah.'

'Apparently he does not know all the words to the song.'

'Is that so?'

'Are your arms aching? No? Then I will just fit this calico to you.

It is the one we used last time, and your measurements have not changed.'

She deftly pinned a few pieces of calico together on the desk, then came behind him again and pressed them flat against his back. Her light voice drifted in his ear then, in a just audible whisper.

Still the angel stars are shining,
Still the rippling waters flow,
But the angel-voice is silent
That I heard so long ago.
Hark! the echoes murmur low,
Long ago!

What a sad song! Bellman thought. He hadn't realised it was sad. Had he remembered he would not have sung it – yet in Lizzie's soft voice the sadness was enticing. He was glad when she continued.

Still the wood is dim and lonely,
Still the plashing fountains play,
But the past and all its beauty
Whither has it fled away?
Hark! the mournful echoes say
Fled away!

Listening, he felt a sensation in his chest. The readiness to release of something held taut for too long, the welcome letting go of a burden too tightly clutched ... . What was happening to him?

Lizzie came to stand in front of him. Shy or embarrassed, she did not meet his eye and fell silent. She took the calico pieces for the front of the waistcoat and laid one on his chest, pinning it at the shoulder to its corresponding back half.

'Go on with the song. Please.' His voice was gruff to his own ears.

The red in her cheeks deepened. She was so close he saw the moist inner part of her lips as they opened and closed.

Still the bird of night complaineth,
(Now, indeed, her song is pain,)
Visions of my happy hours
Do I call and call in vain?
Hark! the echoes cry again,
All in vain!

She pressed the other half of the waistcoat front to him, and when her voice broke and missed a word or two, Bellman discovered that he did know the words after all. A song taught by drunks so long ago in the Red Lion and nine-tenths forgotten, now emerged from the past. Words that had evaded him came to his lips one after another, at the exact moment he needed them. Conscious of Verney in the next room, he murmured with as much tune as he could muster under his breath:

Cease, oh echoes, mournful echoes!
Once I loved your voices well;
Now my heart is sick and weary—
Days of old, a long farewell!
Hark! the echoes sad and dreary
Cry farewell, farewell!

Lizzie had finished her pinning. She was watching him sing, as he had watched her, and her hands were clasped at her breast. It would be the easiest thing in the world to take her hands between his own.

I should ask her about Black, he thought. He had been meaning to do it for . . . oh! a long while.

'When I met you before,' he said, 'the night before the shop opened,' and his path diverged unexpectedly from his intention, 'there was a baby's crib in your room.'

He saw her flinch, under the skin. 'I had a little girl, once. Her name was Sarah. She—'

Lizzie halted and swallowed. Her eyes filmed with water; it was held tense, trembled. The tear dropped and glazed her cheek, then another, and her face was brilliant with sorrow, and at the same time – Bellman was utterly dazzled – she smiled. Whatever it was she might have said was quite unnecessary for her face was radiant with the memory of joy and pain and he was spellbound. The glance she gave him then was a gift, beautiful and frightening, and he longed to accept it.

Something was brimming in him. He felt a twitch at his lips. What sweet relief there would be in weeping now, with a song to speak for him and a woman to weep with . . . His eyes ached, the pressure behind them increased and at the moment his vision broke into a brilliant dazzle, he saw – or thought he saw – movement at the window.

'What was that?' he asked.

'What?'

'At the window. A bird, was it?'

'I didn't see.'

In the moment of surprise, his hand had found hers.

There had once been a William Bellman who knew how to kiss a woman. Who knew how to offer and receive the comfort of an embrace. Who could draw another human being close to him and feel a heart that was not his own beat against his chest.

But I am with Black now, he thought as he scanned the sky for whatever had interrupted them. The comfort of grief was out of bounds and it was too late for sorrow.

He released Lizzie's hand. She turned away to her sheet of measurements.

'Will you have the pockets as before, Mr Bellman?'

'I think so, yes.'

'Be careful of the pins then, as I take it off you.'

He stood without moving while she edged the pinned pieces down his arms. She folded the model loosely and rested it over her arm. 'I can do it by tomorrow. Will lunchtime be soon enough?'

'There is no rush.'

Lizzie went back to the sewing room and Bellman went back to work.

23

'Will!'

It was so long since anyone called him by this diminutive – or even by his Christian name come to that – that at first he didn't realise it was he who was being addressed. He almost walked right by, and it was the expectation in her gaze that slowed him. Then the use of his name caught up with him, and he halted.

Her face was familiar and unfamiliar. At Bellman & Black he knew everyone, but this was Whittingford High Street. He couldn't think for the life of him how to go about attaching a name to this face that clearly knew him so well. She smiled at him, asked him how he was, and he struggled to reply till he knew who . . .

'It's Jeannie Armstrong. Jeannie Aldridge as I used to be . . . What a long time it's been. I can't blame you for not knowing me. I've changed.'

The Jeannie he used to know was visible in this woman. She was older, fatter, greyer. It wasn't only time that had changed her though. Some other thing had happened to darken her eyes and line her face.

He listened to her speaking of her children. Rob, the eldest, who now delivered the bread to the mill and to Mill House. 'Thank good-ness we have him, that's what I say. Though he's still only a lad he's taken on the whole running of the bakery, deliveries and the lot, and I don't know how we'd have coped without him. Your Dora has been a godsend. She has been teaching him the bookkeeping, and more than that, in truth she is doing it for him, till his brother leaves school and can help him more. I can't be in the bakery and looking after Fred, can I? And now that he needs me more and more, I can hardly leave his side. Our daughter is with him now, while I came out to fetch . . .'

From her talk he put together the facts: Fred was sick, Rob the son was moving prematurely into his father's shoes, his own daughter was helping them out. He faintly recalled one of Ned's reports, he had an idea he had been told the baker was unwell but that deliveries were being maintained. He seemed to remember reading that Dora had learned bookkeeping from Ned and was making herself useful in the mill office a few mornings a week. The reality of it seemed somehow unexpected.

Jeannie's chatter had come to an abrupt halt as she was struck by an idea.

'Why don't you come and say hello? "I always knew he would make something of himself, that Will Bellman." That's what Fred always says. Saw it in you, he reckons, when you were boys together. And you gave him that big chance, the bread for the mill breakfasts. It was the making of us, that was. He never forgot that.'

The blue of her eyes was no longer the cloudless shade it had once been.

An image came to him out of nowhere: the river, sedges grown to their tallest, Jeannie's white legs spread on the green of the riverbank, and her black boots still on her feet.

He saw her remember it too. She saw he had remembered.

'Come and see him, Will,' she said. 'It would mean a lot.'

'Yes,' he said. 'I will.'

'So you are working with Ned in the mill office now?' he asked Dora at breakfast.

'I have been for the last year and a half.'

He nodded. 'Do you like it?'

'I do.'

'And the bakery bookkeeping?'

She nodded more slowly, frowning. 'The Armstrongs were thinking of taking young Fred and Billie out of school to help out. I can see why they felt it necessary, but it seemed short-sighted to me. With another year or two of education they can be so much more useful in the future. Rob can manage the bakery side of things in the meanwhile if he has someone to take care of the paperwork for him.'

'So you are doing it. Are you being paid?'

She smiled. 'We don't pay for the household bread. And we have the bakery's delivery cart for expeditions on Sundays. And when Rob falls asleep at a picnic or in your old chair when he brings the invoices over, I have a model to draw for an hour at least and he doesn't move an inch. That seems a fair exchange to me.'

He nodded. 'In any event, it would be a costly annoyance to have to get a new baker for the mill if Armstrong's went under.'

'I hear that you are going to see Mr Armstrong before you leave for London?' Dora asked, looking up from her marmalade. 'Rob mentioned it to Mary when he delivered the bread this morning.'

Bellman suddenly frowned and stared. She was right. He had promised.

He shook his head. 'I would have. But now . . .' He gestured in the direction of the letter at his side. A letter from Verney, setting out all the numerous and varied issues that had arisen in his short absence, for him to peruse on his journey so that he would arrive fully informed and ready to act. He felt a sudden sense of urgency. It was imperative that he should get back to London at the earliest opportunity.

'I am needed in London,' he explained.

The need to hurry gripped him now. He rose from his chair still wiping his mouth with his napkin, all before he had even swallowed his last mouthful of toast.

'What is the matter with Mr Armstrong, anyway?'

Dora's eye and voice were neutral. 'He is dying.'

'Let them know I'll go next time,' he said, as though she hadn't spoken, and he dropped his napkin on the floor in his haste to reach the door.

He opened the door and fled.

'Next time will be too late,' Dora told the door as it swung shut.

She took another bite of toast.

Bellman made notes in his calfskin notebook and acted upon them. In his next letter to Ned he advised him of his decision to pay for a Bellman & Black's funeral for the baker who had provided the mill's breakfasts for so many years. Would Ned please notify Mrs Jeannie

Armstrong of this, at the necessary time, and also act as intermediary between Mrs Armstrong and Mr Latimer, funeral director in chief at Bellman & Black, to make the arrangements according to the family's wishes. He added a note to the same effect in a regular memo to his funerals man, Mr Latimer.

A few weeks later, Bellman was processing a pile of papers on his desk in his standard fury of activity. One particular invoice brought him up sharp.

What was this? An invoice for a funeral provided free of charge by Bellman & Black? Name of Armstrong . . .

Fred!

His blood jumped in alarm. His heart made ready to beat faster. Something blocked his throat.

With a scrawl that was even hastier and less legible than usual he signed the invoice off and moved quickly on to the next item.

He concentrated hard, very hard on his papers. He worked fast and then faster still. Every minute and every second and every fraction of every second he worked. When the pile of papers he was working on was reduced to nothing, he took up an absorbing piece of analysis from his accountant that he had been meaning to evaluate for some time and sat up with it till the small hours, making notes and listing queries. At the end of it he wrote a full assessment of the argument. Then he found a few other bits and pieces to do. By the time it was morning and Verney came knocking, he had forgotten all about his blood and his heart and his throat, and Fred's funeral was a detail from the distant past.

24

Verney placed the month's accounts summary on his desk together with the related files. There was a touch of hesitancy, reluctance even, in his manner. 'And I thought you would want to see this,' he said, placing a printed paper on top.

Bellman glanced at it: the broadsheet was folded so as to show a letter from one of the literary names of the day, criticising the excesses of funeral spending.

'Another one?' Bellman cast his eye over it. 'It only serves to dissuade people from going to the charlatans and brings them to our door. All to the good.'

Verney nodded. 'I'll be off then, if you have no further need of me.'

They said goodnight.

It was the last day of October and, ignoring the bursts of rain against the dark window, Bellman sat down to his desk with relish. Every last Friday of the month his heads of department wrote their accounts of the last four weeks' trading: the rises and falls in sales of different lines, the factors that had influenced the takings. Most of this was known to him already, from his thrice-daily tours of the shop in trading hours; still he enjoyed this hour after closing time alone with the reports. Whether bonnets were up or down, and why; the sudden run on serpent motif jet; stationery takings up and the difficulties with an Italian supplier of gloves – his interest in these bread-and-butter aspects of the business was unflagging. A big funeral – two months ago it had been the funeral of the Earl of Stanford – could boost the profits of almost every department. As he read, questions occurred to him, points of action, things to follow up, so here and there he noted something in the margin: a question mark, an arrow, a word or two. He forgot nothing.

From the written reports he proceeded to the chief accountant's figures. He needed do little more than glance at the page. If there was an error it would jump out at him, obvious as a statue in the middle of a dance floor. He looked over the rows and columns, everything looked all right. It was only the bottom line that gave him pause for thought. He peered at it more closely, then held the paper a little further away. He dropped the paper onto his desk and stared at the point where wall met ceiling. What was going on?

It had been another good month, hadn't it? An endless stream of customers who grieved, purchased, paid and left consoled. For every customer who left the store, another entered. For every customer who came out of mourning, another was just entering it. Those that came out of mourning would, as likely as not, one day go into it again. There was a strong feeling – and why discourage it? – that to keep mourning garb 'for next time' was asking for trouble. And when his customers died and could never spend another penny, why even then – especially then – they contributed to the success of Bellman & Black . . . Let the poets and the novelists write what letters they would, let *Household Words* print a dozen such letters a week, it made no difference. People continued to die and when they died the bereaved wanted their mutes and their lined coffins and their new black gowns . . .

Nothing had changed. Boys had used thousands of yards of paper and of string to wrap parcels to send to all corners of the country. Girls had stitched thousands of yards of black thread into black crape and merino and cashmere. He had seen the invoices for the thread and the string. All was well.

He picked up the figures and looked again. Level sales. No increase on last month.

Bellman frowned. Was this levelling off the effect of the market having reached its natural limit? If so, it would be no great disaster. They could go on for ever at this level. Was it possibly – his chest contracted – the sign of something else? Was this flat month the precursor to a downward turn?

Bellman stood by his chart, pen in hand. He rose to ink in his takings and hesitated. It couldn't be! Verney's balletic fingers must have made a mistake. A decimal point astray somewhere. A three that wanted correcting to an eight. He would get him to right it tomorrow.

He put his black pen back in its holder.

What target should he set for next month? What was happening in London? The temperature was falling. It was cold and soon it would be colder. People would try and stretch their fuel and the poor would have to do without it altogether. It would be a choice between logs for the fire and something for the pot. Snow would cut people off in the country. Food would be harder to come by in isolated areas. The well-off were not immune to winter. Even in their furs they would shiver through Sunday services. In icy streets, feet would fly out from under people; bones would be broken; infections would set in. Illness would harness the weakening effect of winter to its own ends.

Bellman took up his blue pen to fix next month's target. It hovered over the chart. For the first time he imagined the line extending itself into a downward curve. He tried to wipe the image from his mind and decided that, in any case, it was a job that would be better left till morning when he and Verney had had a chance to go through it all properly.

At some black hour of the night the curve of Bellman & Black's sales figures etched itself on the darkness and Bellman found himself study-ing it again. His brain continued making calculations – had never stopped, it seemed. Haberdashery plus millinery plus stationery plus funerals plus . . . March plus April plus May plus June . . . Apoplexy plus influenza plus consumption plus old age plus heart trouble . . . The additions went on and on, he lost his way in the lists of figures, had to go back and start again, because he had lost count . . .

But what was it that he had forgotten?

The curve rose and rose and rose, ever more steeply, July, August, September, every month above and beyond Bellman's most ambitious predictions. He went to place his sales target on the graph and an invisible hand closed over his, forced it down, beyond where he meant it to go.

So low? That's impossible! he thought. But a dark certainty bled into him: the sales would fall and fall again.

Down and down went the figures, one transaction after another, half a yard of ribbon and a baby's tombstone, a jet hatpin and two dozen yards of black merino, four servants kitted out in mourning, and mutes, eight, for the funeral of an earl, and . . . what had he forgotten?

Down and down, the curve drawn smoothly on the endless sky over Whittingford, down and down, towards the old oak tree . . .

Bellman was awake.

His heart was beating fast and he had an obscure sense of something unpleasant receding from his mind as sleep retreated.

The match spat and flared and he was grateful for the company of the little candle. He drank some water. He would get up for a while till he felt better. Perhaps the room was stuffy.

In his nightshirt and nightcap he stood looking out. All was quiet, all was dark. Beyond the grand façades of Regent Street were other streets, smaller, more modest, with rooms over the shops where butchers and booksellers and tobacconists slept with their wives and their children. And further out, the densely populated areas where whole families shared a single room and a house might be home to a hundred people. People. Living and dying, it made no difference, they were all customers.

Bellman's back felt stiff and his feet were painful. He knew he was tired but he didn't feel sleepy. It was the accounts. It wasn't like Verney to make a mistake. His boys were accurate and he had a method where everything was checked and double-checked. But somewhere a mistake must have slipped through. What other explanation was there?

He would fetch the workings and go through it all himself.

Bellman did this.

It all worked out just as before.

His face grave, Bellman lifted his candle to illuminate the graph on the wall. He moved his candle so as to illuminate the entire curve from the first month's trading to now.

Something struck him.

Ten years! he thought. *For ten years I have been drawing this graph on this office wall.*

How could that be? Had ten winters come and gone? He had not seen it happen. But that would make him . . . forty-nine! He did the sums and to his great perplexity found that he was indeed forty-nine. He peered at himself in the window glass. Against the background of night his white self was spectral. His hair was grey. He looked tired. He was tired.

He shook his head in wonderment at the man in the risible white nightcap and gown. How was it possible? Ten years, and he hadn't noticed. He who noticed everything! He who forgot nothing!

His stomach lurched, as if the ground beneath his feet had suddenly given way.

That, again, he thought.

The nausea came first, the dizziness a second later.

He drank a brandy and the trembling subsided somewhat.

Come on, he chided himself. Focus on the numbers.

They added up, didn't they? Yes. And at the same time they didn't.

Fashions in bonnets. Coffins in Lancashire. The Earl of Stanford.

Or was there something else behind it?

One thing only affected the profits of Bellman & Black: death.

So, Bellman wondered wearily, whose hand was it that nudged his own and placed the monthly target always a bit higher than he intended? Was it the same hand that covered the mouths and pinched the nostrils of the sick? That applied pressure over the trigger finger of the sick at heart? That pressed laudanum into the hand of the love-lorn?

Whose was it?

Black.

The quaking took hold of him again; he placed a hand on the desk to steady himself. He remembered with a sense of foreboding that he had never completed that contract.

In his anxiety to find the draft he opened one drawer after another. He turned out papers, which slithered between his trembling fingers

265

and onto the floor. On hands and knees he riffled through them by candlelight, squinting, panting with frantic effort.

How much, William wondered, do I owe?

He couldn't find it.

Well, never mind. He could write it out afresh. The essential thing was to get the sums in order.

He fretted over calculations, jotted extraordinary figures into his notebook, added things up one way and another and squinted at the results.

It was too much. Far too much.

And nowhere near enough.

The next morning Verney was astonished to find his employer asleep at his desk with papers strewn on the floor all around him. He was still in his nightshirt, his white nightcap stained with ink where his head had come to rest on a set of wild and unfathomable calculations. Without waking Bellman, Verney gathered the papers together before tiptoeing from the room. Outside the door he orchestrated a prolonged burst of sound – heavy footsteps, much jingling of keys and jiggling of lock – before re-entering the office. By that time Bellman had removed himself and his fantastical calculations into his bedroom.

25

Mr Anson of the Westminster & City nodded.

'Well, it's a bit short notice, but I dare say I could call by and see Mr Bellman this afternoon if it's urgent.'

The young man swallowed. 'I believe that Mr Bellman is . . . hoping – expecting, I should say – to see you sooner than that.' He coughed. 'If it can be managed, sir.'

George Anson stretched his legs out under his desk and looked over his glasses at the young man.

'If I understand you correctly, Mr Bellman would like me to step over to his office now, is that right?'

'Yes, sir.'

Mr Anson had a hundred things to do but curiosity and concern conspired in him. What is the good of being the manager of the Westminster & City Bank, after all, if you let your diary tell you what to do?

He rose from his chair, ignoring the dismay of his secretary. 'That's my coat, if you would. Behind the door. We'll step over there now, shall we?'

Relief broke onto the young man's face.

On entering Bellman's office, Mr Anson saw immediately that the great businessman was not quite himself. His eyes were red-rimmed and there was a slow, lumbering aspect to his movements as if he were in pain.

'It's about the sleeping account.'

Mr Anson understood what Bellman meant, though he had never heard him use this term for it before. It was his second personal account. Over the last ten years Bellman had transferred one-third of his personal income into it. He had never drawn a penny out. It now represented a large – a very large – fortune. From time to time Anson had suggested investments to his client, but while Bellman was happy enough to risk the funds he held in his other account, and had seen significant returns, he had always refused absolutely to touch this money.

'Glad to hear it,' Anson now said. 'Where are we to put it, then?'

'Nowhere.'

'Nowhere?'

'I want to make an additional transfer of funds.'

'What sum?'

Bellman named a figure.

Mr Anson took a breath that did not adequately disguise his surprise.

'That would amount to – some seventy-five per cent of your personal liquid wealth . . . Of course it is possible, anything you wish is possible . . . Your intention would be to maintain the funds in cash?'

'It is.'

Anson brought his fingertips to his lips while he thought. The role of a bank manager was a delicate one. It was not for him to know what his clients meant for their money. How much they spent and on what was no concern of his. But sometimes he sensed something troubling in his clients' money and one part of his job, as he conceived it, was to act as go-between when his clients and their money had a falling-out, a failure to understand each other. He allowed silence to grow in the room, while he considered the matter.

It was logical to conclude that Bellman kept it apart from his other wealth for some special purpose, but no word had ever been spoken to indicate what that purpose might be.

'To see money sitting with its feet up by the fire when it could be put to work earning a good return – it goes against the grain with me, Bellman.' Anson spoke with a grimace, shaking his head sorrow-fully.

Bellman was unmoved. He did not answer but only sat, staring through the window, blind to the street but seeing, Anson thought, something fearful in the far distance of the mind's eye.

It couldn't be debts. He knew Bellman. Not as a friend exactly – they had never had any conversation that you might call personal – but he knew the habits of the fellow's life. Bellman only worked. He did not gamble, nor did he frequent brothels. Not a breath of scandal, financial or moral, had ever attached itself to his name. He lived for his work only and his work was a success. The haberdashers knew every last detail of the financial affairs of Bellman & Black and you only had to see their smiling, contented faces in the bar at Russell's to know that all was well there. He knew the accounts like the back of his hand and it was as clear as day that Bellman did not live expensively. In fact, his personal spending was as restrained as that of the most modest country vicar.

Was it possible that the man was being blackmailed? Had some villain got a hold over Bellman and was extorting money?

'Are you expecting to be in need of the money in liquid form at some time in the near future?'

Bellman put a hand over his eyes as though the light was hurting them. 'Perhaps. I don't know.'

'Bellman, I am your banker and one who has known you these last ten years and has your best interests at heart. Seeing you in this state, I am obliged to ask a difficult question: tell me, are you acting as a free man in making these arrangements?'

Bellman stared at him. 'Free?'

'If some person is extorting money from you, there are things that could be done . . . Lawyers . . . With perfect discretion. It could be dealt with by others, your name need never be mentioned.'

Then Anson saw a thing he had never expected to see. Bellman squeezed his eyes closed and a tear welled out of them.

'No lawyer can get me out of this. I am bound.'

When Bellman's eyes opened, Anson saw melancholy of the blackest tint.

Bellman took a breath and went on, as if the tear had never been shed. 'Furthermore, the quarterly payments into the account are to be made on a monthly basis henceforward. And from thirty-three per cent they will rise to fifty per cent. All clear?'

Anson walked back to the bank a troubled man.

26

Tick!

What ghastly watch is this, counting down the seconds so painfully?
Tick!

What an eternity of time between ticks. Any tick might be the last.
Tick!

He must not let the watch run down.
Tick!

But how to wind it? He feels for the watch in his breast pocket . . . But what is this? The watch is not in his pocket! It is ticking inside his chest!
Tick!

And any tick might be the last . . .
Tick!

Bellman awoke leaden-hearted. Something foul and chilling had enveloped him while he slept; it clung about him with the sheets. He escaped by rising immediately and plunging into activity: he shaved too quickly and cut his chin, was too nauseous for breakfast, gnawed at a piece of bread to try and settle his stomach. In his office he did two hours' letter writing before his first meeting of the day. He could do two jobs at once – or three. He piled task upon task, crammed every hour, every minute with ceaseless challenge. He prolonged his day beyond even his own excessive habits, and when he had worked nineteen or twenty hours, the despair he met in the bathroom mirror could not prevent him falling into an exhausted sleep. He did not emerge rested though: his mind, ever on guard, continued its grim battle through the night against a vaguely formed, forbidding foe, and when he woke it was to the same clinging foulness.

There were nights when he sank into his usual exhausted coma, then found himself wide awake an hour later. His conscious thoughts were no better than the sick horrors that assailed him in his sleep. Awake or asleep, it made no difference: trapped birds, the panicked flapping of wings, the brush of feathers close to his ear . . . He lay awake, sweating and breathing heavily, while his heart beat fit to wake the dead.

Insomnia took its toll.

Jerking into consciousness, as if from sleep, it was full daylight and there was Miss Chalcraft opposite him.

'Yes,' she was saying, 'the new girls we took on from Pope's, when they closed, are wonderfully quick.'

He was in his office, seated at his desk, entirely unable to remember his senior seamstress's arrival in the room, nor anything that they had spoken about prior to this moment. Her manner was entirely normal. Clearly she had noticed nothing out of the ordinary.

Not only did he have no memory of her arrival in his office, but their last meeting – had he really agreed to take on Pope's seamstresses when his competitor closed? Was that wise, when his own sales figures were so uncertain?

And later that same day, when Dixon reported smilingly that he had sold three reticules in an afternoon, thanks to the display suggestion that Bellman had made the day before – he had nodded approvingly, what else could he do? – but had he really made that suggestion? It was news to him.

It was undermining to realise that he must be sleepwalking through his working day, unconscious of three-quarters of his actions while, at night, his mind was painfully alert to every horror of the dark. He wondered whether he had been replaced by a usurper, another Bellman who made surprisingly effective suggestions about pricing and displays and employed his rival's redundant seamstresses while he, the real Bellman, remained trapped in a dark netherworld, neither awake nor asleep, neither living nor dead.

*

Click!

   Click!

   Click!

The remorseless beads of an abacus.

Thirty-eight.

Thirty-nine.

Forty.

How many does he owe? How many tens and how many hundreds and how many thousands?

   Click!

   Click!

   Click!

But there was no abacus and it was only his heart, adding up his debts, incurring new ones with every beat, and he could only endure helplessly as the tally mounted.

27

'Why don't you have a look?'

Dr Sanderson stood back and passed the magnifying glass to Bellman. The father leant over his child. Her large eye, five inches wide, blinked at him, through the lens. Her finger, skin imprinted with a pink whirl, a shiny white sliver of nail embellishing the fingertip – held open the lid, along which was a row of tiny blisters or beads, like fish roe.

'Don't rub or scratch,' the doctor was telling her. 'It is good news: your eyelashes are growing back.'

The eye blinked, then the finger recaptured the lid and the wide eye was once again offered to the magnifying glass.

Fascinated, Bellman stared. Dora's iris, blue as a summer sky, was flecked with dark marks. They appeared to him as a flock of distant birds.

'Will my hair grow back too?'

'Give it a few months and I wouldn't be the least bit surprised.'

Bellman accompanied Sanderson to the door.

'Why now?' he wanted to know. 'After all these years?'

'If I may take the liberty – Miss Bellman seems happier now. Science would scoff at the idea that happiness makes the hair grow, but the heart can work miracles on the body. I have seen it time and again. The opposite too: sorrow makes people sick.'

Sanderson eyed Bellman with worried curiosity. 'I suppose you consult one of the well-known London doctors for yourself?'

'I? I am never ill, as you know.'

The doctor looked doubtful. He overcame his hesitation to speak again.

'You have lost weight though?'

'I have been meaning to have these suits taken in, yes. I've had more important things to do.'

'Appetite all right? Sleep?'

It was impossible to describe accurately the horror of his nights. Bellman was loath to admit, I am tormented by dreams. Birds tap at my window in the night with their black beaks, they are trapped inside my lungs and leave me gasping for breath, they feed on my heart and when I shave in the morning I can see them looking out at me through my own eyes.

'My breathing seems shaky at times. I sometimes wake in the night – quite often actually. And my heart . . .'

'Your heart?'

'Is it normal for it to beat so fast? So hard?'

In the mild, untroubled voice that doctors adopt when they have not yet made up their mind whether a thing is serious or not, Sanderson asked a series of questions. Bellman answered and Sanderson listened, noting too the red rims of his patient's eyes and the grey tint to his skin. There was hoarse agitation in his voice and his hands shook. He noticed how verbose strings of words tumbled too fast from Bellman's lips; he paid attention to the momentary lapses in which Bellman seemed aware of nothing but only stared into space before coming to life again with a jerk.

'May I check your pulse?'

They sat and Sanderson held Bellman's wrist.

Then Sanderson let go of his wrist and when he spoke his voice was surprised and relieved. 'Well, there's nothing seriously wrong with you. A good rest will set you right. You have been working too hard. That kind of life is all very well for a young man – you always had prodigious energy – but even you must take account of your age. Take a holiday and when you go back to work you'll be fit as a fiddle. There's no reason why you shouldn't go on for another twenty years, if you take a day off once a week!'

A holiday? Regular days off? Bellman was astounded.

'Go on as you have been and it will be the death of you. I'll give you some sleeping draughts to start you off, but you'll find you won't need them long. Once you are in a more rested frame of mind your sleep will take care of itself.'

Bellman had little faith in sleeping draughts, but he took the laudanum and was surprised. He lay his head down on a feather pillow and opened his eyes to morning. The seven hours he had passed in bed between those two moments were as nothing. No fear, no wakefulness, no thoughts, no dreams. Nothing but blackest unconsciousness. For a week he slept the whole night long and rejoiced in it. The insomnia, he persuaded himself, had been a minor, fleeting thing. Now it was over he would not need the laudanum any more.

On his first night without the drug, the full force of the torment returned instantly to him.

He returned to his nightly dose but needed a little more to achieve the same effect.

After a little while, though, Bellman began to realise that medicated sleep was not true sleep. It had not the same capacity to restore. For one thing, the very second after he laid down his head to sleep, he was awake again and it was morning. Where were the ebbs and flows, the waves of deeper and lighter sleep of his earlier years? Where the fruitfulness of sleep, where he could close his eyes on a problem and wake in the morning to a solution? All this was gone. The moment he put his head on the pillow he was swallowed, engulfed into a dead blackness from which he woke unrefreshed, lethargic, downcast. The profound unconsciousness did not reassure him. He imagined dark-winged creatures of the night bending over his sleeping body and feasting on his soul while he lay oblivious to the danger, vulnerable as an infant. He was reluctant to go to bed, sat up later and later, afraid of sleep, afraid of wakefulness. To take the sleeping draught or not? He took it sometimes and sometimes not. He slept or he didn't. When he had no more of Dr Sanderson's laudanum he consulted a London doctor. Obtaining more was not difficult, and it could be combined with other potions besides. He became adept in the mixing of different medicines and learned how to poison himself to sleep at will.

It was not only sleep that was irregular. He was never hungry, except when he was starving. He ate at dawn or midnight or not at all. Time came adrift. The hands of his watch turned always too fast or too slow. He took it to a watchmaker to be checked over; the man insisted it was in good working order. He did not always know whether he had turned the leaves of his desk calendar. Was it today or already tomorrow? Perhaps it was still yesterday. Sundays came at what felt to Bellman like irregular intervals. Even the seasons lost their moorings: more than once he found himself looking from his window at one of those colourless London skies, wondering with acute anguish whether it was April or September.

Bellman got used to living his life curdled and sour from lack of sleep. Inside he was hollow, but he smiled and shook hands and added and multiplied and divided. None but he knew what it all cost.

28

Perhaps there was a solution.

Bellman was not in the habit of asking for help, because for the most part he knew how things ought to be done. But faced with one particular difficulty he felt himself at a loss and sought assistance.

'Verney, how would you go about finding a person?'

'A person?' Verney thought hard. He knew a hundred ways of locating a mislaid shilling, understood the numerous devious ways a decimal point might go astray. He was an expert in restoring overlooked digits to their rightful place in the ledger. But a person . . .

He shook his head. 'I wouldn't know where to begin.'

At Russell's, in conversation, Bellman tried again.

'There's someone I want to trace. How do you suppose I might go about it?'

'Ask at his club. Leave a letter for him there.' The haberdasher made it sound so easy.

'He's the solitary type. I don't believe he has a club.'

'No club?' The haberdasher's eyebrows rose. In his world a club was indispensable, and a fellow without one was a peculiar fellow indeed. He scratched his head. 'Damned difficult, then.'

'What's his name?' asked Anson, when he applied to him for help. 'If he banks with us, I'll send a letter on.'

To answer that would lead into explanation, and he wasn't up to explaining anything. Besides, what if Black's name wasn't Black at all? The more he thought about it, the more likely it seemed that he had made a profound mistake.

On his rounds at Bellman & Black, he dropped the question in here and there.

'Lawyers look for people, don't they?' the messenger boy suggested.

'I'll keep an eye out,' offered Pentworth the doorman. 'Everybody in the world walks past this door sooner or later. What does he look like?'

Which is all very well, thought Bellman, if it wasn't that looking for Black was simply not like looking for anyone else. How to explain, without sounding like a madman, that you are looking for someone whose appearance hovers at the edge of your mind, evading memory? Whose name you cannot be certain of? Who you have not seen for a decade but whose influence you feel in every guinea earned? Whose aura slinks in like a shadow, attached to the feet of every customer at Bellman & Black?

Tinkering with the printing press, he asked the typesetter the same question.

'If a man owes you money, you'll never find him, though you look high and low,' the man remarked, with a sorrowful shake of the head. He spoke from what sounded like sad experience.

'It's the opposite way about, really,' Bellman told him.

The typesetter laughed aloud. 'Mr Bellman, if you owe this man money he will come to you. Mark my words! And he won't be long about it!'

And then the driver of the brougham made a suggestion that might be some good. 'Go back to where you saw him last. People don't stray far.'

'That man . . .' he began.

'What man?'

Lizzie frowned, taking pins from the cushion strapped to her wrist and inserting them in his waistcoat. 'I only made this waistcoat a few months ago. You are wasting away, Mr Bellman.'

'I saw you with him.' His voice was hoarse. 'Do you remember? The night before the grand opening.'

She bent her head, carried out some complicated fiddling with the pins. 'I don't remember any man. I had come from my child's grave. It was a long time ago.'

'What street was it?'

'They called it Back Lane then. It is all gone now.'

279

'Gone?'

'Knocked down and built over. The whole area.'

'Oh.'

Her arms encircled his waist briefly to place the tape measure around him. She did not touch him, there was a decorous one inch gap between her arms and his body. Hold onto me, he wanted to say. He wished that he might rest his head in the crook of her neck. He wished he might weep while she stroked his head. If she would only stay close to him, watch over him, he might sleep at last. True sleep. The real thing.

Too soon the embrace of her arms was over. She sighed as she noted the new measurement of his waist.

'Are you eating enough, Mr Bellman? Have you lost your appetite?'

The kindness of her question made his eyes dazzle. He blinked and a sudden image came to mind: Turner's field flooded, the water held at brimming point by the reservoir walls. The surface used to tremble in captivity, he remembered; no one could see it without imagining an overspill. There was Crace, of course, who used to release controlled volumes into the mill race as and when necessary. The pent-up field of tears was overfull in Bellman today. What deluge would ensue if he released it now? What corpses float within it?

There came a firm knocking and Verney's face appeared, urgent, in the gap of the door.

'Forgive the interruption, sir. It is Mr Critchlow.'

Bellman turned to Lizzie. 'Come back later, will you?' And to Verney, 'Show him in.'

Verney's eyes widened in shock. 'It's not that, sir. Mr Critchlow is *dead*.'

29

Bellman oversaw the arrangements personally.

'It is,' he told Mrs Critchlow, 'the least I can do.'

He put Lizzie and another seamstress into the brougham and sent them to the house for three days and nights to stitch the widow and daughters into their crape; he ran down the stairs to the basement to the printing press to instruct the printer and give him the address. 'Caslon? Baskerville?' the typesetter wanted to know. Bellman ran back upstairs to fetch a sample of Critchlow's letterhead, took it down again. It was neither, it was Clarendon. The order given, he raced back up to his office, barely out of breath and before ten minutes were out he was back in the stairwell, on his way to collect the catalogue of coffin decoration. He did everything in his power to remove the weight of decision-making from the grieving family, planned every detail on their behalf. There was not so much as a fringe or ribbon that was not personally selected by him, and he selected only the most fitting. Earls and dukes might have more costly funerals (though this one was costly enough, and it was Bellman & Black that would foot the bill) but none had been provided with closer personal attention. Everything had to go without a hitch.

With all these arrangements to be made, there was not a moment to sit and pray by the corpse. This passed without comment. It was a decade since that dinner, and the family had altered their expectations of him since. He was simply Mr Critchlow's business partner and, given the nature of his business, they took for granted now that he expressed his sympathy and respects professionally.

'What am I to do about the business, Mr Bellman?' Mrs Critchlow asked in the middle of a conversation about velvet for the coffin cloth. 'We have no son to take over my husband's interests and my sons-in-law . . .' Her sons-in-law were too grand – she didn't need to speak the words aloud – for anything so sordid as retail.

'Don't worry about it. I will buy you out.'

'Really? Is it as simple as that?'

He didn't even need to see Anson about a loan: the money was ready and waiting in the sleeping account. He called at the Westminster & City on his way back to the shop.

'Is it the right time to extend your exposure in the market place?' Anson wondered aloud.

'Whyever not?'

'The way things are going . . . The judge has found in favour of the Welsh doctor, you know. It is not against the law in England to dispose of a body by cremation.'

'What difference does it make to us whether a body is buried or burned? It is still a funeral. There must still be a coffin, attendants, mourning clothes.'

'It is change, Bellman, and change never comes singly. Every day more voices are raised against the expense of funerals. Powerful voices too. People are spending less, you must have noticed? This funeral for Critchlow . . .' He didn't say the words, but what he was thinking was that such a funeral would never be seen again. The days of such lavishness were on the wane.

But Bellman's instructions were firm. Anson did the paperwork for the transfer of funds though he was not happy about it. As for his own capital, well, he had come out of crape a few months previously and put the money into the new crematorium they were building at Watford.

As Bellman made these preparations for the funeral, there was an excitation underlying his activity. Energised, renewed, he was his old self once more. The days contained their usual complement of hours, hours were made up of sixty minutes, no more, no less. His thoughts were ordered, he felt hunger at appropriate times and though his nights were short, he slept without artificial aid. He lived and worked with the expectation that these worries of his were about to be set right. The day and time of the funeral were fixed; the procession would be a fine one; Bellman & Black would make the event as gravely beautiful and as expensively solemn as any earl or duke's, and the example would be an inspiration to all who saw the procession pass.

More important than all the rest: Black was sure to be there.

On the day, Bellman was ready early. He joined the procession and walked with a flutter of trepidation in his chest. Today, he told himself, things would be settled once and for all. For good or for ill, he could not say, but there was at least one thing he could count on: no longer would he live in a state of uncertainty.

The passers-by stopped out of respect for the funeral procession. Some bowed their heads in prayer for the stranger whose death interfered briefly with their day. Others whispered, wanting to know who it was, enclosed in that ebonised box with its brass eternal-serpent fittings and ivy-engraved plaques. All heard the grateful voice inside that said, *It is not I who dies!* Some heard it continue, *Not today, at any rate.* The plumes bobbed and floated impressively above the six black horses, finely turned out and groomed till they shone. The polished hearse, the sober mutes, the blackest crape . . . Nothing in heaven could be finer, Bellman thought, than this spectacle of death, and the crowd watched it pass with sadness and admiration and sympathy in their eyes – and one or two, Bellman observed, wore another, new expression: cool judgement.

Entering the church, the mourners bowed their heads. Each mind, in each still living skull, considered the eternity that Mr Critchlow had already entered into, and which awaited them. All except one, that is, for Bellman's head was raised and he looked about him with intent concentration. Those who had entered ahead of him were already seated. He studied the backs of their heads, frowning and staring, trying to identify each scalp, each pair of shoulders. Was that him? No. Nor that one.

Some stranger – not Black – turned his way and sent a frowning rebuke. He bowed his head apologetically, mimicked the subdued demeanour of the other mourners, but could not quell the intensity of his curiosity. As soon as the man looked the other way he could not help but raise his head and continue his search.

All through the service, while he sang and prayed and knelt and stood and sat, his eyes were too vigilant, and his turning of the head this way and that, caused no little disturbance to those who had the misfortune to be placed by him. It was plain to all that Mr Bellman had forgotten why they were gathered together in church today. His mind was elsewhere. The frowns grew more pointed; certain mourners turned to each other and tut-tutted their disapproval.

Bellman grew agitated at realising that Black was nowhere to be seen. He even turned to look behind him: rows of black-suited mourners glared at him. They were angry, disconcerted, disapproving – but they were not Black. Where was he? Where?

Then he exclaimed aloud. 'Of course!' Black would not come here, to the church! He would be there for the burial! Had he not seen him always on the way in or out? Or at the very graveside? Critchlow was to be buried not at this church's overcrowded graveyard, but at the cemetery, in leafy peace, on the edges of the city. He must go there immediately!

'Excuse me!' he muttered, in his impatience, and he shuffled his way to the end of the pew, not minding whose toes he crushed, and he half ran back along the aisle to the door which he opened noisily before escaping.

No athlete nor any thief could have covered the distance as fast. Bellman drew all eyes as he raced through the streets. Red-faced and panting heavily he came to the cemetery gates and staggered in. He knew the spot – he had selected it himself.

Here was the grave. A beautiful position, with views and greenery all around. He himself had selected the design for the tomb that was to be erected here: a grand and elaborate affair with three angels, scrolls describing Critchlow's paternal and civic virtues and a small spaniel, its likeness taken from the painting of the one Critchlow had loved as a young man. It would be magnificent.

Today it was just a pit in the earth.

No one was there.

'He will come!' Bellman muttered. 'He will come.'

He paced all the paths, a hundred yards in each direction. Coming back to the grave site he peered into it. Just in case. Seeing a large tombstone not far off, he clambered up, hoping for a better vantage point, but slipped in his haste, grazing his hands and losing a button or two from his jacket. He brushed at the stains on his trousers, but only added blood to them and muddied his hands further. On his second attempt he achieved his objective and got himself a clear view of the area around the burial spot. Not a sign of anyone approaching.

'Black!' he hollered. 'Here I am, waiting for you! Make yourself known!'

There came a rustling in a patch of bushes. Branches swayed, and – Bellman's heart leapt – a figure stepped out onto the path. But it was only a grubby young fellow roused from sleep, a gardener or gravedigger or other such person, yawning and rubbing his eyes, and on seeing Bellman he looked alarmed and backed away, then turned and sprinted in the direction of the gates.

Bellman sighed and sat down. His arm was aching. He must have landed badly when he slipped. The pain brought sudden tears to his eyes and wiping them away, he added a smear of dirt and grass and blood to his sweating face.

There was time yet. Black wouldn't be expecting him so early, he reflected. In half an hour the others would come and that would be the moment. He was at the end of his energy now. He could only sit and attend to his modest, frail hope that Black would take pity on him. In this mood of passivity he allowed time to pass. He took out his watch from his breast pocket and saw that it had stopped. He wound it and held it to his ear. Nothing.

He reached automatically for his calfskin book but he had forgotten it. He didn't even have the energy to marvel at having forgotten the one thing he took everywhere with him. Dulled and dazed he remained there, still as a mannequin at Bellman & Black, and did absolutely nothing until the others arrived.

It was Anson who separated himself from the crowd of mourners and came to Bellman's side.

'Whatever is it, my friend?'

He took Bellman's arm, and though he did it gently, the action made him wince.

'Come, let me see you home. You are not well.'

But Bellman would not move, nor did he even look at or seem to hear Anson. He kept his eyes on the funeral party, scarcely blinking. Anson was aware that Bellman's behaviour in the church had been awry, and he noted that here, for all the eccentricity of Bellman's appearance and unnatural alertness, he was at least quiet and still. Rather than risk agitating him by bringing him away now, he resolved to stay with him and wait until after the interment to get his friend to a doctor.

Bellman looked. If he did not pick Black out of the crowd around the grave, he would see him afterwards. As the mourners departed in pairs and small groups there would be one solitary figure left, and it would be him . . .

His eyes shifted restlessly, always on the move. Every shuffle, every tilt of a head caught his attention. He expected from one moment to the next to see the face he was looking for. The face he would know instantly, that would be looking for him. His feet were ready. Before Black was even aware of his approach, there he would be, at his side.

And now all was over. There was a bit of handshaking, back-patting. The exchange of consoling words. Bellman wished the mourners would stand further apart, so that his view might be unoccluded.

At last the first of them departed, then others.

When all but the last few mourners were gone, Bellman remained there, staring.

'Are you coming?' Anson asked him. He placed a hand gently on Bellman's shoulder but Bellman appeared not to notice, so he took his arm and tried to lead him to the path.

'Let me take you home,' he suggested. But Bellman had no home. 'Why don't you go to your daughter for a few days—'

With a bellow of rage, Bellman threw off his hand. Anson leapt hurriedly out of the way. The last lingerers eyed them in alarm, casting

286

wary glances over their shoulders at the staring man with blood on his face, then hurried away.

Now alone with Bellman, Anson considered what to do for the best. He would go to the guardian of the cemetery, he decided. It needed two of them to get Bellman safely into a cab and to a doctor. Briskly he went to fetch help, leaving his friend staring into the grave and weeping, as though his own soul were buried in it.

When he returned with a burly fellow to help, Bellman was nowhere to be seen.

30

Bellman & Black was closing. The last customer departed and Pentworth bowed in deep sympathy as he closed the door behind her. As he was about to lock the door a familiar silhouette appeared out of the evening shadow and came up the steps. Mr Bellman. Pentworth opened the door again. It was not his place to notice his employer's unusual appearance, so he feigned not to see it.

As the office door opened, Verney looked up. Mr Anson had called this afternoon with an unlikely story about the funeral. He found it hard to credit it. Clearly something had happened, but it couldn't be as he had been told . . . On seeing Bellman's face, he put his questions away.

'The figures are on your desk,' Verney said uncertainly, and Bellman only raised a hand to silence him. Without even a glance in his direction, he entered his office and shut the door firmly behind him.

Verney supposed that if Bellman wanted him he would let him know. In the meantime he got on with his regular work. His fingers danced uncertainly; more than once he had to start a calculation over again for loss of concentration.

Half a dozen times someone came knocking: a handful of senior staff worked on well beyond closing time. 'Is Mr Bellman back? I wanted . . .' and each time Verney shook his head.

'Come back another time.'

At the end of an hour he didn't dare knock and interrupt his manager. For another thirty minutes he occupied himself with things that didn't need doing and when at the end of it Bellman's door was as firmly closed as before, he put his coat on and left for home.

Behind the closed door, habit made Bellman pick up the monthly figures from his desk. Sales were down – for the third month running

– but Verney's neat figures and ruled lines marshalled disruption and trouble into an appearance of order and harmony. Slowing sales and growing losses were neatly aligned, columns and rows still worked out, whichever way you added and divided. It was scant consolation to know that the falling profits were so impeccably recorded. Bellman sighed heavily and the prospect of the long evening weighed painfully upon him. *I am abandoned*, he thought. The one he was looking for could not be found. What was he to do with the rest of his life?

Outside the window a rook flapped ragged and unsettled over the rooftops of Regent Street. Bellman turned his back on it and, resigned to the task, stood before his chart, pen in hand. With the black pen he entered a black cross to mark the month's sales. The parabola had a quality to it that he recognised. *I could have predicted this degree of drop*, he thought, and then corrected himself. How on earth could that be the case? But it was true. He had seen this curve before.

He switched to the blue ink. Next month. What were people dying of now? There was Critchlow, dead of old age. There were thousands like him. He thought of Fred, dead of having lived and loved and made bread for – what? Fifty years? How many like him? A good many.

Fred was the same age that he was, wasn't he? Staring at the curve on the wall, he suddenly realised that he and Fred were almost exactly the same age. They had birthdays in the same month. Fancy thinking of that, now! His cousin Charles too. Poor Charles. And that other boy . . . Luke. Whom he himself had . . . So long ago.

He blinked.

He could see the whole trajectory of the arc. The apex of the curve. The exact spot where it loses velocity. He could foresee the terminal point. He entered his cross with certitude. He knew. He had seen it before.

A sudden anxiety made him wonder about the rook he had seen over the rooftops a moment ago. What was it doing now? He moved urgently to the window. The sky was deep blue, not yet so dark that he would not see the outline of a rook against it. *But it is too late for a rook*, he thought. *I can't have seen it. They will all be gone to their treetops by now.*

Scanning the roofline for the silhouette of a rook, he felt it. A tingle at the back of the neck, the stirring of the bone marrow when someone has their eye on you . . .

He turned and spoke in the same moment: 'There you are!'

Seated comfortably in the armchair by the fireside, Black looked pleased to see him. Even in shadow, the mild amiability of his smile did not fade in the face of Bellman's startled vexation.

'What kept you? I've been looking everywhere!'

'Me? I've been here all along.'

'All along?' Bellman wondered whether he had misheard.

Black inclined his head with grace, without explanation.

'I suppose it doesn't matter. You're here now.'

Black was peaceable, at ease. His curious gaze settled on Bellman as if he was expecting him to take the lead. Flustered, Bellman seemed to have forgotten all his negotiating skill. 'I have drawn up a contract for you,' he began, somewhat flustered. 'It's here, some-where.' He opened a drawer and rummaged. How many years ago had he written it? He extracted a sheaf of papers that dated from the right period, fanned them out on his desk but the contract wasn't immediately obvious. Blast! Why hadn't he kept it separately some-where? His hands trembled as he grasped another bundle of papers. 'I know it's here! I can find it, if you give me a few minutes. It's just a question of time.'

'Of course.'

Bellman glanced up. With an easy gesture, Black seemed to indicate that he was not in any great hurry.

'Perhaps you would like to see the ledgers while you are waiting?' Bellman took them two at a time from the shelf to make an armful. 'You'll find the records are up to date, very complete, nothing for-gotten!'

'Nothing forgotten?' Was there a touch of irony in Black's voice?

Crossing the room to place the ledgers on the side table within reach of Black, he had the odd sensation that Black's silhouette grew darker the closer he got.

'Not a thing! It's all there! Bank statements too, if you want! They're here, look.' He was already at the shelf where the bank documents were archived, pulling out box files when he stopped. 'Forgotten what? What kind of thing do you mean?'

And before Black could answer, Bellman, suddenly suspicious, asked another question: 'Who let you in? Verney?'

Black shifted in his chair. His face was in shadow. 'The safe . . .' Bellman said, with a mouth so dry the words were as feathers in his mouth. 'I can advance you part of your share as soon as you like. Tonight. Here and now.'

The safe's dial was stiff; the effort of turning it helped calm his quaking hands. The door swung open on the day's takings, counted out in a heap of felt bags. He spilled money from the felt bags onto the desk, talking ten to the dozen all the while. 'Sales have dropped a little lately. It is nothing to be concerned about. The public sentiment is wavering in the matter of death ritual. In a little while habits will reassert themselves, and we shall know where we are again. Death never goes out of fashion. It is the one sure thing!'

He was talking too much, he knew it, his jollity smacked of over-confidence; no one but a novice would be persuaded. But Black's silence was full of questions that he did not know the answer to and preferred not to hear, so on he babbled. The new cremations, ex-changing one style of ritual for another. 'There is always the same need for consolation, you see! Some things never change!'

In a great hurry he emptied bag after bag on the desk. The money made a small mountain, so that the topmost coins began to slide down the heap to the edges. Some rolled off the edge to the floor. 'Look! Even with this decline – temporary, of course – we are doing well. It can't be said the business is failing. Far from it.'

The coins on the floor had their own velocity. They rolled in all directions, under the cupboard, towards the door, under the chair.

'Twenty-five per cent, that's what I envisaged. It will make you a wealthy man. But that's open to negotiation, of course. It's just a starting point. We can talk it all through. I'm not an unreasonable man. I want to see your contribution amply recognised. If fifty per cent seems more appropriate, make your case. I'm more than happy to listen.'

Black said nothing. Bellman's heart was beating so fast he could barely get his breath.

'Fifty per cent it is, then. I told you I was prepared to be generous, didn't I? Shall we agree to that?'

He sat and dipped a nib in the ink. 'I can rewrite this contract here and now, as we speak . . .' and he could too, except that there was nowhere to put the paper to write. He swept an arm across the table to clear a space. More coins fell streaming from the desk. Some of them rolled in Black's direction. One came to rest at his feet and his cloaked arm reached down from his chair to retrieve it from the carpet. Bellman felt a small relief at the knowledge that some part of his debt at least was in the hands of his debtor. It was a start.

But as Bellman started to write, out of the corner of his eye he saw Black place the runaway coin indifferently on the unconsulted ledgers.

So far as he could make out in the thickening gloom, Black looked bemused. Or sad. Or else was smiling kindly at him, as though he, Bellman, was a young boy who had failed to understand something.

'Seventy-five per cent,' he proposed, gabbling. 'It's not as if I need the money myself. I'm quite wealthy enough . . .'

When he got no response his nerve failed him. 'Eighty?' It seemed a lot, but he sensed the beginning of the relief that would come from having the matter at last settled. It would be worth it, for Dora's sake. Worth more, even.

'Or ninety? You were the one who recognised the opportunity, after all.'

Ink was leaking from his pen. The contract was nothing more than an ink blot, a shape that could have been anything.

'The opportunity?' Black queried, gently.

'Of course!' Bellman stared. 'That night when we entered into partnership. Bellman & Black! You must remember!'

There came a soft rustling and a movement that Bellman interpreted as a shrug. 'I thought it was your idea.'

' "I see an opportunity!" That's what you said!'

Black was looking into the fireplace. 'And you thought I meant this.'

'What did you mean, then?'

Bellman could see almost nothing of Black in the shadows. He appeared only as a darkly shrouded form. The faint gleam of his garments suggested there was light somewhere to be reflected, but where it was coming from Bellman couldn't say. And there was, too, the gleam of his black eyes, intelligent, not unkind exactly, but intransigent. Never had Bellman felt himself so keenly seen.

'I will transfer ownership entirely to you,' he said. 'For that I will need your full name.'

The silence told him he had gone astray somewhere. He was on the wrong track. He placed his pen on his desk.

'Why have you come? I should have made it clear at the time, I realise that now, but Dora . . .' He felt foolish and ignorant, as he hadn't felt in years.

'This is not about your daughter.'

'No?' Bellman tried to make sense of it. So Black didn't want Dora. He looked around the room. There was money everywhere. Black didn't want money either. It was no good, he felt more bewildered than relieved. What on earth *did* Black want?

'I've come to say goodbye.'

Bellman rose from his desk. 'But where are you going? And why? I've hardly even got to know you! If anything, I knew you better in the old days at Whittingford. Why is it that I know you so little? I had hopes at one time that we might be friends . . .'

'We've not got long.'

Bellman had crossed the room towards the fireplace. He placed a hand on the back of the second armchair. Should he sit down or not? He had the obscure feeling that he ought to wait to be invited.

'Time is short, eh? But if there's one thing I have learned it's that there is always more time than you think. And I could learn a lot from a man like you. All this time I've been waiting for you to come, and now, at last—'

'I've been here all along.'

'Did I hear you right? All along, you say?'

Black nodded. 'Right behind you.'

Bellman paused. He peered doubtfully into the shadows. 'Was it Verney who let you in?'

Black let the question pass.

'I offered you an opportunity. I'm not talking about Bellman & Black. That was your idea. What I was offering you in your bereavement was an opportunity of another kind. I offer it to you again now. Before it is too late.'

'Too late for what?'

As Bellman spoke, the silhouette of his visitor seemed to darken, and an answer – astonishing, obvious – occurred to him.

'Oh,' he said. 'I never thought . . .'

Weariness suddenly overwhelmed him and he sat down. He put his head in his hands while the world seemed to spin, and when it came to a stop he discovered a clarity that had been missing before.

'So there is no deal then?'

'There is no deal.'

'And the money . . .' he gestured helplessly at the coins.

Black shook his head.

'So this opportunity . . . ?'

'Thought.'

'Thought? Is that it?'

'And memory.'

Bellman nodded. Thought and memory. Time slowed while he applied himself. Here at Bellman & Black, he had thought of nothing but death for the last decade. Yet he had failed to devote a single moment to the thought of his own mortality. It was – almost – ludicrous. However had he come to forget such an important thing?

He tried to remember. Turning his mind's eye to his past, he could see only darkness. It was something he recognised from his dreams and filled with menace. 'I can't remember,' he said, shaking his head. He looked into the darkness and it shifted and altered to make shapes that figured the horrors he had lived. His wife, racked by illness, appeared to him and he trembled painfully. His sons calling for him, bewildered by his inability to lift them out of their agony. His baby daughter crying with rage and incomprehension at the first incursion of suffering into her short life.

The pain of contemplating such pain and loss was hard to endure. 'But what good can come of it?' he asked Black. 'It is more than I can bear.'

'Remember!'

The blackness contained more. Luke's head of copper hair bright on snow. Charles, lost far away and never mourned. Fred – he should have gone to see him! Why hadn't he gone?

He twisted his face. 'Don't make me do it . . .'

'Remember!'

There was an image he had buried for years, and it returned to him now: his uncle, dead but bolt upright in his study chair. 'I can't!' he cried, for it terrified him now as it had terrified him then.

'Remember!'

The Misses Young and a white china bowl stained with blackberry juice. That damned grave. That damned coffin. That damned Reverend Porritt speaking his mother's name . . .

Memories of all his unmourned dead pierced him. The grief of an entire lifetime entered his heart in a single moment. He thought he would collapse. He thought the pain would crush him. He thought he would die of it. But it was not yet the end of him.

'Remember,' Black told him softly.

'I am.'

'There is more.'

Fearful of what might await him, Bellman looked once more into his past. He saw – he seemed to see – a curving line. A parabola. Marked out on the graph paper, traced on the sky over Whittingford, a perfect curve with a boy and a catapult at one end of it – and a young rook on a branch at the other.

He was beyond trembling now.

The stone traced its perfect curve in the sky and, his tongue thick in his mouth, he wished only to cry out, to startle the bird into taking off. There was time, still time, for it to release its grip on the branch and rise, laughing, into the sky . . .

The stone completed its trajectory.

The bird fell.

William dared not look at Black. He felt more than saw Black rise.

'I am afraid,' he whispered.

'Remember!' he heard.

'I have remembered all. All!'

'Remember!'

'There is nothing more!'

'Remember!'

When Bellman looked up, it was so dark he could see nothing at all, until a shimmer of purple and blue and green shifted and radiated through the darkness.

Now all kinds of things emerged from the darkness of his buried past. Children's faces grave with responsibility, pouring vinegar over a bowl of coins and mixing the contents, a cow in a ditch, wet boots, and a grinning girl with a gap in her teeth, a good piece of cheese and a dish of stewed plums, Uncle Paul plucking a rose from his mother's hat with a penknife, Poll at the Red Lion stroking his hair as if he were a pet dog and pulling up her nightdress, the joy to the eye of a field gashed with crimson cloth, two boys in his lap laughing at their father, a seamstress singing a sad song, her face illuminated with joy and memory . . .

'What a life I have had!' he told Black, wonderingly. 'Why I could spend half a lifetime just thinking about it!'

'Remember!'

He remembered. Scene after scene, moment after moment, joys and sorrows and pleasures and loves and losses of all sorts streamed out of the place where he had entombed them, a flow of days, hours and seconds that seemed as if it would never end.

I am cold, he thought and instantly he remembered that once, years before, he had shivered in blankets by the fireside of a small cottage, his daughter heavy on his lap. Gravely she raised her hand and he felt the mysterious touch of her fingertips drawing down his eyelids.

31

At the top of the emporium in Regent Street, a draught slipped under a door and into one of the seamstresses' bedrooms. It found a gap between neck and blankets, insinuated itself into the space between body and bedclothes. It chilled.

Lizzie stirred in her bed. She turned over, seeking a bit of warmth, but found only coolness. Her forehead and her nose were cold. Her eyes flickered and she was awake. This, her sleepy mind knew, was not right. She rose and padded across the chilly room thinking to close her window, but it was not open. The draught was from elsewhere.

On the walkway outside her bedroom door, the chill was evident. A cold breeze was coming in from above. Who on earth had raised the glass ceiling? It was opened to its full extent and there was a clear three-foot gap all around the edge of the glazing, giving onto a cloudless sky of midnight black, with stars bright all over. It was the kind of sky that you might stand and stare at, entranced, only Lizzie's bare feet were cold on the walkway and she was too tired for enchantment.

There was only one thing for it. She would have to go down and tell Mr Bellman.

Her coat was behind the door; she put it on over her nightdress. She felt for her shoes in the dark, buttoned her naked feet into them by feel alone.

Rising and turning in one movement, Lizzie stepped onto the walkway where an unexpected sound made her halt.

The beating of wings.

There came a feather-rush of air, it touched her eyelids, cheeks and neck. Blackness she had never seen the like of before, flapping upwards right in front of her. Something there and gone again. Craning her neck, she made sense of it: could it be a bird?

It was! A rook.

An ungainly repositioning mid-air, then an adeptly gauged flap propelled it through the gap in the ceiling. Out! Black on black, it was almost invisible, yet for a few seconds she followed it with her eyes, for it blocked out the stars where it flew. Then it was gone.

She stood looking up, hands to collar, unaware of the cold, unaware of the hour. The rook was written blackly on the sky, on her eye, miraculous.

PART THREE

On the crow

. . . he does not know what care is,
he does not know what sorrow is,
he does not know what remorse is,
his life is one long thundering ecstasy of happiness,
and he will go to his death untroubled,
knowing that he will soon turn up again as an author or something,
and be even more intolerably capable and comfortable than ever he
   was before.

Mark Twain, *Following the Equator: A Journey Around the World*

THE MOURNERS HAD remembered William Bellman, and they had buried him. Now they had gone back to their lives. Only the household and its familiars remained in the reception room at Mill House, which is to say that along with Dora and Mary and Mrs Lane, you could count Ned and Grace from the mill and Robert who made the bread for the mill and who had lost his own father not so long ago. The only newcomers were George and Peter, orphaned nephews of Mary, lately taken in by Dora.

'Your father killed a rook once,' Robert told Dora. 'When he was a boy. My father was there and never forgot it. Your father's catapult was the envy of all the boys back then.'

He told her the story.

'My father never liked birds,' she said. 'And yet they are so fascinating. There is a river of rooks that passes over this mill twice a day.'

He nodded. 'The Flytesfield rooks.'

'Flytesfield?'

'It's what they call it. Where the parish congregates.'

He saw the idea born in her expression, and she spoke it the very next moment. 'Let us go there!'

It was nearly an hour's drive to Flytesfield, and an uphill walk at the end of it, so that by the time they arrived, only a sliver of sky separated the white sun from the horizon. All carried things: the men carried Dora who could not keep up over the rough ground; Mary and the children carried the oilcloth and cushions. When they arrived, they organised their cargo and themselves on the sloping ground, and settled, swathed in blankets.

It was no artist's country, only a broad band of field, a stripe of trees and above it the vast whiteness of an early winter sky.

'Where are they?' Mary's nephew George was keen to know. 'We can't see them.'

'We're the first. They'll be on their way.'

Dora looked at her watch; peered at the sky through her binoculars.

'Look that way,' she suggested, pointing to the west.

Dots in the sky, too far away at first to even see that they were moving.

There they were, the first, from over Stroud way. She turned her binoculars this way and that and saw what the others could not yet see: more groups arriving from every direction. She dropped the binoculars to her lap, put a warming arm around George's shoulder and abandoned herself to the spectacle to come.

They came from north, south, east and west. In groups of twenty or thirty they had set out from their different departure points, then found each other en route, and formed larger and larger parties, until now they converged on Flytesfield in long streams. After a few minutes the first of them dropped low, flapping and swooping, claws outstretched as they landed heavily on braced legs. More were coming behind them, and in no time twenty, a hundred, three hundred birds were strutting and cawing on the field beneath the spectating humans. The sky was thick with flight: the birds flowed towards their destination like black rivers, thousands of them, intent, purposeful, moving as one, and they funnelled ceaselessly from air to land, an endless flood of them.

The sky was so full you might easily think all the rooks of the world were congregating here. They came and they came and they came. The landing rooks extended their spread on the earth like spilt oil, and before long the field was more black than brown. The cawing of the birds in their hundreds and thousands was an entirely different sound from the noise of a few. The individual cries melded together into a sound effect that was not musical, nor like the noise any living creature makes, but more like the sound of the planet itself. Now the field was three-quarters filled, and now more than that, and the spaces for newcomers grew smaller and smaller. Sometimes, by misjudgement or overcrowding, the birds came to land on top of each other, toppling and tumbling to the ground.

At last the sky thinned, the light reasserted itself overhead. There came a gap in the syphoning of birds to ground, then another, and in a few more minutes the last birds flapped to earth, and there was a separation between empty sky above and the seething field below.

Now the world paused. The sun sank one degree lower in the sky. The air cooled a little. Five pairs of human eyes did not blink and thirty thousand rooks stilled their chattering tongues.

All was quiet. All was still.

Somewhere, invisibly, at the heart of the mass, a single rook readies its muscles. Now it flaps and rises. A thread of birds is drawn up, out of the mass, a line that rises, coiling and twisting into the dusky air. It thickens at its base, spirals up, and paints shapes on the sky: swirls and eddies, like black dye dropped into water. Endlessly and unexpectedly shifting, it is hard to believe that these are individual birds, it seems to be a single force that animates these fantastical forms in the sky.

The dark lake of birds shrinks as the black mass flows upwards from its centre, more and more joining the whirling dance flight until the last birds leave the ground and the entire parish is twisting and writhing as one force in the air. There is no time. Future and past are banished, and this moment is all.

These are shapes, Dora thinks, that she has seen before, a million years ago, in another world. They are incomprehensible, but she has known them in the past, and the day will come when she will know them again. For today she watches, holding her breath. She forgets the others, forgets herself, forgets everything but the bliss of the shapes that paint themselves on her soul as they paint themselves on the sky.

The watchers are so caught up in the spectacle of the black air that roils and dances over Flytesfield that no one notices the first birds dropping out of the sky and into the treetops. But it becomes clear as the light falls that the numbers of birds are thinning. The shapes grow pale and lose some of their vitality. Then they break up altogether and all that remains of them are a few hundred birds flapping their wings, waiting to drop down onto a branch. The winter branches are thickly foliated with rooks and you have to peer through the darkening evening to see the last birds settle.

When the mysterious sky dance is over, the spectators blink and breathe and come to themselves after their long enchantment. They feel mild surprise at finding themselves contained in their bodies on this sloping hillside: for the last half-hour they have been elsewhere. Their souls resettle in their bodies. Fingers stretch and toes wriggle experimentally. Their ribcages and unfeathered flesh feel faintly foreign to them.

George looks without seeing: his little mind is overfull of rookery and nothing else can make an impression. He yawns, then, without speaking, falls abruptly into deep sleep. Dora holds him while the others gather cushions and fold the oilcloth. No one in the party speaks but when eye meets eye, there is a powerful sense of something shared.

Dora glitters, serenely exultant. It is what a rooking escapade does to a human. She looks as if she has gathered all the glory of the world into herself. To see it once is never to be without the feeling for the rest of your life. It is the rook whirl of excitement in the blood that lingers, the spirals of rooks still turning in the brain, in the eye, long after the actual rooks have settled on their branches.

Dora has been set right inside herself. Tomorrow and in the days afterwards she will paint and paint well. The rooks unleash a freedom of the painting arm and of the mind that makes things possible . . .

Dora will be sad and happy and ill and well. She will live the best she can for as long as she can and when she can do that no longer, she will die. And rooks will paint mysteries on the sky at dawn and dusk for as long as the world exists.

&

There are numerous collective nouns for rooks. In some parts people say *a storytelling of rooks*.

All stories must come to an end. This one. Everyone's. Your own.

The rook is a great lover of stories. He has been harvesting them for as long as there have been stories to harvest, which means for as long as there have been gods and men and rooks. And he has a good long memory for them.

When your story comes to an end, a rook will harvest it, as I harvested William Bellman's story. So when you arrive at the last line of the last page, it is Thought or Memory or one of their many descendants who will be waiting to accompany you as the book closes on your story. En route, over the last blank page and beyond the covers to that other unknown place, your rook will harvest your story. Later, he will make his way back without you. And then, when the time is right, he will make his way to the white page of sky where he will partake in the most important rook ritual of all.

All will be gathered together in an inkpool of black. First one will rise, then others, then hundreds, then thousands until, ink-black marks on a paper-white blank, the descendants of Thought and Memory will dance together in a passionate and spectacular act of collectiveness: a storytelling, of gods, of men, of rooks.

Incidentally, we have a collective noun for you too. You are, to us, *an entertainment of humans*.

Sources

A writer of fiction is entitled to take liberties with history and fact, and I have taken full advantage of this freedom. I remain nonetheless indebted to the following for their reliable knowledge of mill history, Victorian funerary practices and the habits of the corvid family.

Jennifer Tann, *Wool and Water: the Gloucestershire woollen industry and its mills*

Pat Jalland, *Death in the Victorian Family*

James Stevens Curl, *The Victorian Celebration of Death*

Tony Mazluff, *In the Company of Crows and Ravens*

Mark Cocker, *Crow Country*

Furthermore, thank you to Robin Mitchell who showed me round Gigg Mill where he demonstrated various historical processes and looms, and to Judy Faraday and Linda Moroney of the John Lewis archive for valuable information on Victorian mourning emporia.

The hymn sung in chapter 1 is Charles Wesley's *Oh Come and Dwell in Me* and the song sung by the seamstresses and later by William Bellman and Lizzie is *Echoes* by Adelaide Ann Proctor.

Acknowledgements

The first thank you must be to Toppen Bech and Håkon Langballe, whose friendship and generosity to me and to this book is without parallel. Tusen takk!

Thank you also to Mark Cocker for his beautiful book *Crow Country*. My book would not be what it is without Mark's passionate and poetic account of the fascination rooks exert on the human mind and soul.

Thank you to Jo Anson, Mike Anson, Jane Bailey, Cathrine Bakke Bolin, Gaia Banks, Emily Bestler, Erin Catley, Fergus Catley, Paula Catley, Ross Catley, Janet Cook, Judith Curr, Marianne Downie, Jenny Jacobs, Anna Franklin, Nathan Franklin, Vivien Green, Douglas Gurr, Guy Julier, Mary Julier, Jean Kirk, Susan Lamb, Caroline Lemarechal Stüwe, Bill Massey, Gary McGibbon, Stephanie Ross-Russell, Noël Ross-Russell, Mandy Setterfield, Jo Smith, Julie Summers, Sarah Thomas, Silvia Querini, Gina Wilson, Zofia Zawisza.

Thank you to Owen Staley who was there when this book was just a few paragraphs old and to Margaret Nicholson (aka Margaret Yorke) who encouraged me. I wish you were both here to see it complete.

Finally, thank you Uncle Neville for telling me about the time you killed a black bird with a stone, even though you never meant to and didn't think you could.